HULK
DEFENDERS

WRITER: **PAUL BENJAMIN**

PENCILERS: **DAVID NAKAYAMA & MARIO GULLY**

INKERS: **GARY MARTIN & SCOTT KOBLISH**

COLORISTS: **MICHELLE MADSEN & SOTOCOLOR'S A. STREET**

LETTERER: **DAVE SHARPE**

COVER ARTISTS: **JUAN SANTACRUZ, RAUL FERNANDEZ & CHRIS SOTOMAYOR**

ASSISTANT EDITOR: **JORDAN D. WHITE**

EDITOR: **MARK PANICCIA**

COLLECTION EDITOR: **CORY LEVINE**

ASSISTANT EDITOR: **JOHN DENNING**

EDITORS, SPECIAL PROJECTS: **JENNIFER GRÜNWALD & MARK D. BEAZLEY**

SENIOR EDITOR, SPECIAL PROJECTS: **JEFF YOUNGQUIST**

SENIOR VICE PRESIDENT OF SALES: **DAVID GABRIEL**

PRODUCTION: **JERRON QUALITY COLOR & JERRY KALINOWSKI**

EDITOR IN CHIEF: **JOE QUESADA**

PUBLISHER: **DAN BUCKLEY**

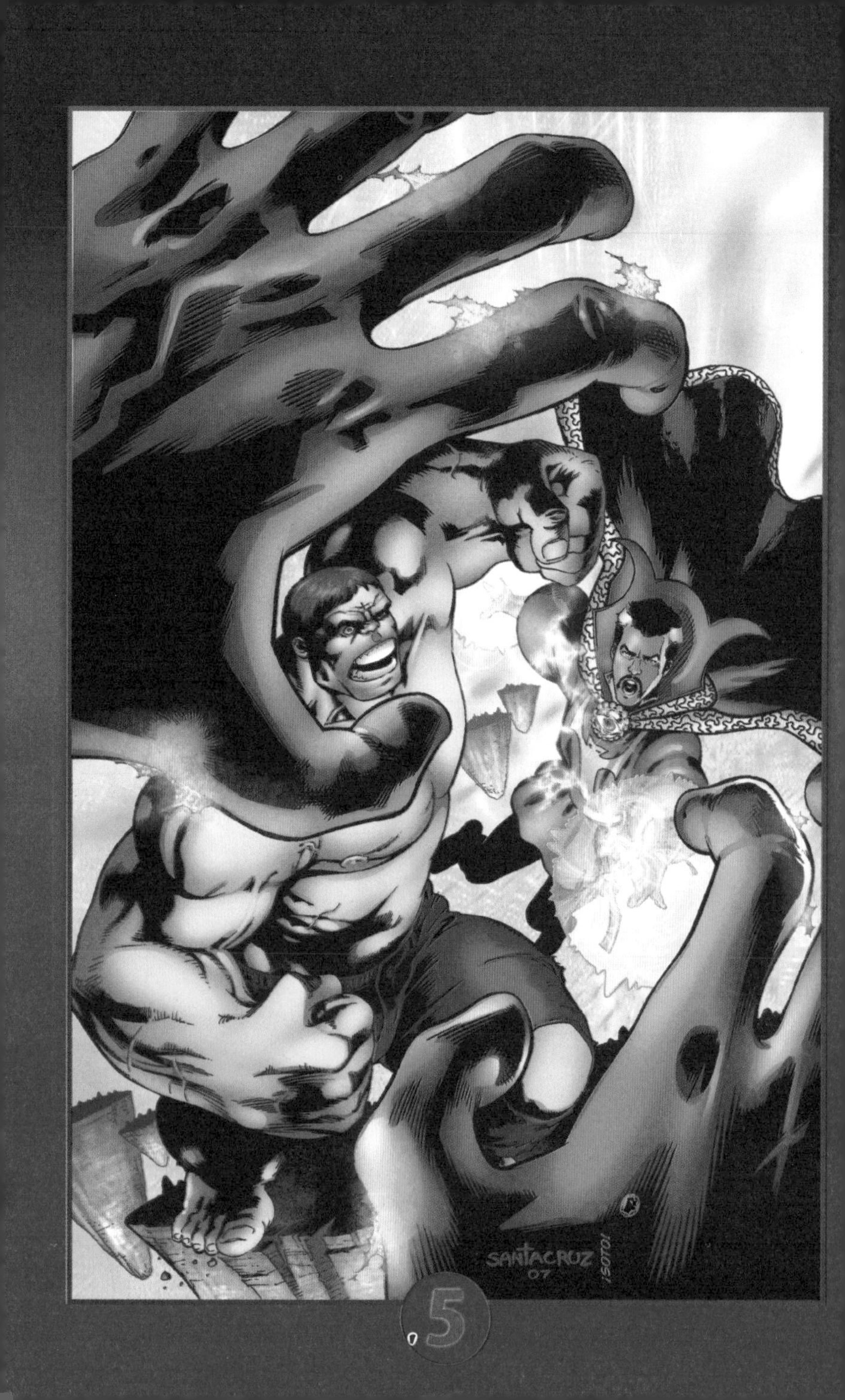
SANTACRUZ
07
¡SOTO!

5

BRUCE BANNER AND THE HALF-MONKEY PRINCE

GREENWICH VILLAGE, NEW YORK.

You sure this is the address the old dude gave, Doc?

As sure as I am that two negative electrons don't make a positron.

It *is* an odd-looking building for a lab.

Caught in a blast of gamma-radiation, brilliant scientist Bruce Banner now finds himself living as a fugitive. The only people he can count on are his devoted assistant, Rick Jones, and the former lab monkey Bruce affectionately calls "Monkey." Bruce Banner is cursed to transform in times of stress into the living engine of destruction known as THE INCREDIBLE HULK.

PAUL BENJAMIN **WRITER** | DAVID NAKAYAMA **PENCILER** | GARY MARTIN **INKER** | MICHELLE MADSEN **COLORIST** | DAVE SHARPE **LETTERER**

SANTACRUZ AND SOTOMAYOR **COVER ARTISTS** | ANTHONY DIAL **PRODUCTION** | JORDAN D. WHITE **ASST. EDITOR** | MARK PANICCIA **EDITOR** | JOE QUESADA **EDITOR IN CHIEF** | DAN BUCKLEY **PUBLISHER**

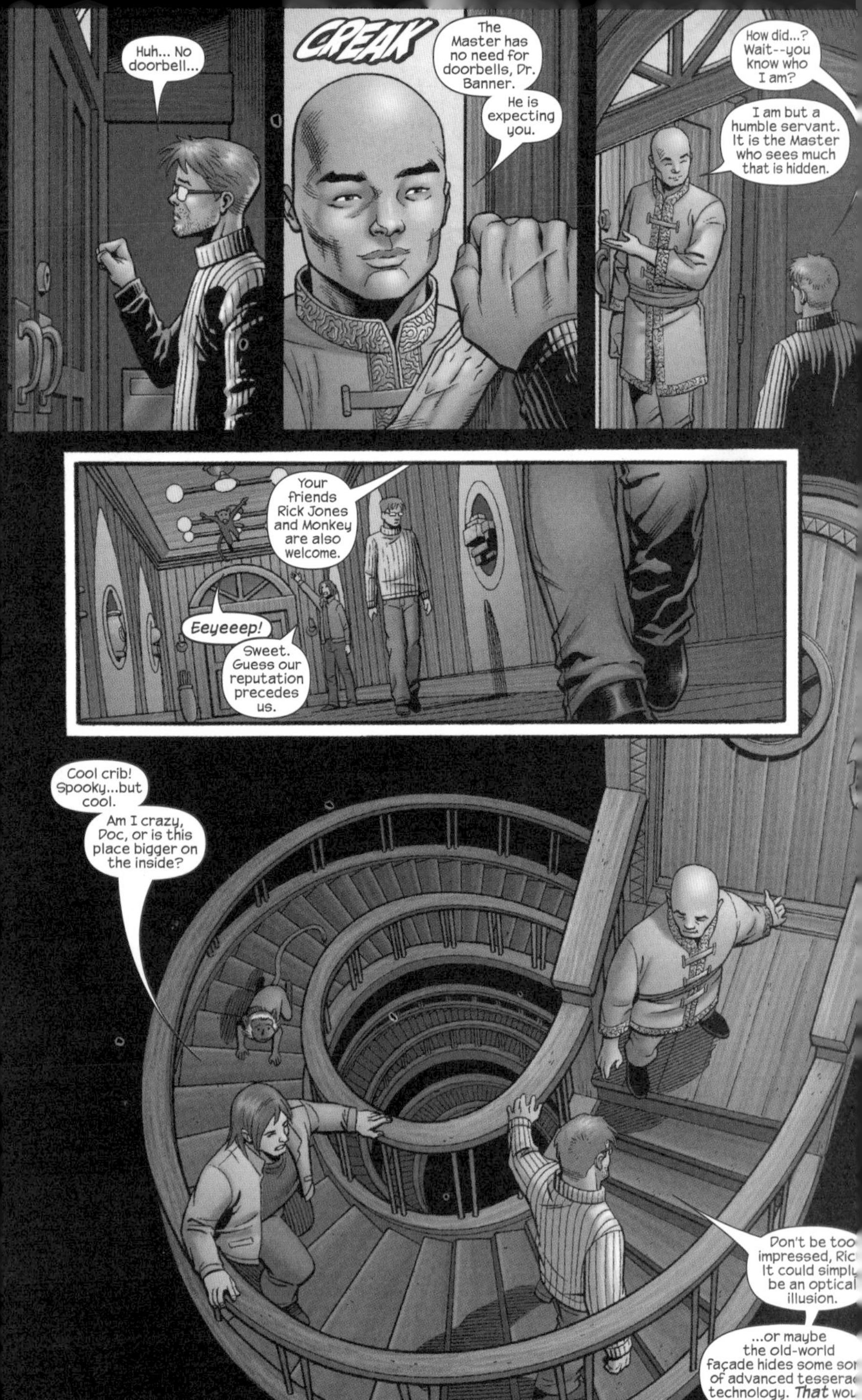

Huh... No doorbell...
CREAK
The Master has no need for doorbells, Dr. Banner.
He is expecting you.
How did...? Wait--you know who I am?
I am but a humble servant. It is the Master who sees much that is hidden.
Your friends Rick Jones and Monkey are also welcome.
Eeyeeep!
Sweet. Guess our reputation precedes us.
Cool crib! Spooky...but cool.
Am I crazy, Doc, or is this place bigger on the inside?
Don't be too impressed, Ric
It could simply be an optical illusion.
...or maybe the old-world façade hides some sor of advanced tesserac technology. That wou be interesting.

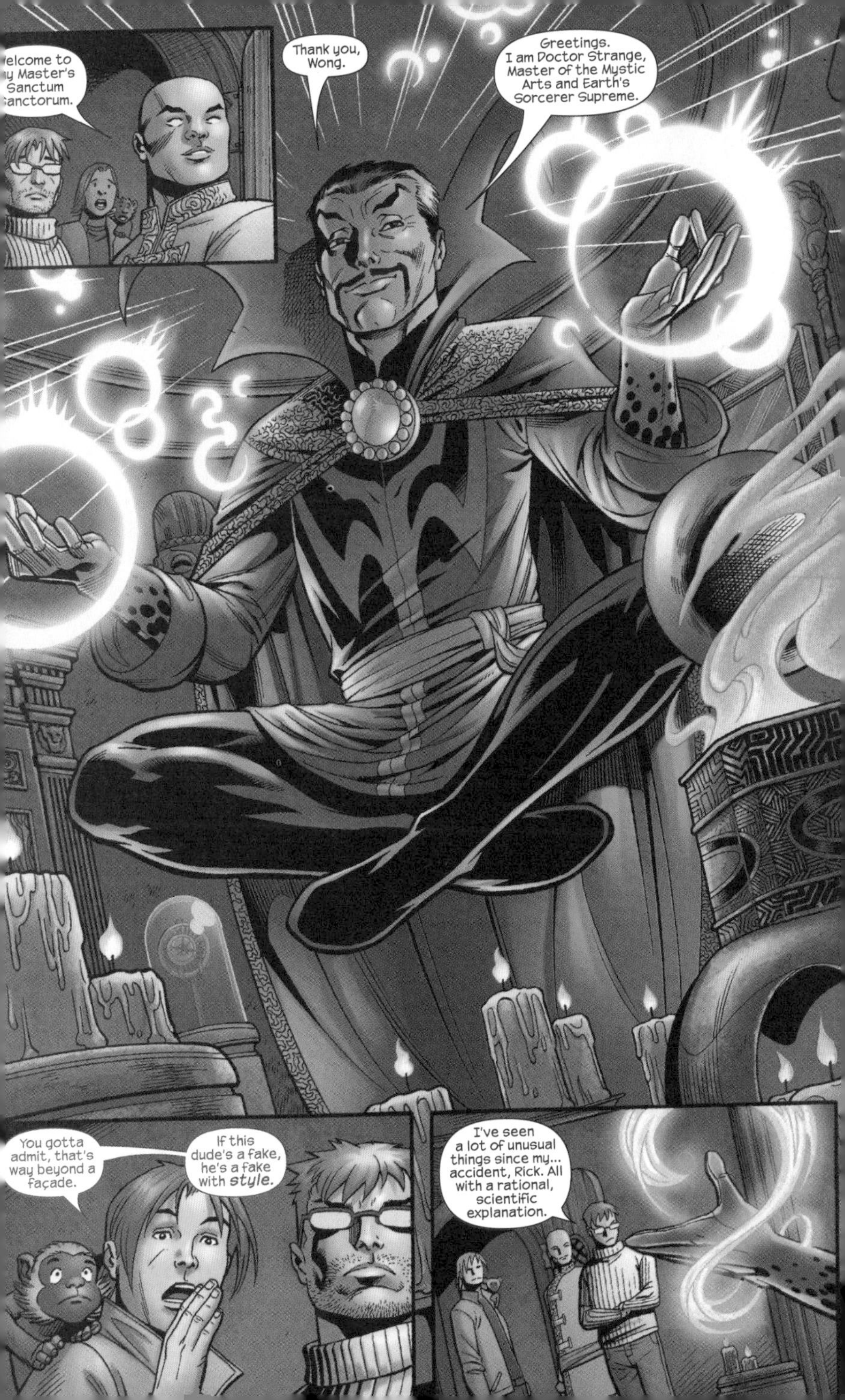
elcome to
y Master's
Sanctum
anctorum.
Thank you,
Wong.
Greetings.
I am Doctor Strange,
Master of the Mystic
Arts and Earth's
Sorcerer Supreme.
You gotta
admit, that's
way beyond a
façade.
If this
dude's a fake,
he's a fake
with *style*.
I've seen
a lot of unusual
things since my...
accident, Rick. All
with a rational,
scientific
explanation.

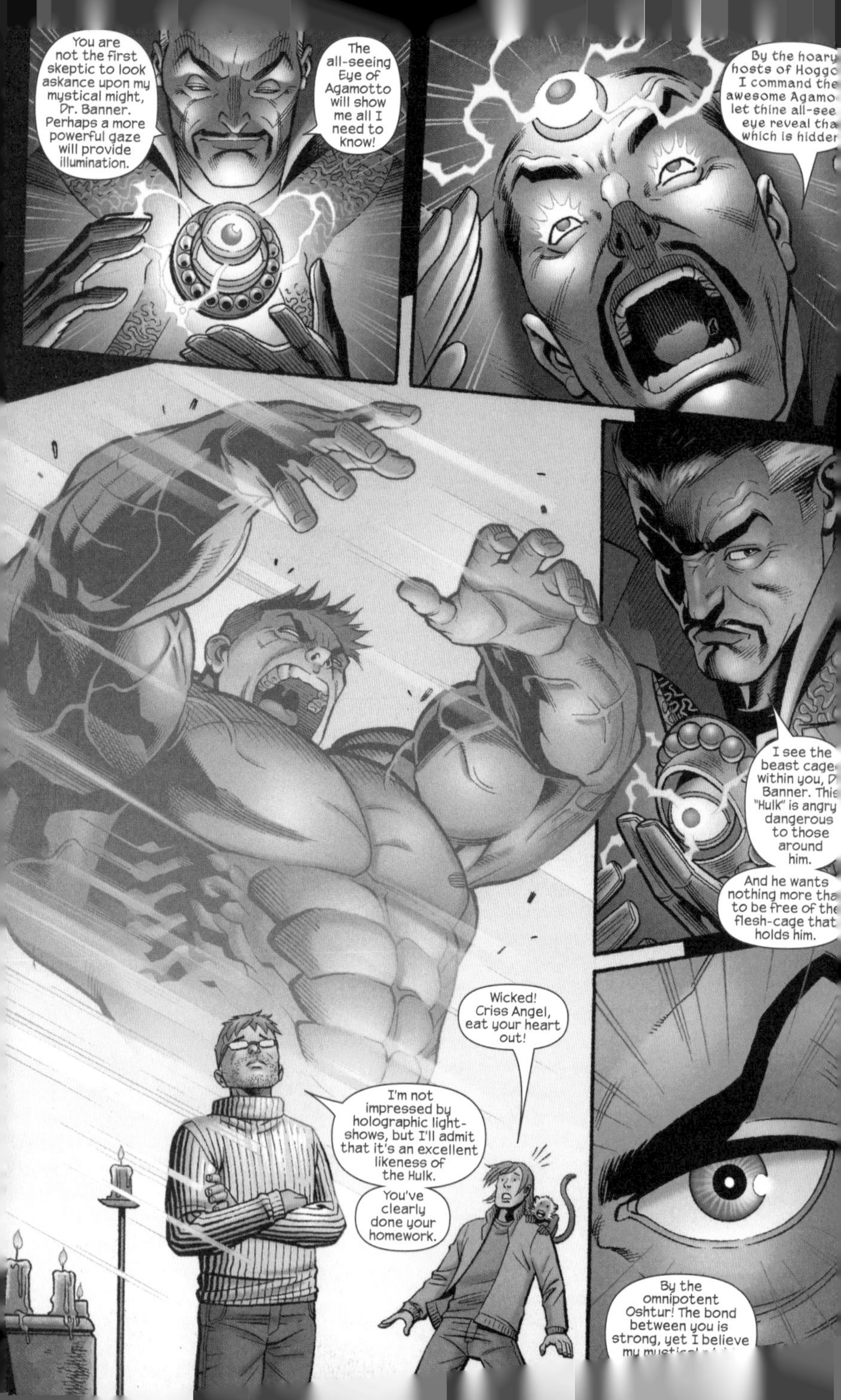
You are not the first skeptic to look askance upon my mystical might, Dr. Banner. Perhaps a more powerful gaze will provide illumination.
The all-seeing Eye of Agamotto will show me all I need to know!
By the hoary hosts of Hoggo I command the awesome Agamo let thine all-see eye reveal tha which is hidder
I see the beast cage within you, D Banner. This "Hulk" is angry dangerous to those around him.
And he wants nothing more tha to be free of the flesh-cage that holds him.
Wicked! Criss Angel, eat your heart out!
I'm not impressed by holographic light-shows, but I'll admit that it's an excellent likeness of the Hulk.
You've clearly done your homework.
By the omnipotent Oshtur! The bond between you is strong, yet I believe

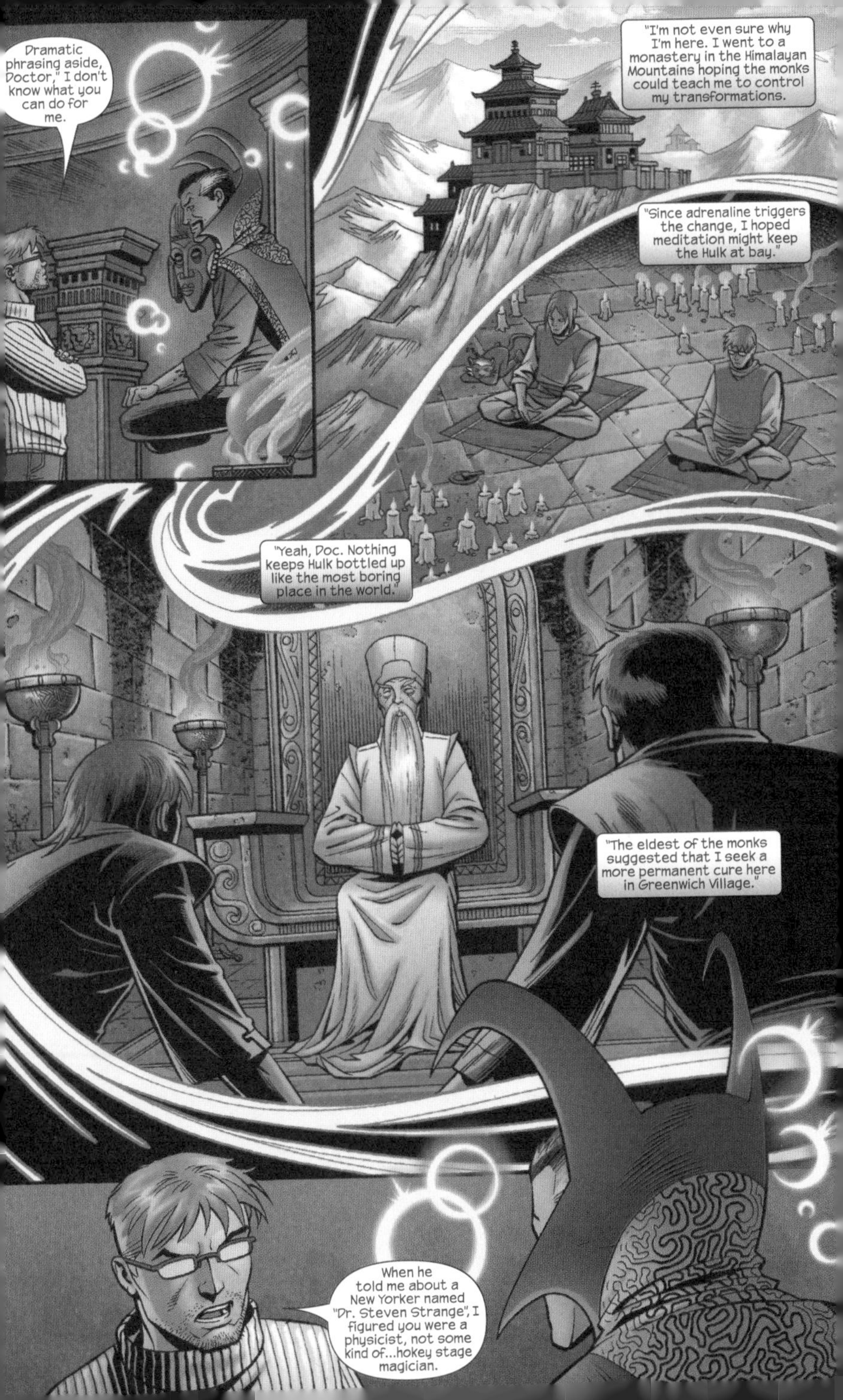
Dramatic phrasing aside, Doctor," I don't know what you can do for me.
"I'm not even sure why I'm here. I went to a monastery in the Himalayan Mountains hoping the monks could teach me to control my transformations.
"Since adrenaline triggers the change, I hoped meditation might keep the Hulk at bay."
"Yeah, Doc. Nothing keeps Hulk bottled up like the most boring place in the world."
"The eldest of the monks suggested that I seek a more permanent cure here in Greenwich Village."
When he told me about a New Yorker named "Dr. Steven Strange", I figured you were a physicist, not some kind of...hokey stage magician.

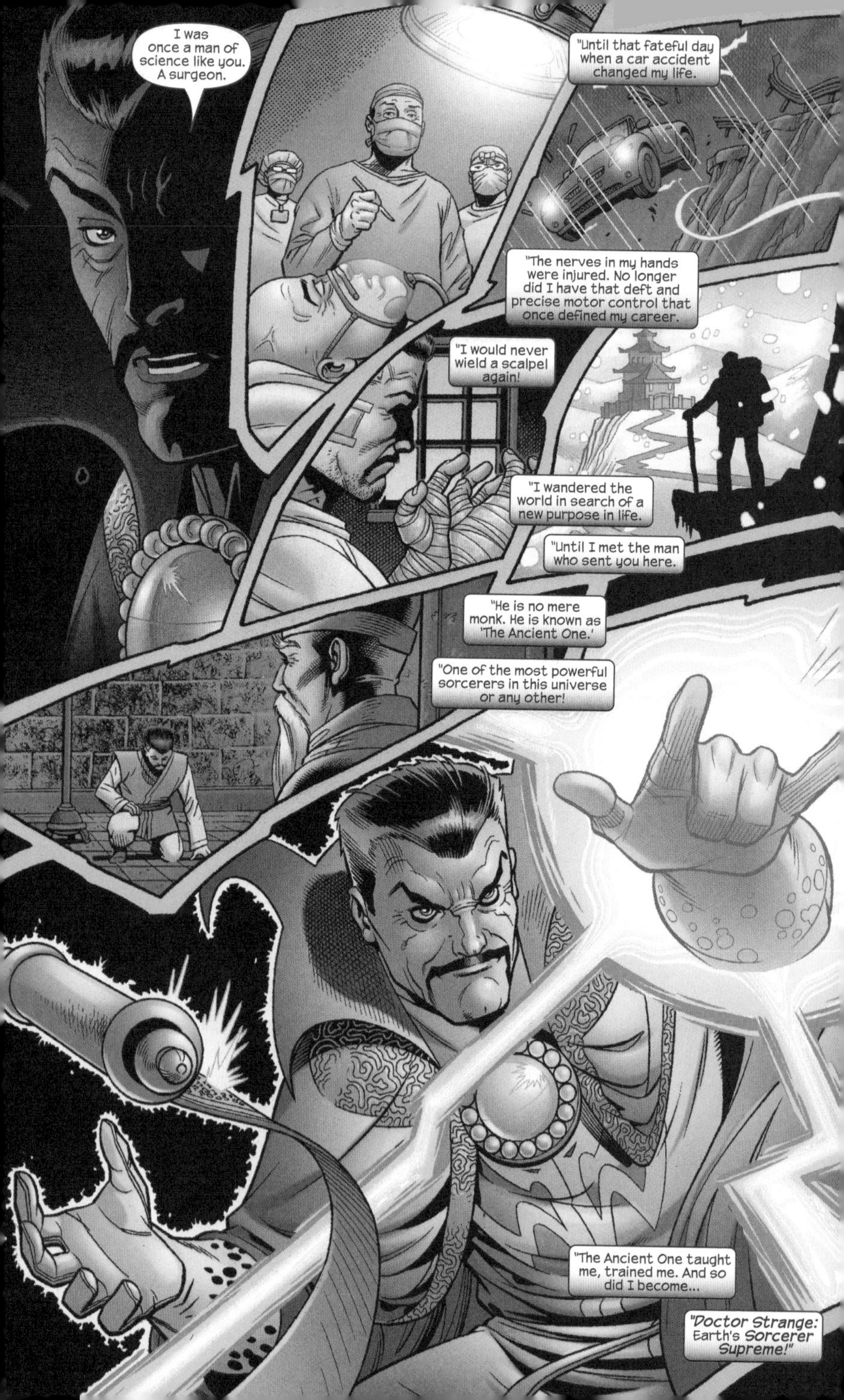
I was once a man of science like you. A surgeon.
"Until that fateful day when a car accident changed my life.
"The nerves in my hands were injured. No longer did I have that deft and precise motor control that once defined my career.
"I would never wield a scalpel again!
"I wandered the world in search of a new purpose in life.
"Until I met the man who sent you here.
"He is no mere monk. He is known as 'The Ancient One.'
"One of the most powerful sorcerers in this universe or any other!
"The Ancient One taught me, trained me. And so did I become...
"Doctor Strange: Earth's Sorcerer Supreme!"

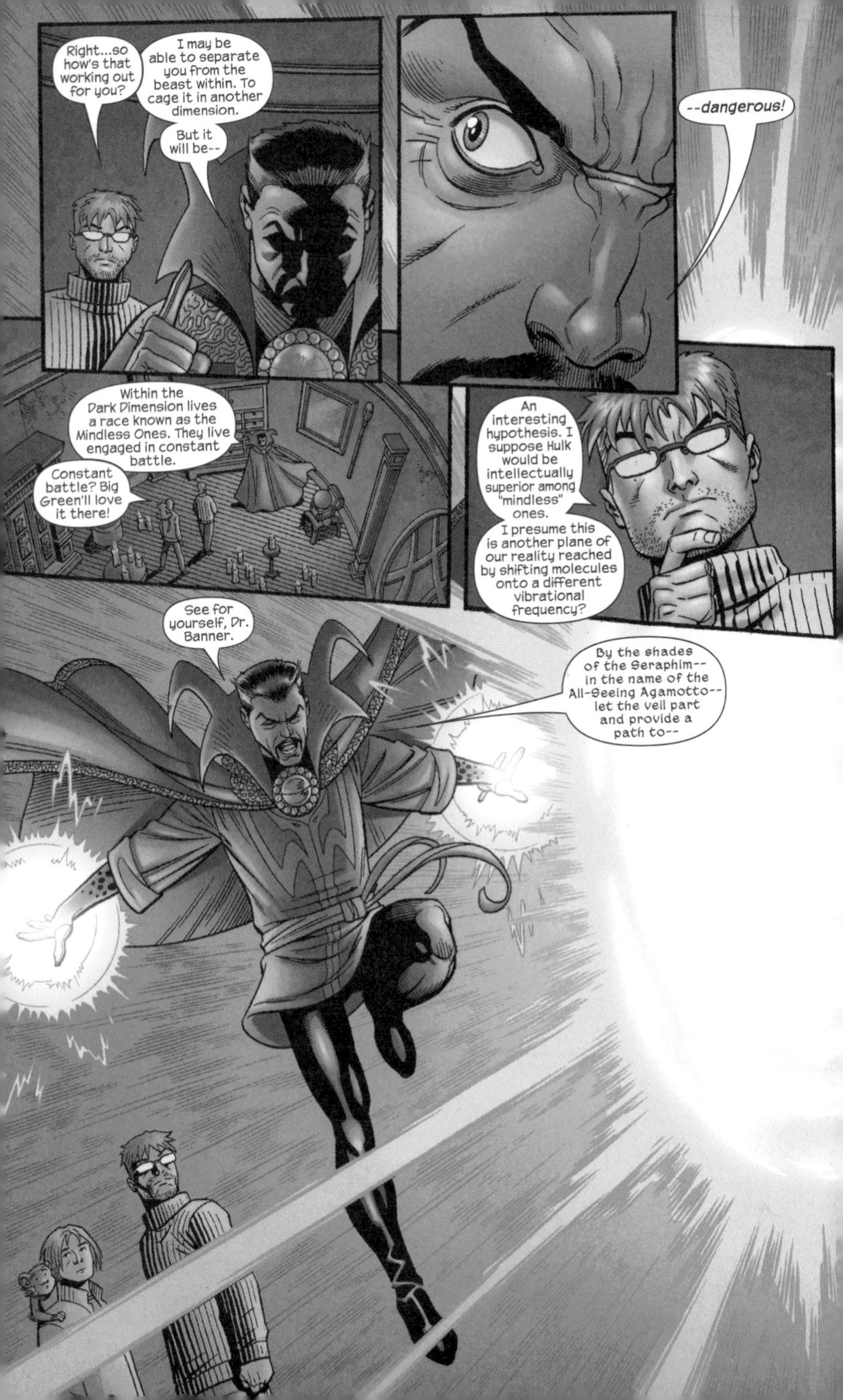
Right...so how's that working out for you?
I may be able to separate you from the beast within. To cage it in another dimension.
But it will be--
--dangerous!
Within the Dark Dimension lives a race known as the Mindless Ones. They live engaged in constant battle.
Constant battle? Big Green'll love it there!
An interesting hypothesis. I suppose Hulk would be intellectually superior among "mindless" ones.
I presume this is another plane of our reality reached by shifting molecules onto a different vibrational frequency?
See for yourself, Dr. Banner.
By the shades of the Seraphim-- in the name of the All-Seeing Agamotto-- let the veil part and provide a path to--

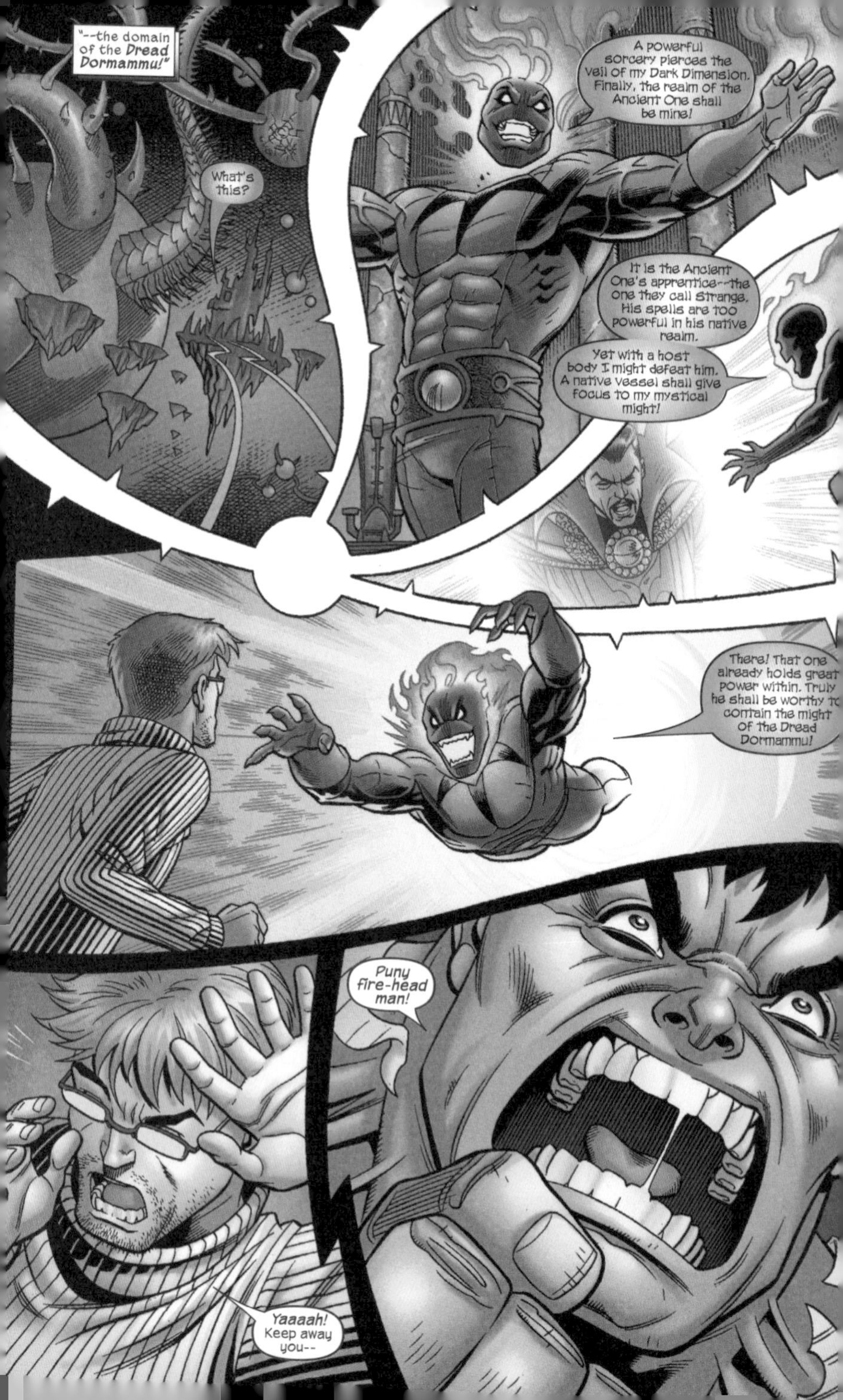
"--the domain of the Dread Dormammu!"
What's this?
A powerful sorcery pierces the veil of my Dark Dimension. Finally, the realm of the Ancient One shall be mine!
It is the Ancient One's apprentice--the one they call Strange. His spells are too powerful in his native realm.
Yet with a host body I might defeat him. A native vessel shall give focus to my mystical might!
There! That one already holds great power within. Truly he shall be worthy to contain the might of the Dread Dormammu!
Puny fire-head man!
Yaaaah! Keep away you--

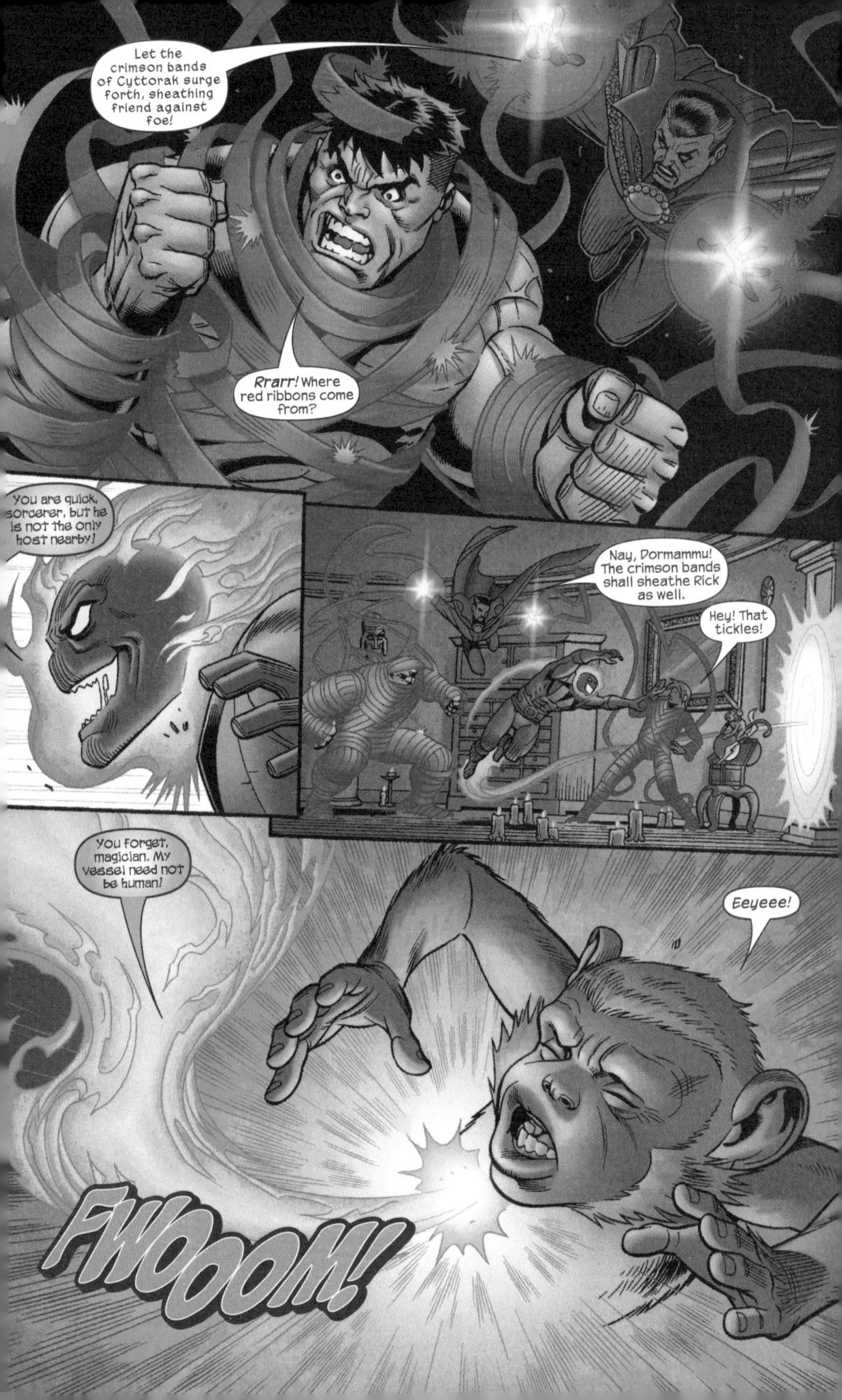

Let the crimson bands of Cyttorak surge forth, sheathing friend against foe!
Rrarr! Where red ribbons come from?
You are quick, sorcerer, but he is not the only host nearby!
Nay, Dormammu! The crimson bands shall sheathe Rick as well.
Hey! That tickles!
You forget, magician. My vessel need not be human!
Eeyeee!
FWOOOM!

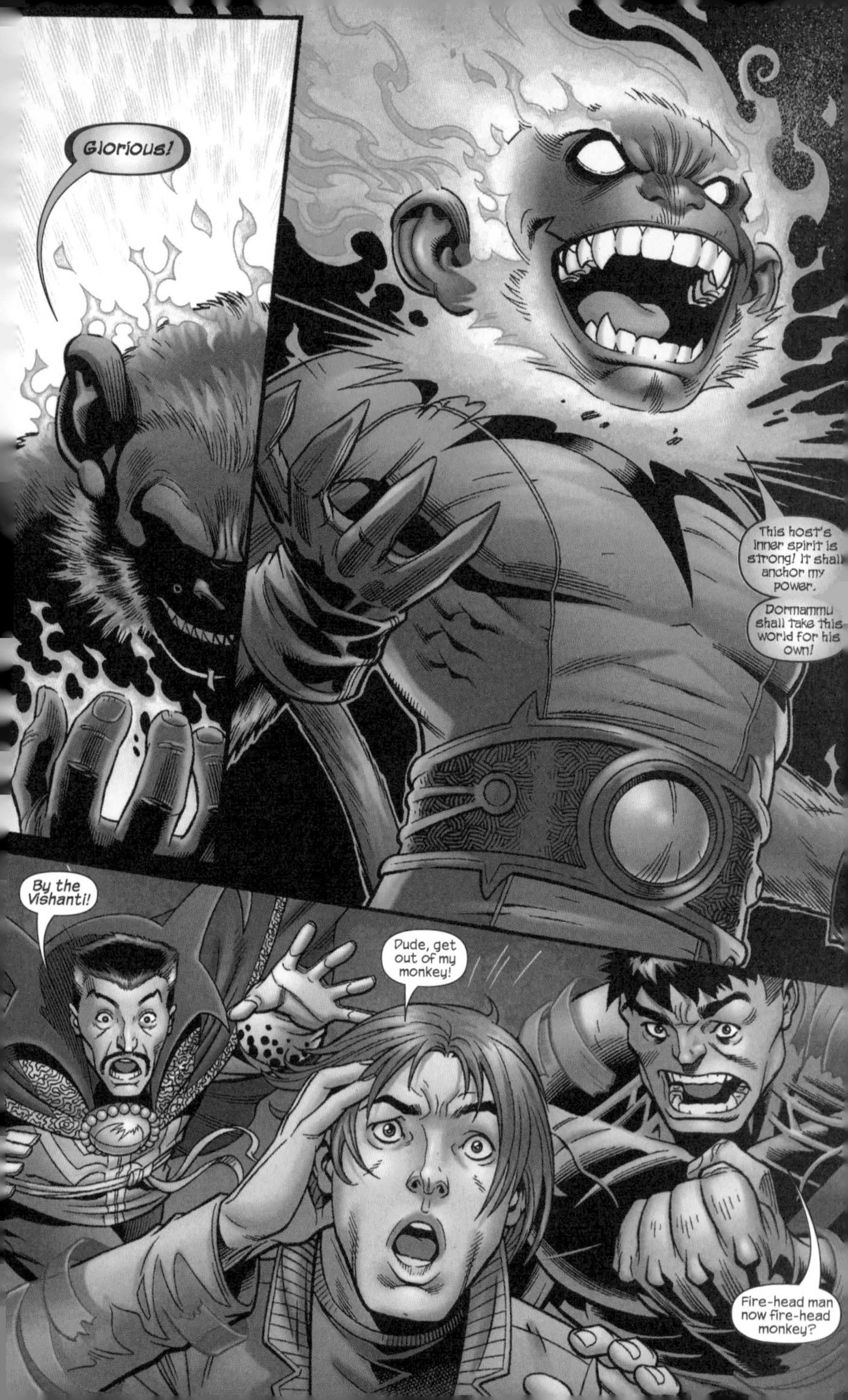
Glorious!
This host's inner spirit is strong! It shall anchor my power.
Dormammu shall take this world for his own!
By the Vishanti!
Dude, get out of my monkey!
Fire-head man now fire-head monkey?

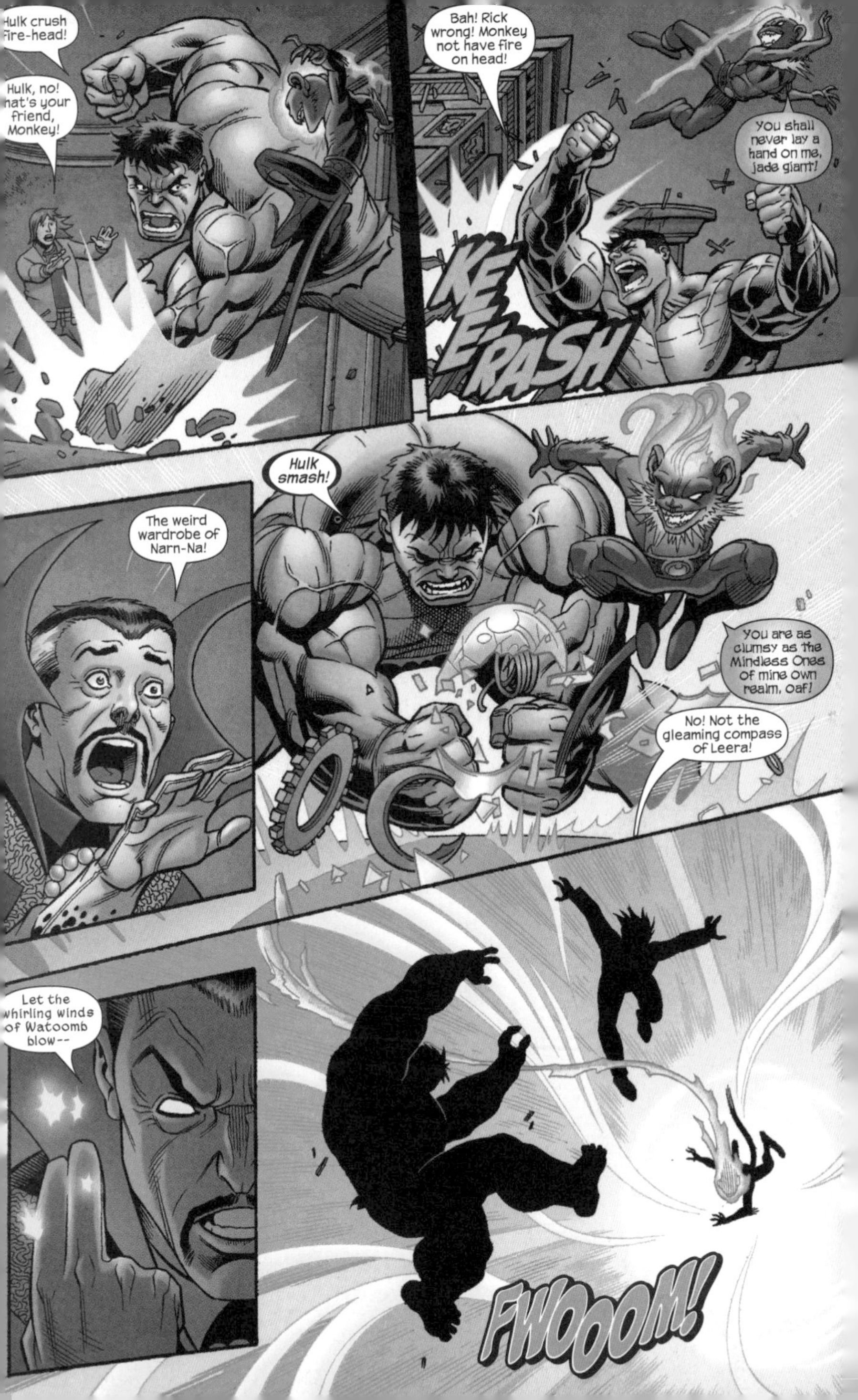

Hulk crush Fire-head!
Hulk, no! hat's your friend, Monkey!
Bah! Rick wrong! Monkey not have fire on head!
You shall never lay a hand on me, jade giant!
KE-E-RASH
Hulk smash!
The weird wardrobe of Narn-Na!
You are as clumsy as the Mindless Ones of mine own realm, oaf!
No! Not the gleaming compass of Leera!
Let the whirling winds of Watoomb blow--
FWOOOM!

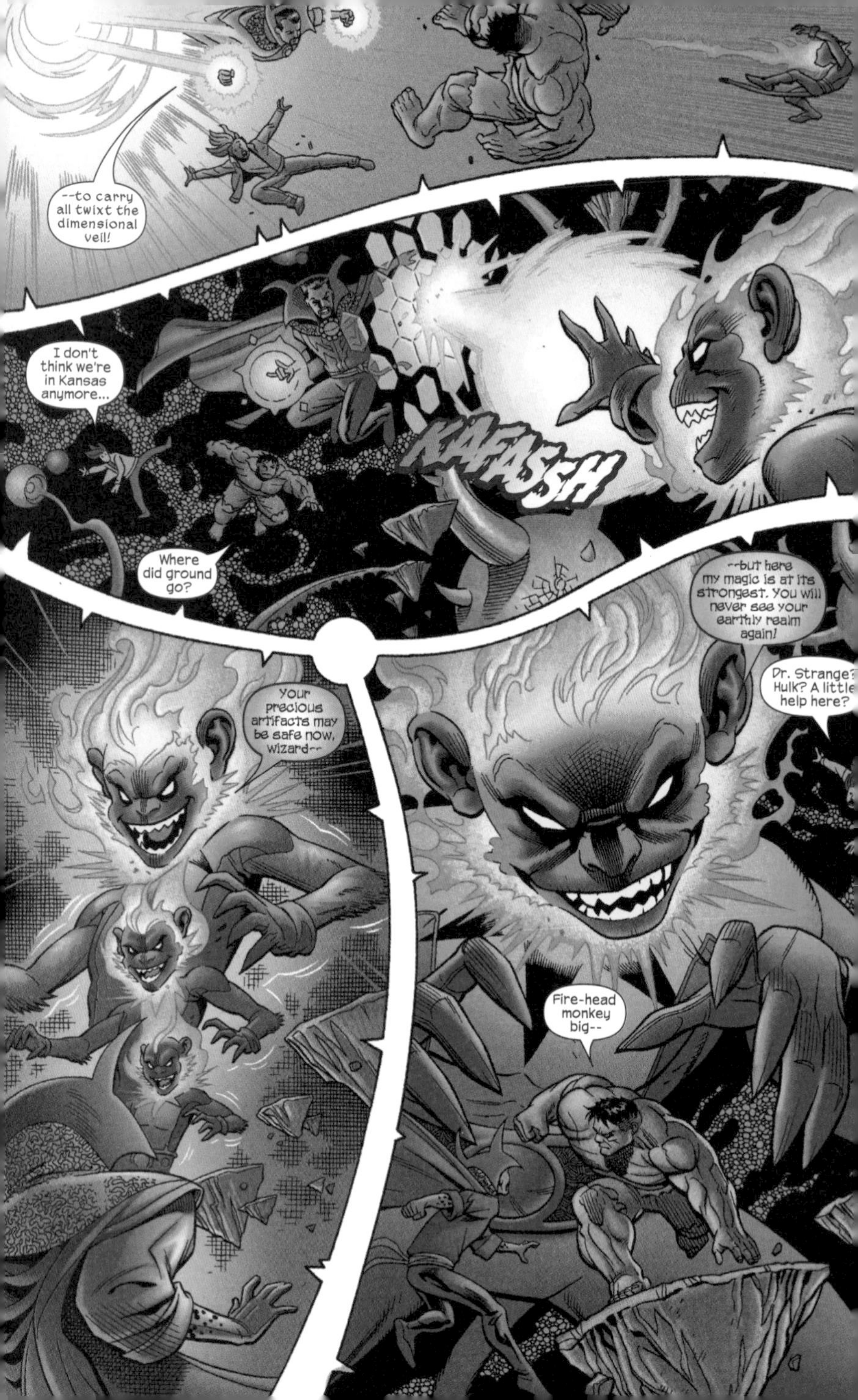
--to carry all twixt the dimensional veil!
I don't think we're in Kansas anymore...
KAFASH
Where did ground go?
Your precious artifacts may be safe now, wizard--
--but here my magic is at its strongest. You will never see your earthly realm again!
Dr. Strange? Hulk? A little help here?
Fire-head monkey big--

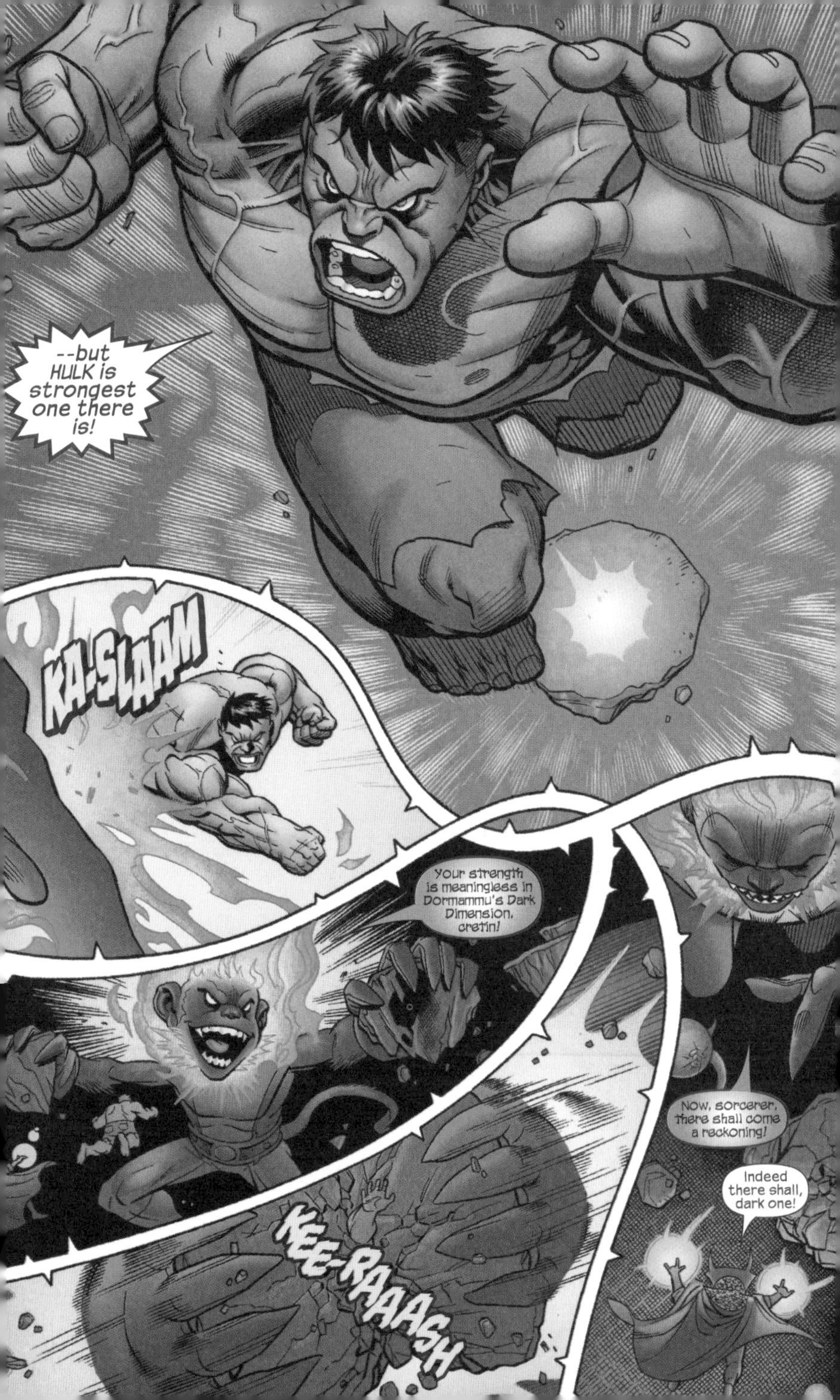
--but HULK is strongest one there is!
KA-SLAAM
Your strength is meaningless in Dormammu's Dark Dimension, cretin!
KEE-RAAASH
Now, sorcerer, there shall come a reckoning!
Indeed there shall, dark one!

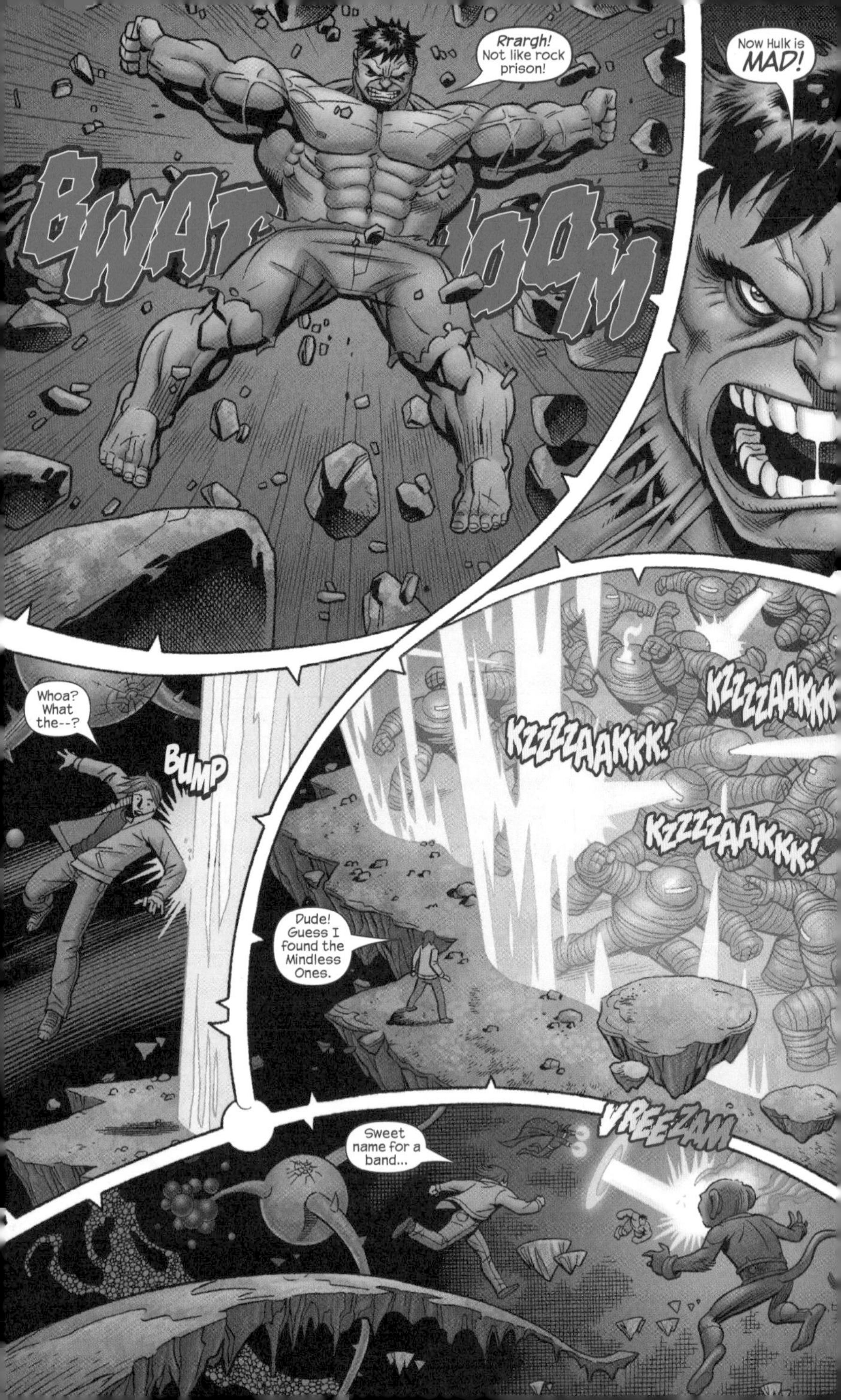

Rrargh! Not like rock prison!
Now Hulk is MAD!
Whoa? What the--?
BUMP
KZZZZAAKKK!
KZZZZAAKKK!
KZZZZAAKKK!
Dude! Guess I found the Mindless Ones.
VREEZAM
Sweet name for a band...

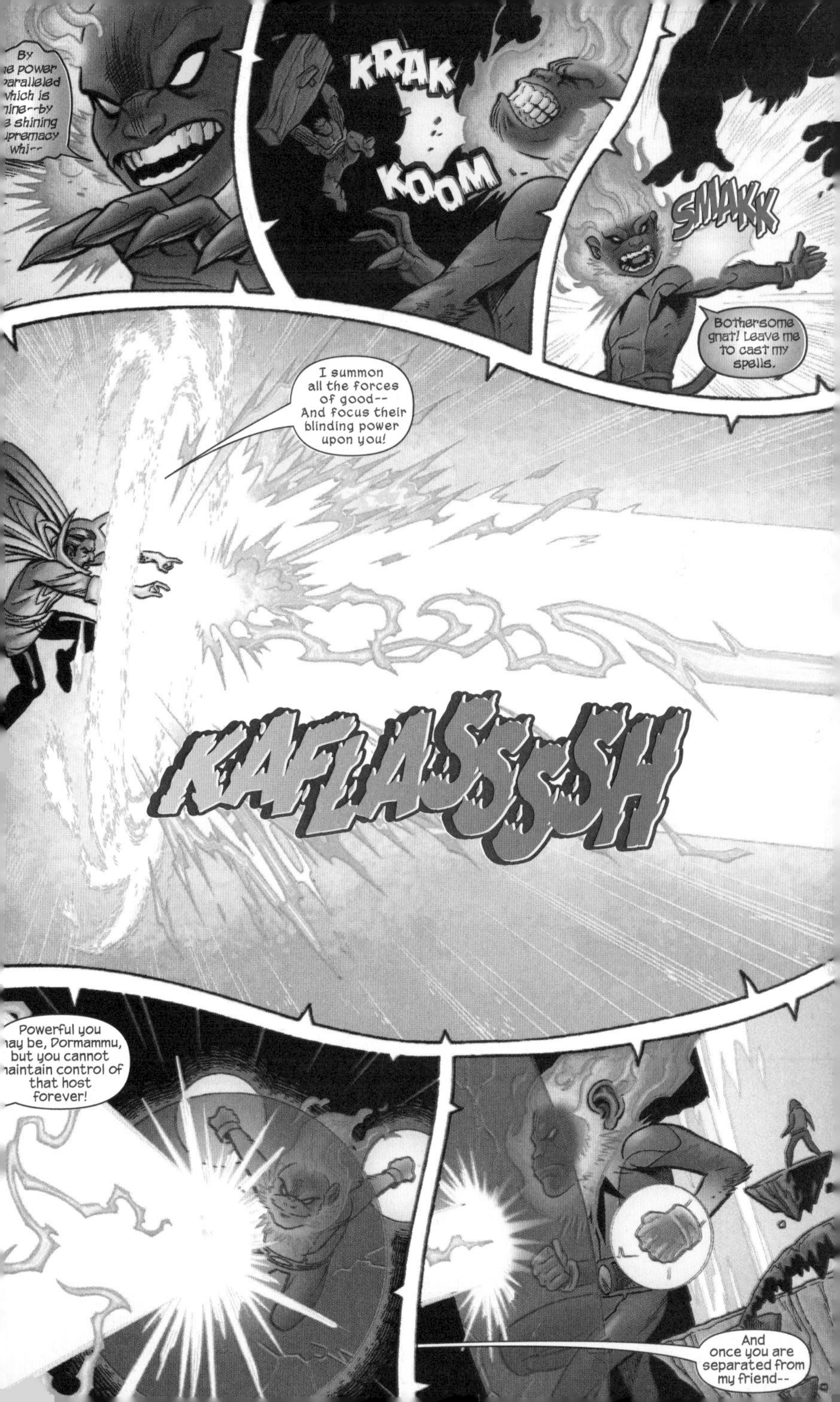
By
e power
arallelled
which is
ine--by
e shining
upremacy
whi--
KRAK
KOOM
SMAKK
Bothersome gnat! Leave me to cast my spells.
I summon all the forces of good-- And focus their blinding power upon you!
KAFLASSSH
Powerful you ay be, Dormammu, but you cannot aintain control of that host forever!
And once you are separated from my friend--

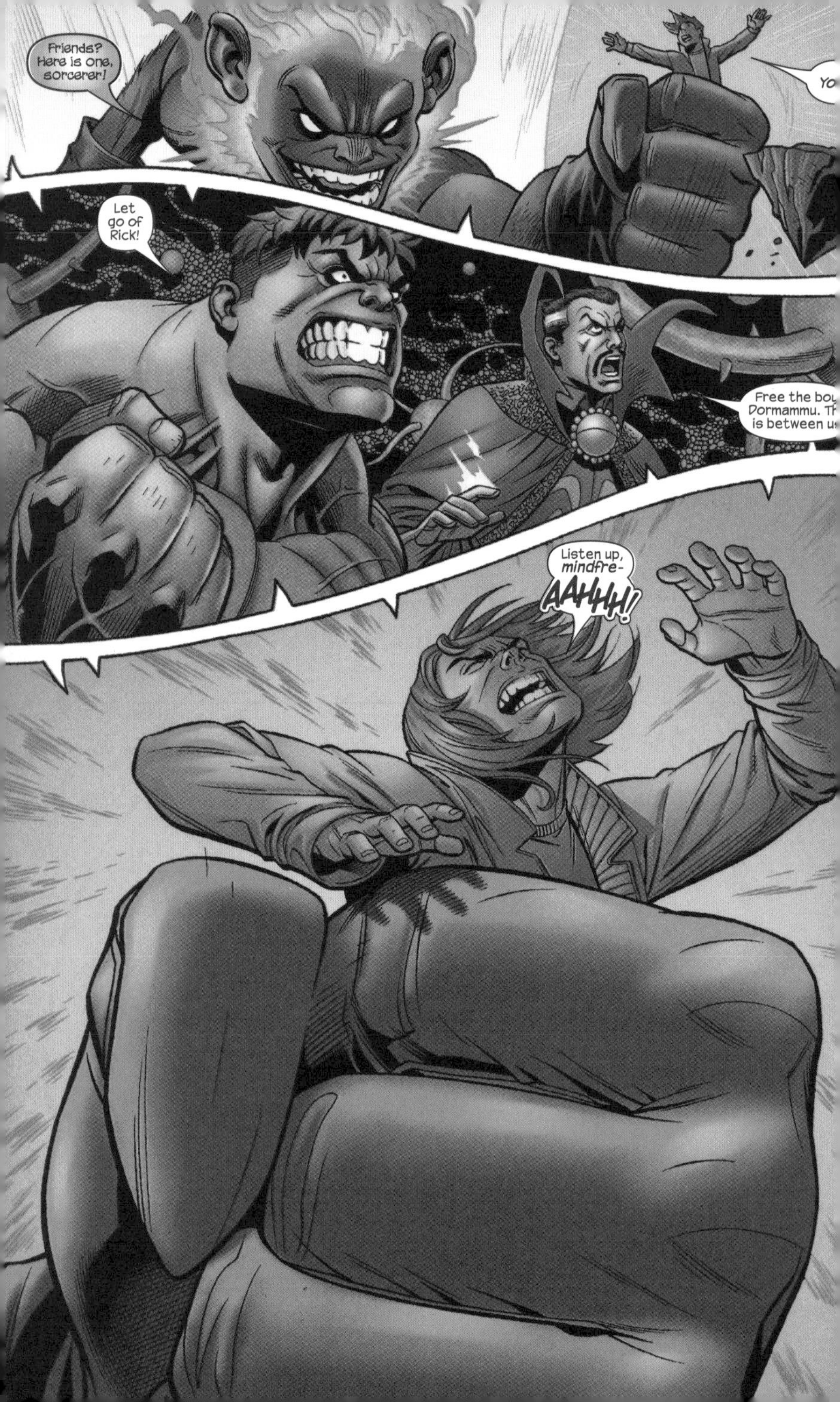

Friends? Here is one, sorcerer!
Yo
Let go of Rick!
Free the bo Dormammu. T is between u
Listen up, mindfre-
AAHHH!

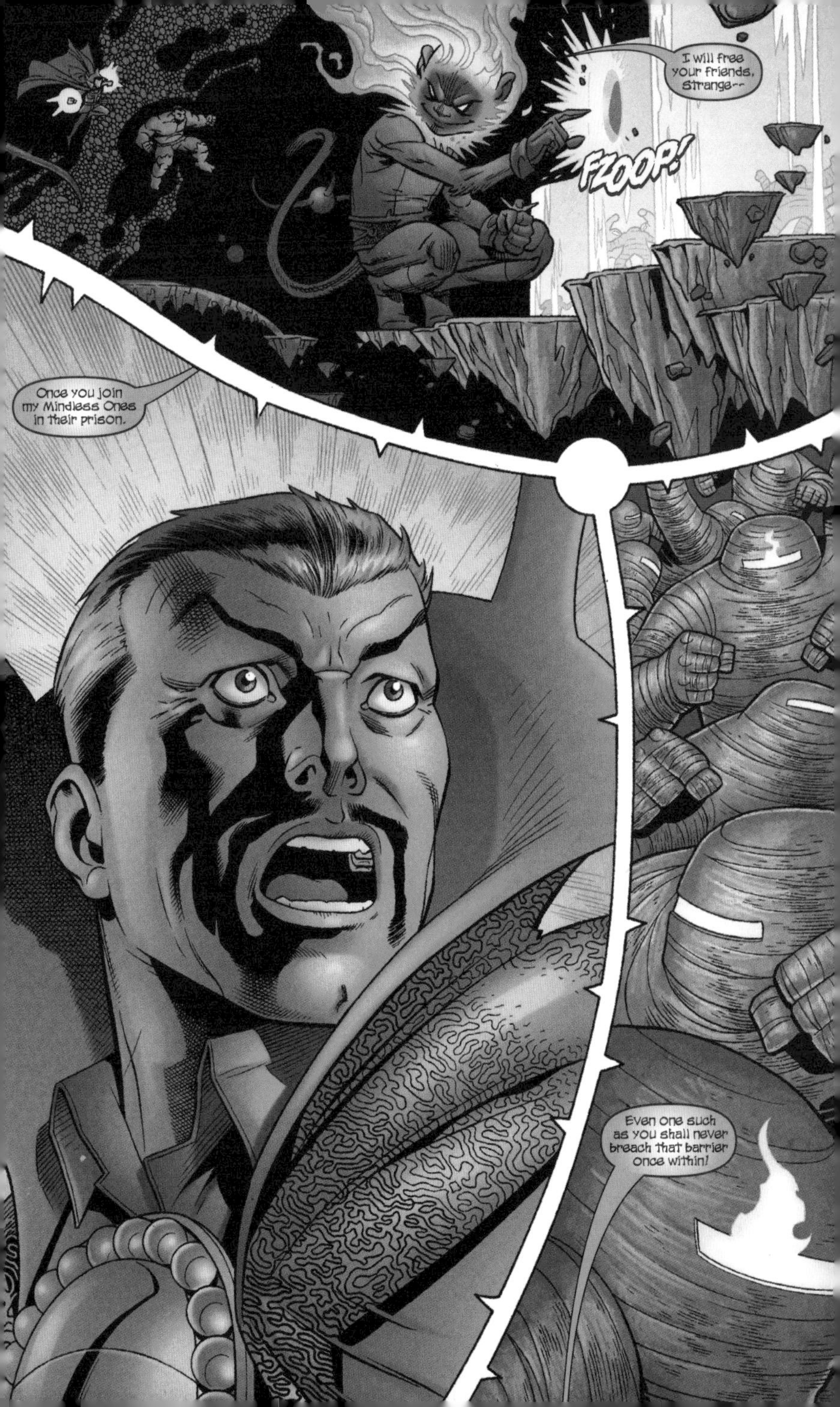
I will free your friends, Strange--
FZOOP!
Once you join my Mindless Ones in their prison.
Even one such as you shall never breach that barrier once within!

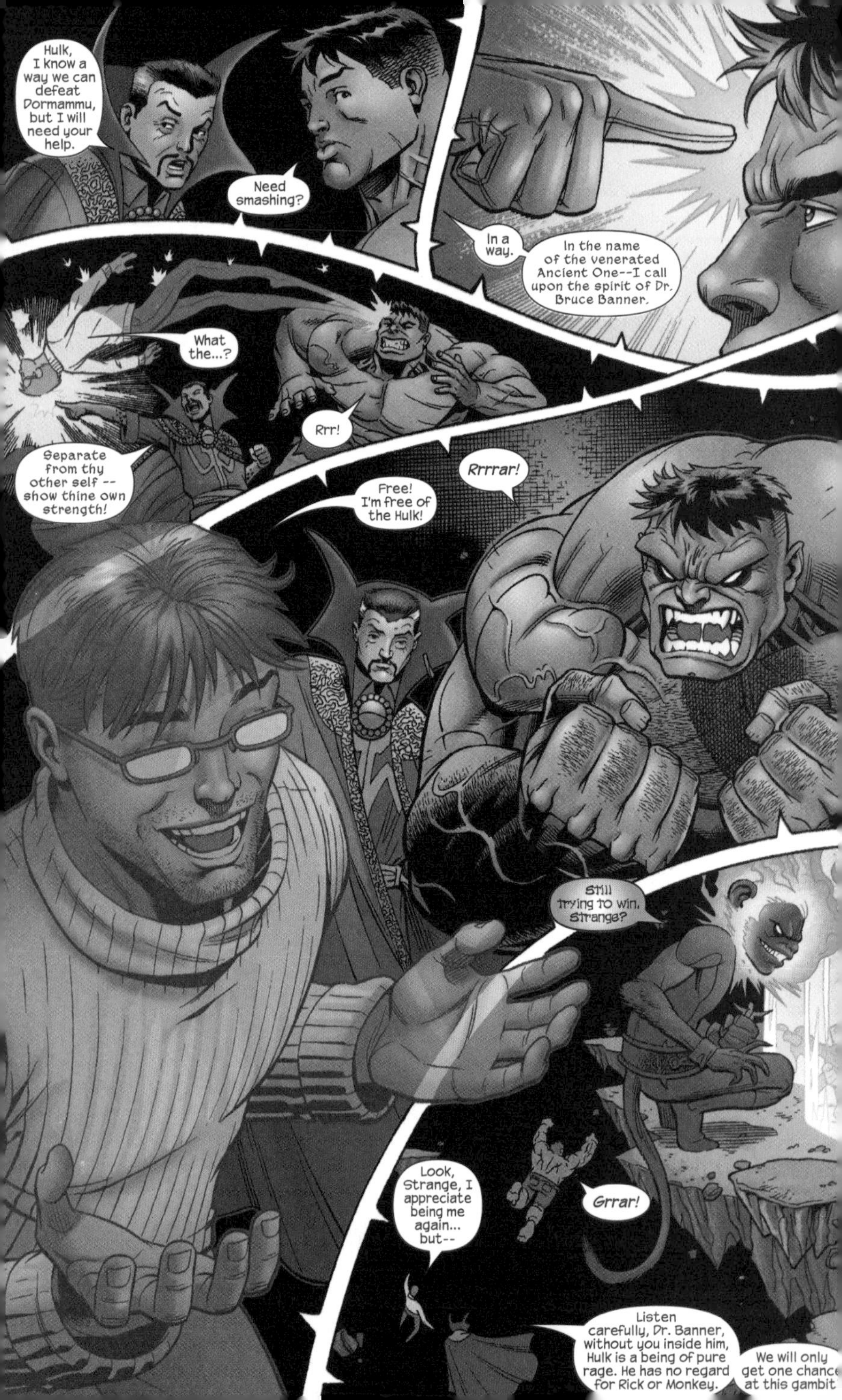
Hulk, I know a way we can defeat Dormammu, but I will need your help.
Need smashing?
In a way.
In the name of the venerated Ancient One--I call upon the spirit of Dr. Bruce Banner.
What the...?
Rrr!
Separate from thy other self -- show thine own strength!
Rrrrar!
Free! I'm free of the Hulk!
Still trying to win, Strange?
Look, Strange, I appreciate being me again... but--
Grrar!
Listen carefully, Dr. Banner, without you inside him, Hulk is a being of pure rage. He has no regard for Rick or Monkey.
We will only get one chanc at this gambit

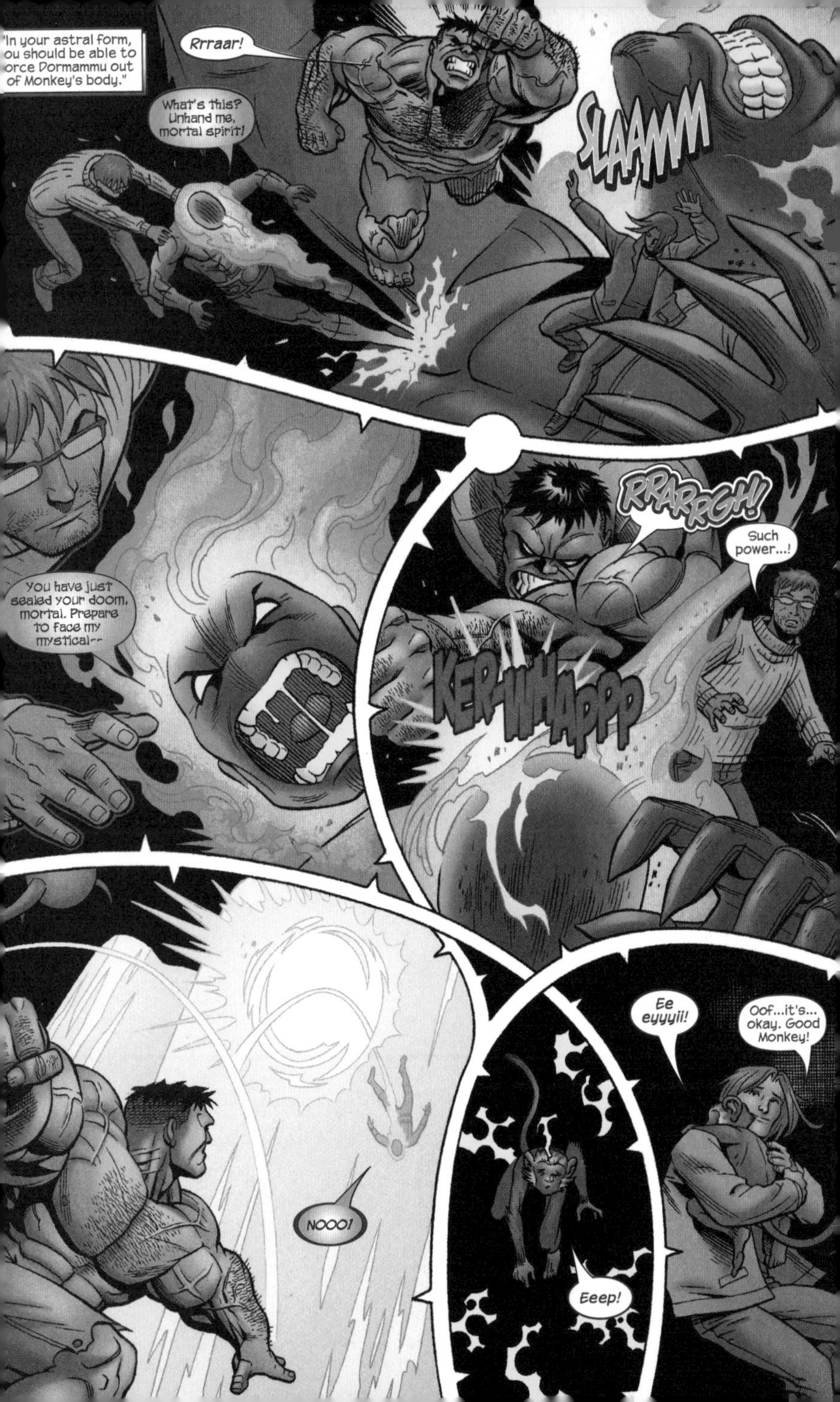
"In your astral form, ou should be able to orce Dormammu out of Monkey's body."
Rrraar!
What's this? Unhand me, mortal spirit!
SLAAMM
RRARRGH!!
Such power...!
You have just sealed your doom, mortal. Prepare to face my mystical--
KER-WHAPPP
NOOO!
Ee eyyyii!
Oof...it's... okay. Good Monkey!
Eeep!

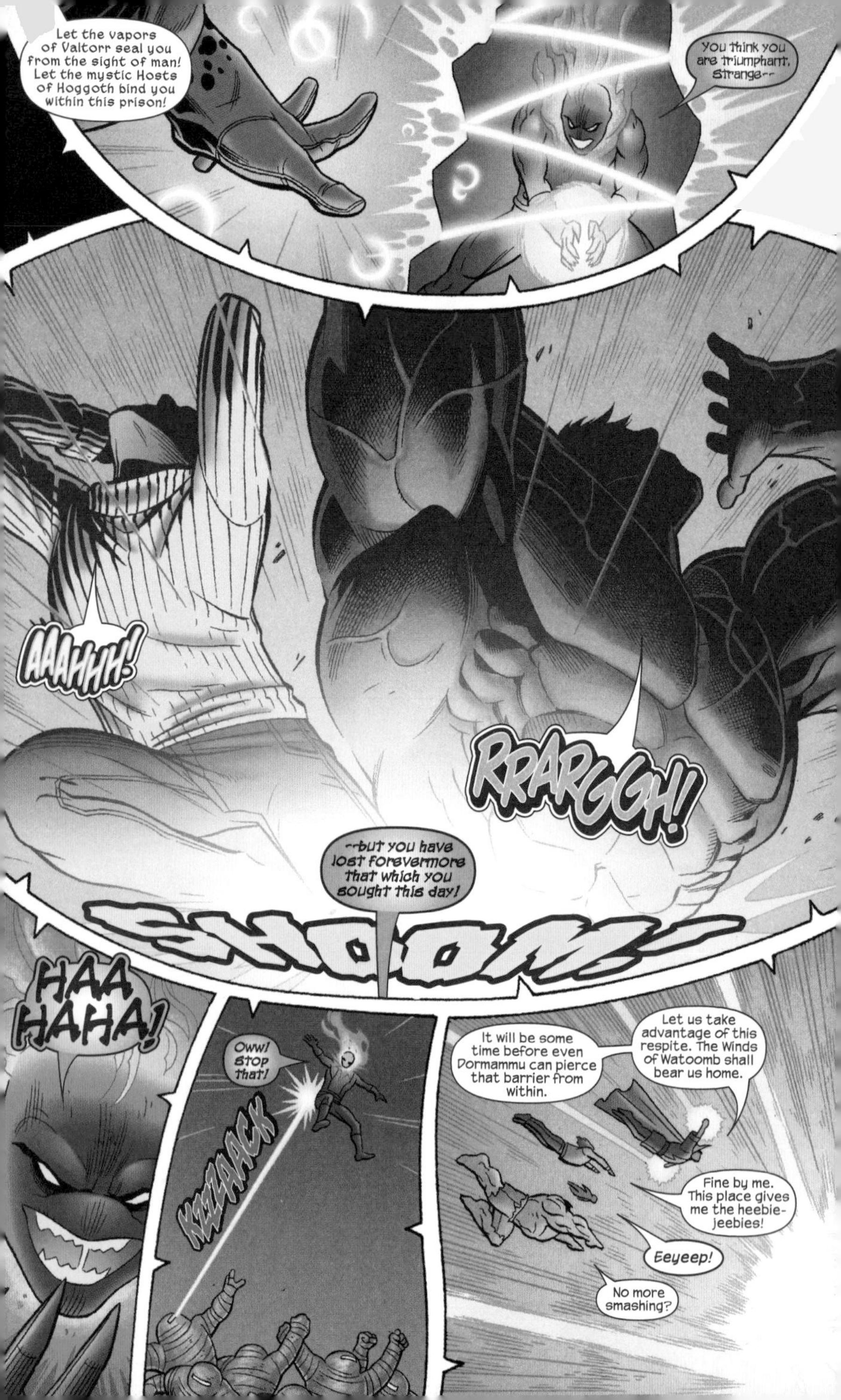

Let the vapors of Valtorr seal you from the sight of man! Let the mystic Hosts of Hoggoth bind you within this prison!
You think you are triumphant, Strange--
AAAHHH!
RRARGGH!
--but you have lost forevermore that which you sought this day!
SHOOM!
HAA HAHA!
Oww! Stop that!
KZZAACK
It will be some time before even Dormammu can pierce that barrier from within.
Let us take advantage of this respite. The Winds of Watoomb shall bear us home.
Fine by me. This place gives me the heebie-jeebies!
Eeyeep!
No more smashing?

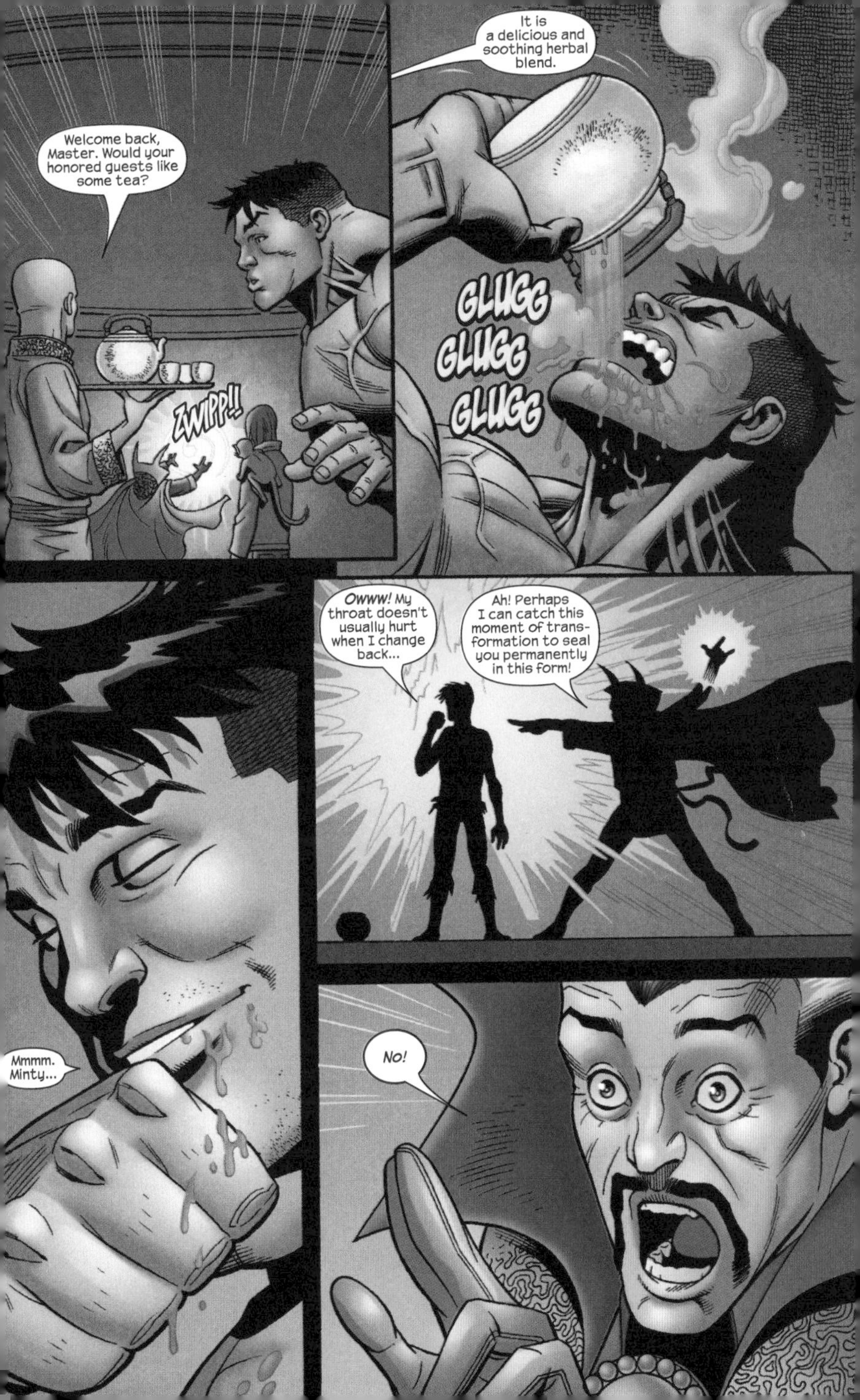
Welcome back, Master. Would your honored guests like some tea?
ZWIPP!!
It is a delicious and soothing herbal blend.
GLUGG
GLUGG
GLUGG
Mmmm. Minty...
Owww! My throat doesn't usually hurt when I change back...
Ah! Perhaps I can catch this moment of transformation to seal you permanently in this form!
No!

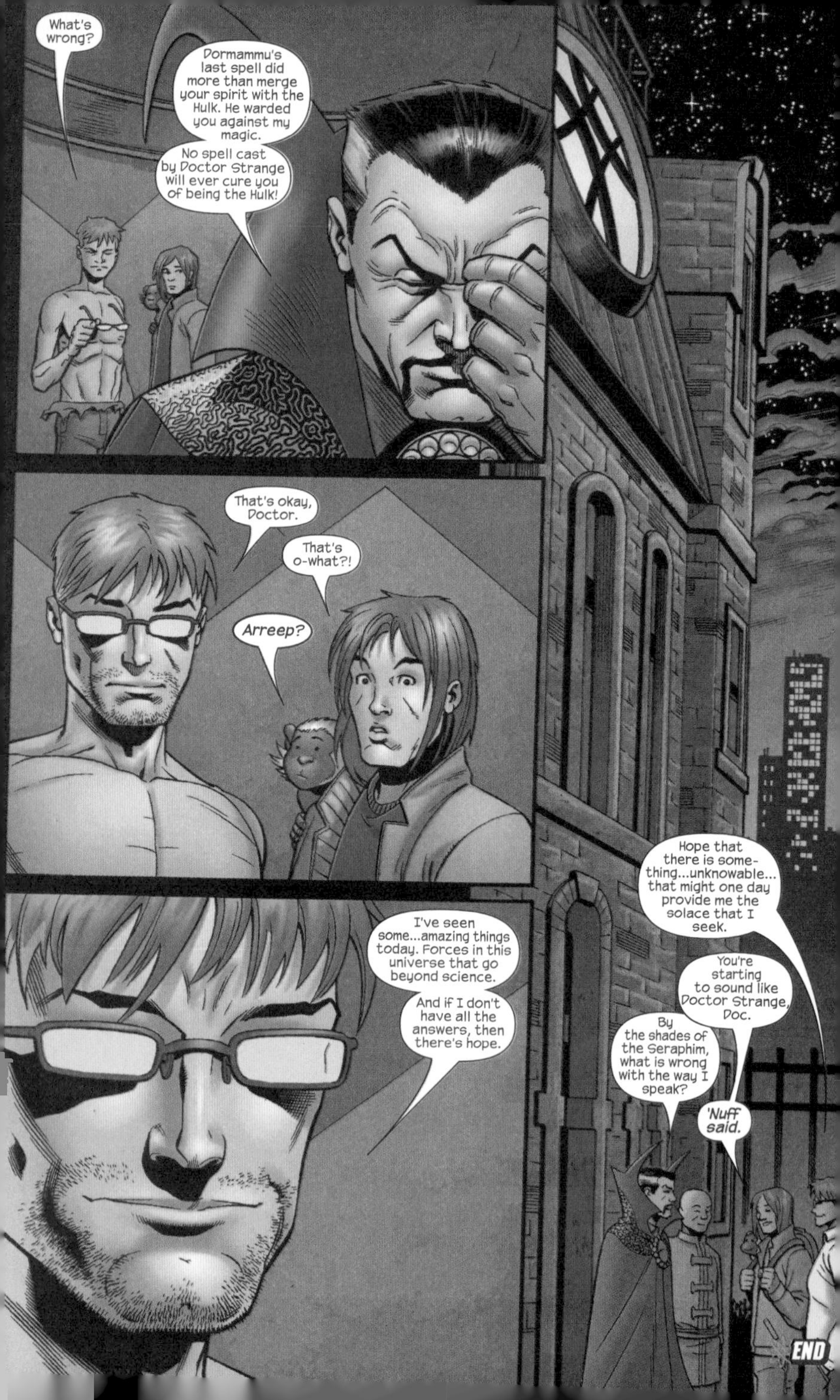

What's wrong?
Dormammu's last spell did more than merge your spirit with the Hulk. He warded you against my magic.
No spell cast by Doctor Strange will ever cure you of being the Hulk!
That's okay, Doctor.
That's o-what?!
Arreep?
I've seen some...amazing things today. Forces in this universe that go beyond science.
And if I don't have all the answers, then there's hope.
Hope that there is some-thing...unknowable... that might one day provide me the solace that I seek.
You're starting to sound like Doctor Strange, Doc.
By the shades of the Seraphim, what is wrong with the way I speak?
'Nuff said.
END

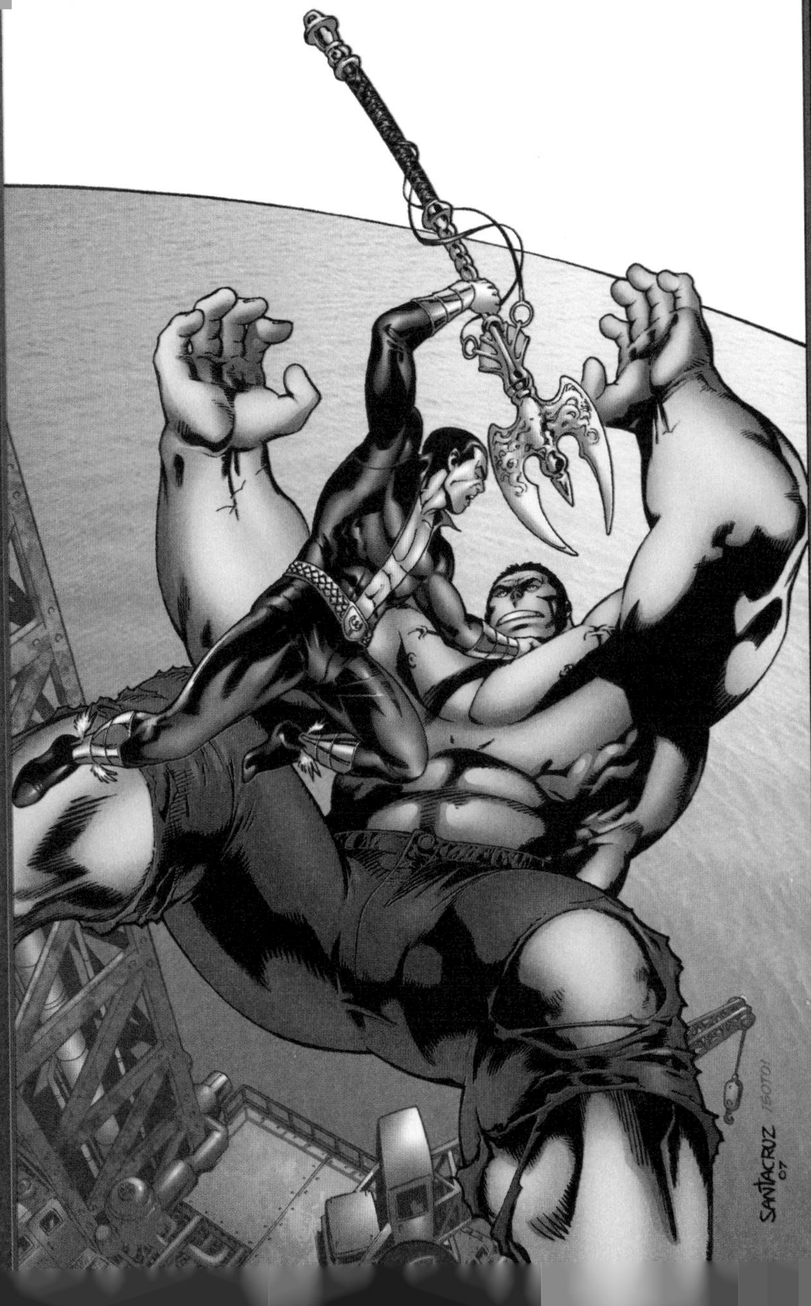
SANTACRUZ
07

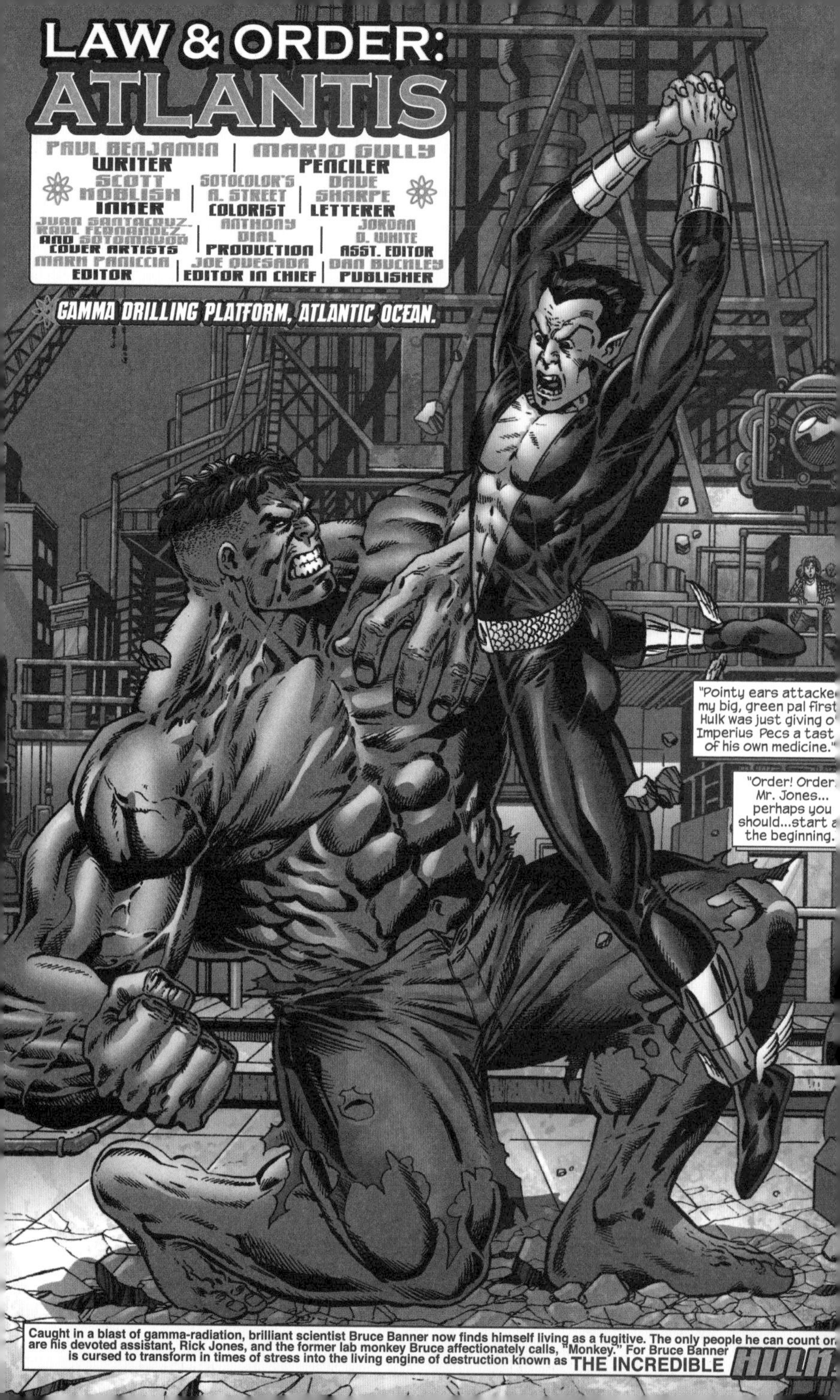

LAW & ORDER:
ATLANTIS
PAUL BENJAMIN WRITER
MARIO GULLY PENCILER
SCOTT KOBLISH INKER
SOTOCOLOR'S A. STREET COLORIST
DAVE SHARPE LETTERER
JUAN SANTACRUZ, RAUL FERNANDEZ, AND SOTOMAYOR COVER ARTISTS
ANTHONY DIAL PRODUCTION
JORDAN D. WHITE ASST. EDITOR
MARK PANICCIA EDITOR
JOE QUESADA EDITOR IN CHIEF
DAN BUCKLEY PUBLISHER
GAMMA DRILLING PLATFORM, ATLANTIC OCEAN.
"Pointy ears attacke my big, green pal first Hulk was just giving o' Imperius Pecs a tast of his own medicine."
"Order! Order Mr. Jones... perhaps you should...start a the beginning.
Caught in a blast of gamma-radiation, brilliant scientist Bruce Banner now finds himself living as a fugitive. The only people he can count or are his devoted assistant, Rick Jones, and the former lab monkey Bruce affectionately calls, "Monkey." For Bruce Banner is cursed to transform in times of stress into the living engine of destruction known as THE INCREDIBLE HULK

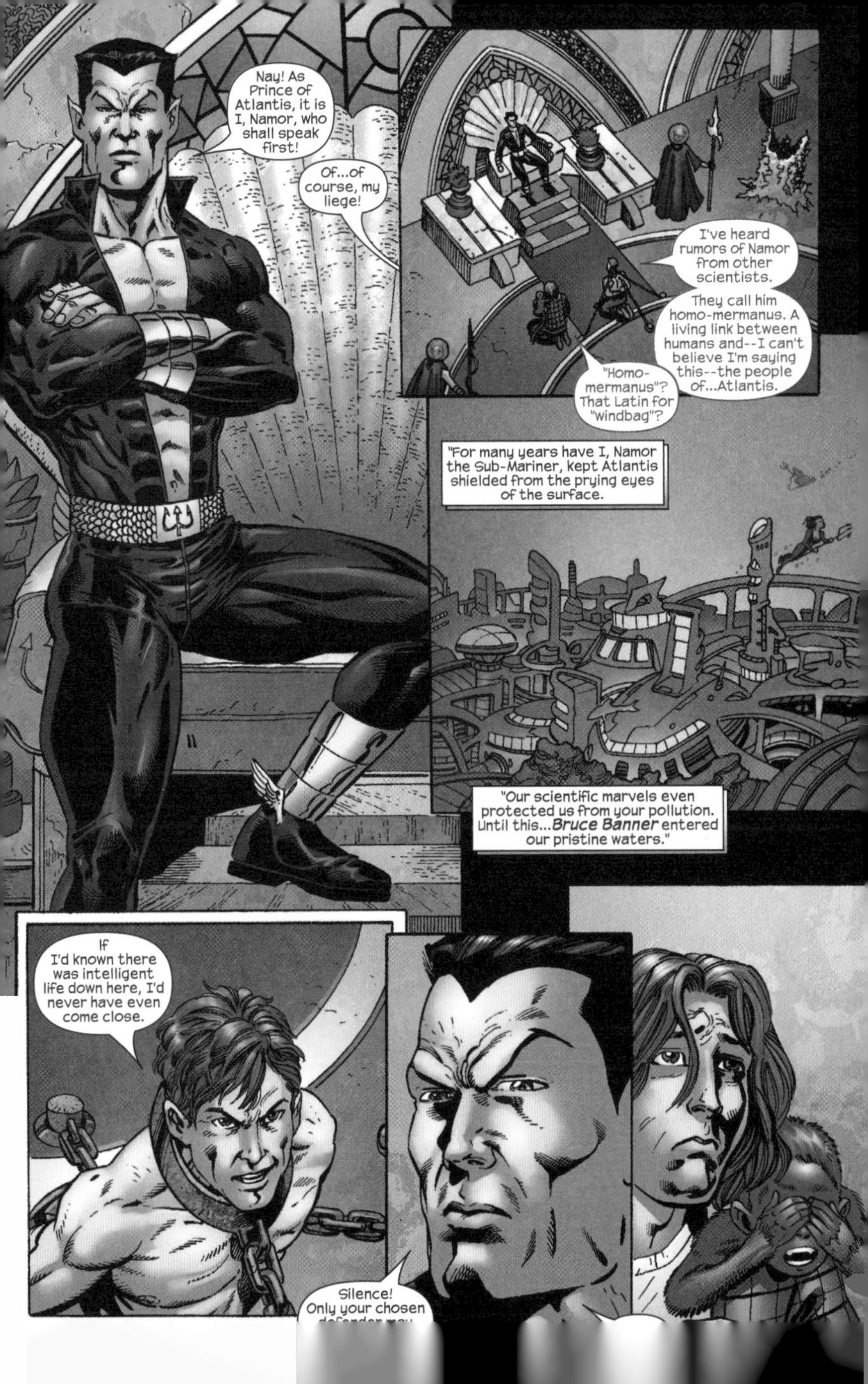

Nay! As Prince of Atlantis, it is I, Namor, who shall speak first!
Of...of course, my liege!
I've heard rumors of Namor from other scientists.
They call him homo-mermanus. A living link between humans and--I can't believe I'm saying this--the people of...Atlantis.
"Homo-mermanus"? That Latin for "windbag"?
"For many years have I, Namor the Sub-Mariner, kept Atlantis shielded from the prying eyes of the surface.
"Our scientific marvels even protected us from your pollution. Until this...Bruce Banner entered our pristine waters."
If I'd known there was intelligent life down here, I'd never have even come close.
Silence! Only your chosen

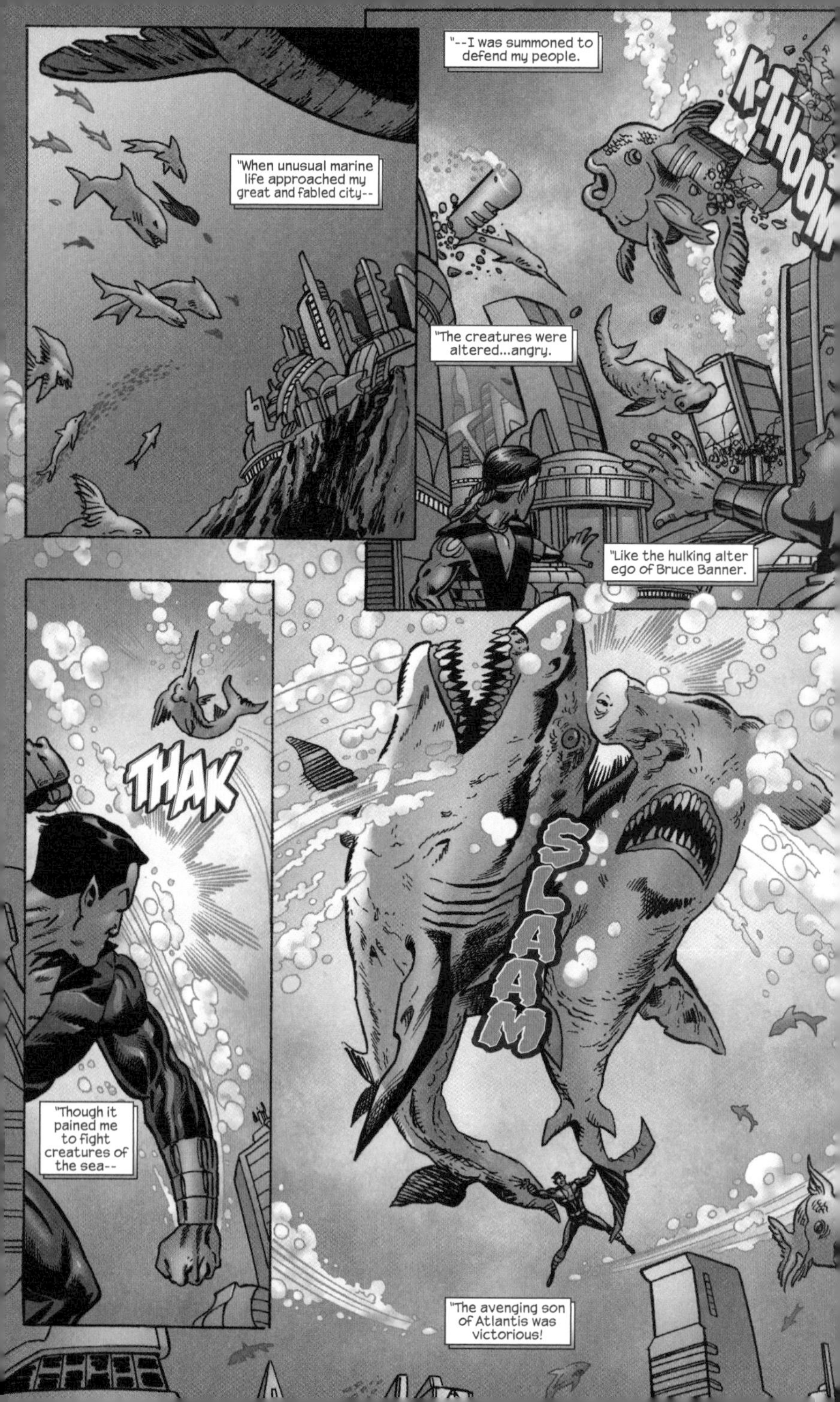
"When unusual marine life approached my great and fabled city--
"--I was summoned to defend my people.
K-THOOM
"The creatures were altered...angry.
"Like the hulking alter ego of Bruce Banner.
THAK
"Though it pained me to fight creatures of the sea--
SLAAM
"The avenging son of Atlantis was victorious!

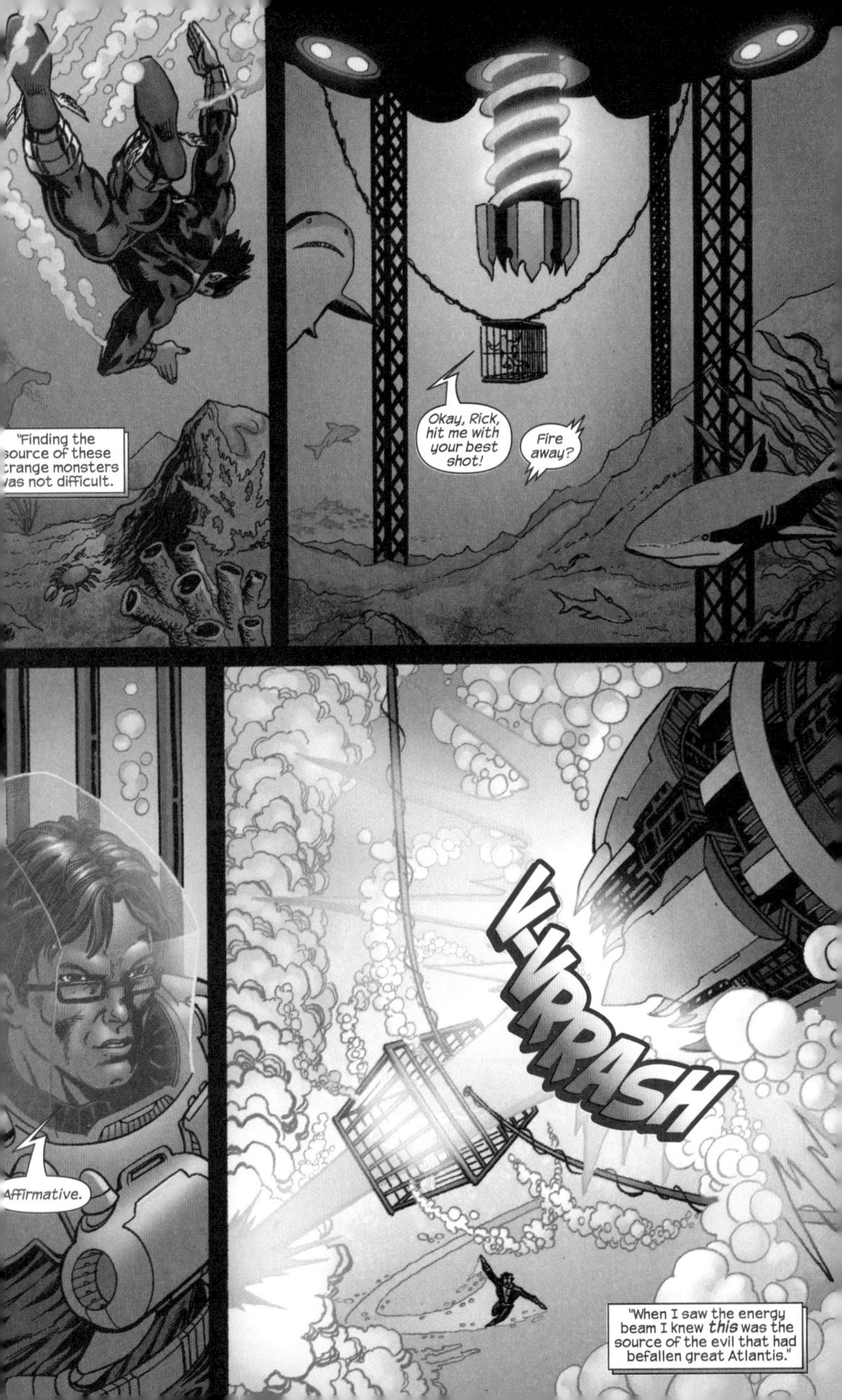
"Finding the
source of these
strange monsters
was not difficult.
Okay, Rick,
hit me with
your best
shot!
Fire
away?
Affirmative.
V-VRASH
"When I saw the energy
beam I knew *this* was the
source of the evil that had
befallen great Atlantis."

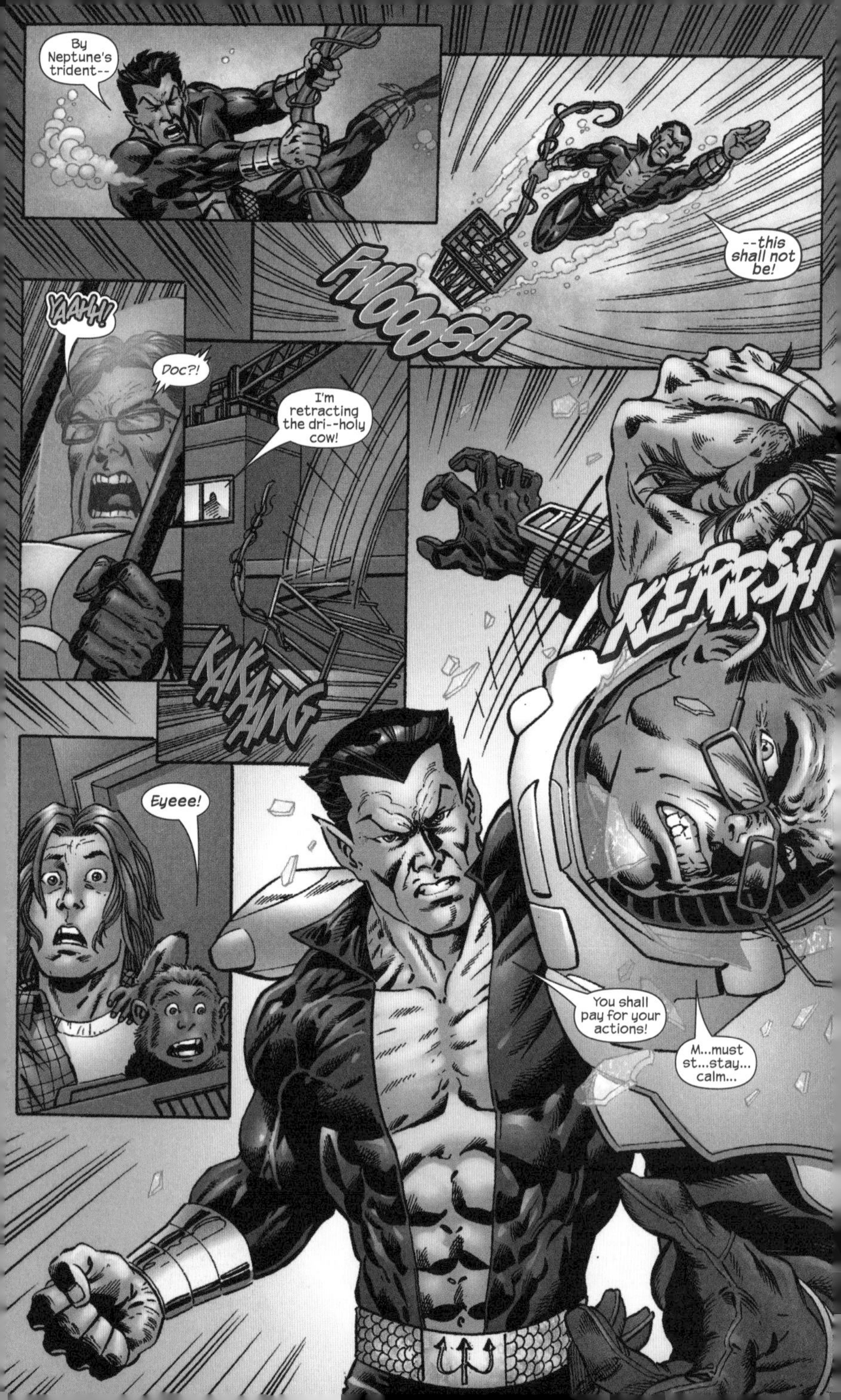

By Neptune's trident--
--this shall not be!
FWOOOSH
YAAHH!
Doc?!
I'm retracting the dri--holy cow!
KAKANG
KERRSH
Eyeee!
You shall pay for your actions!
M...must st...stay... calm...

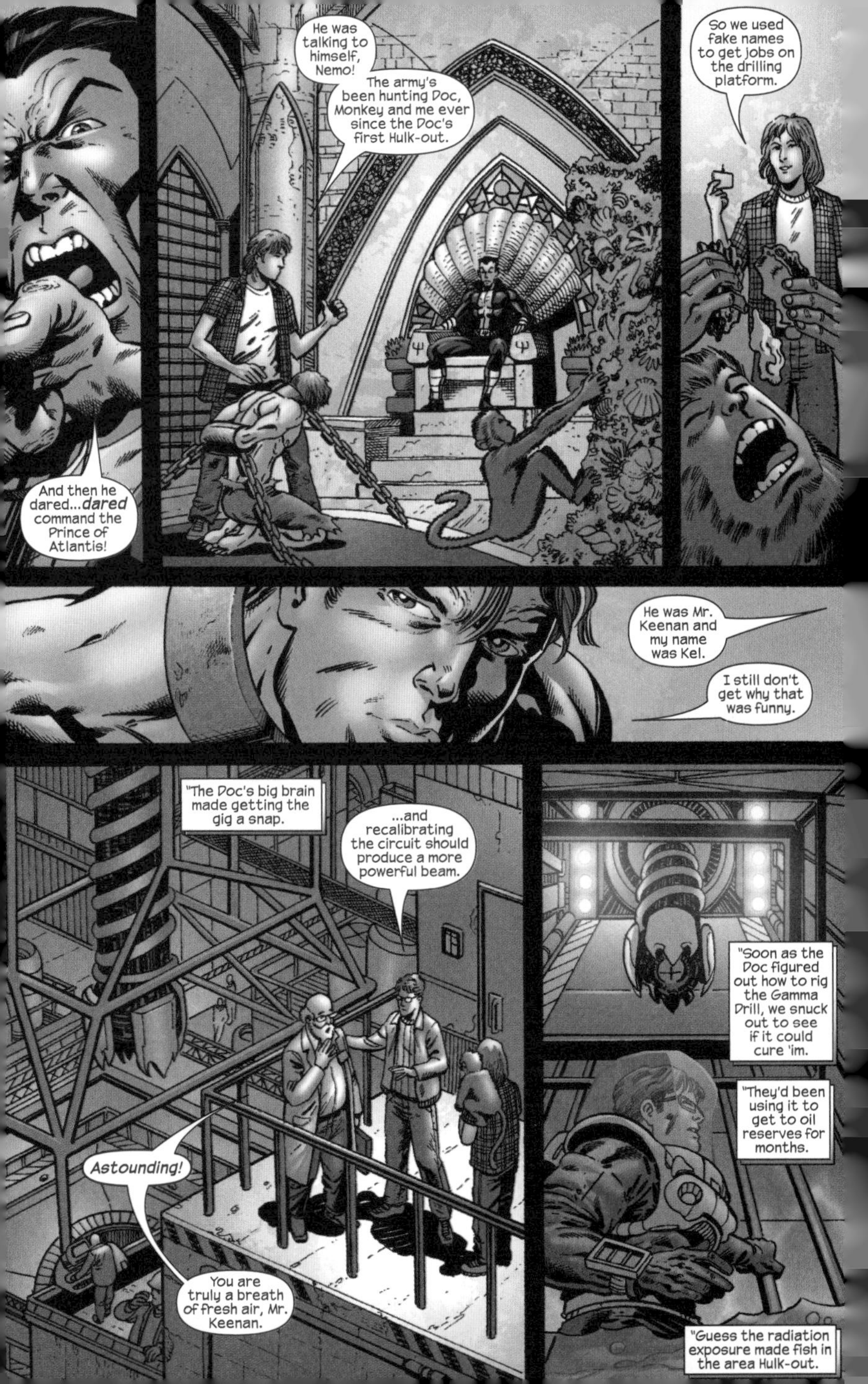
And then he dared...*dared* command the Prince of Atlantis!
He was talking to himself, Nemo!
The army's been hunting Doc, Monkey and me ever since the Doc's first Hulk-out.
So we used fake names to get jobs on the drilling platform.
He was Mr. Keenan and my name was Kel.
I still don't get why that was funny.
"The Doc's big brain made getting the gig a snap.
...and recalibrating the circuit should produce a more powerful beam.
Astounding!
You are truly a breath of fresh air, Mr. Keenan.
"Soon as the Doc figured out how to rig the Gamma Drill, we snuck out to see if it could cure 'im.
"They'd been using it to get to oil reserves for months.
"Guess the radiation exposure made fish in the area Hulk-out.

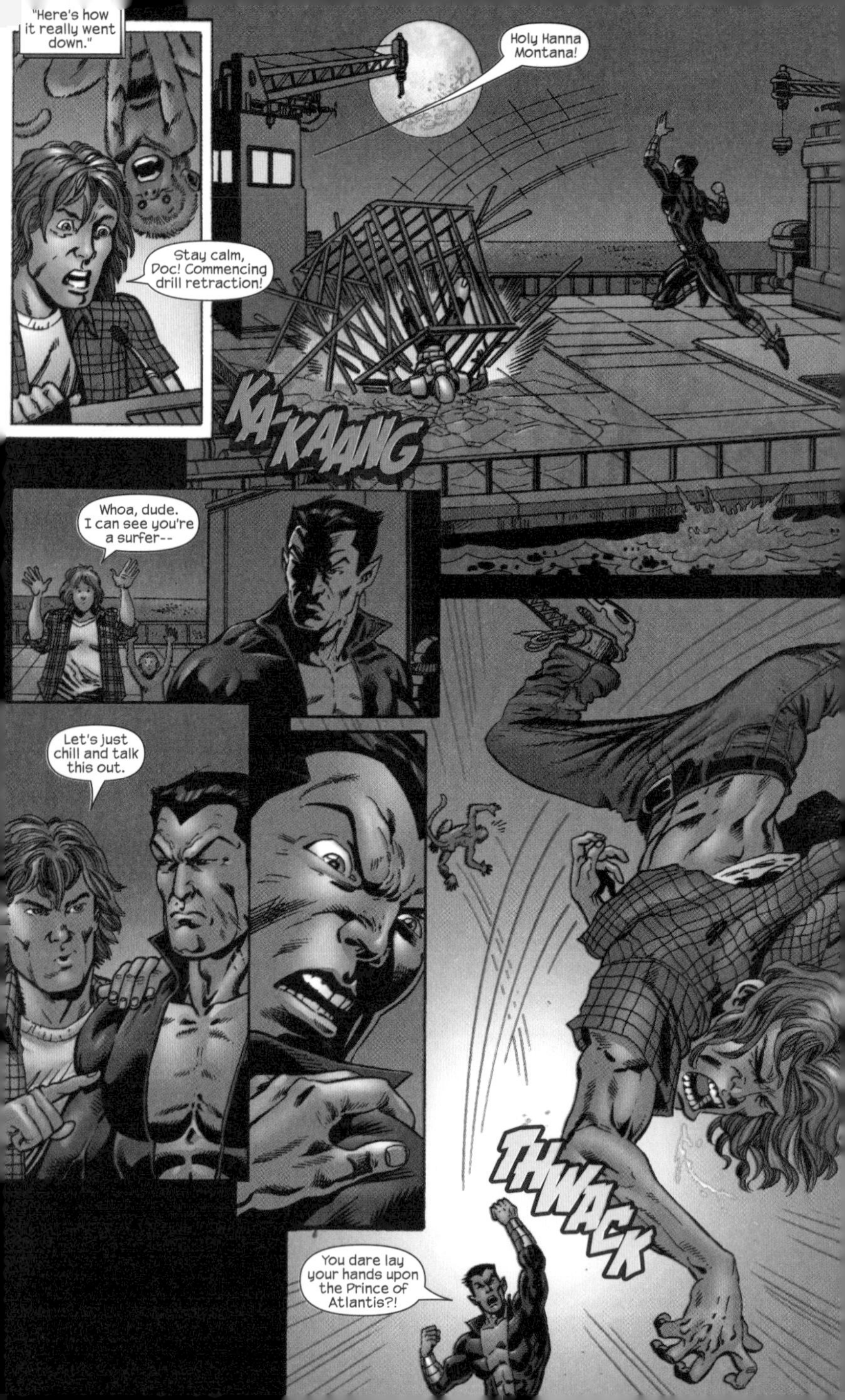
"Here's how it really went down."
Holy Hanna Montana!
Stay calm, Doc! Commencing drill retraction!
KA-KAAANG
Whoa, dude. I can see you're a surfer--
Let's just chill and talk this out.
THWACK
You dare lay your hands upon the Prince of Atlantis?!

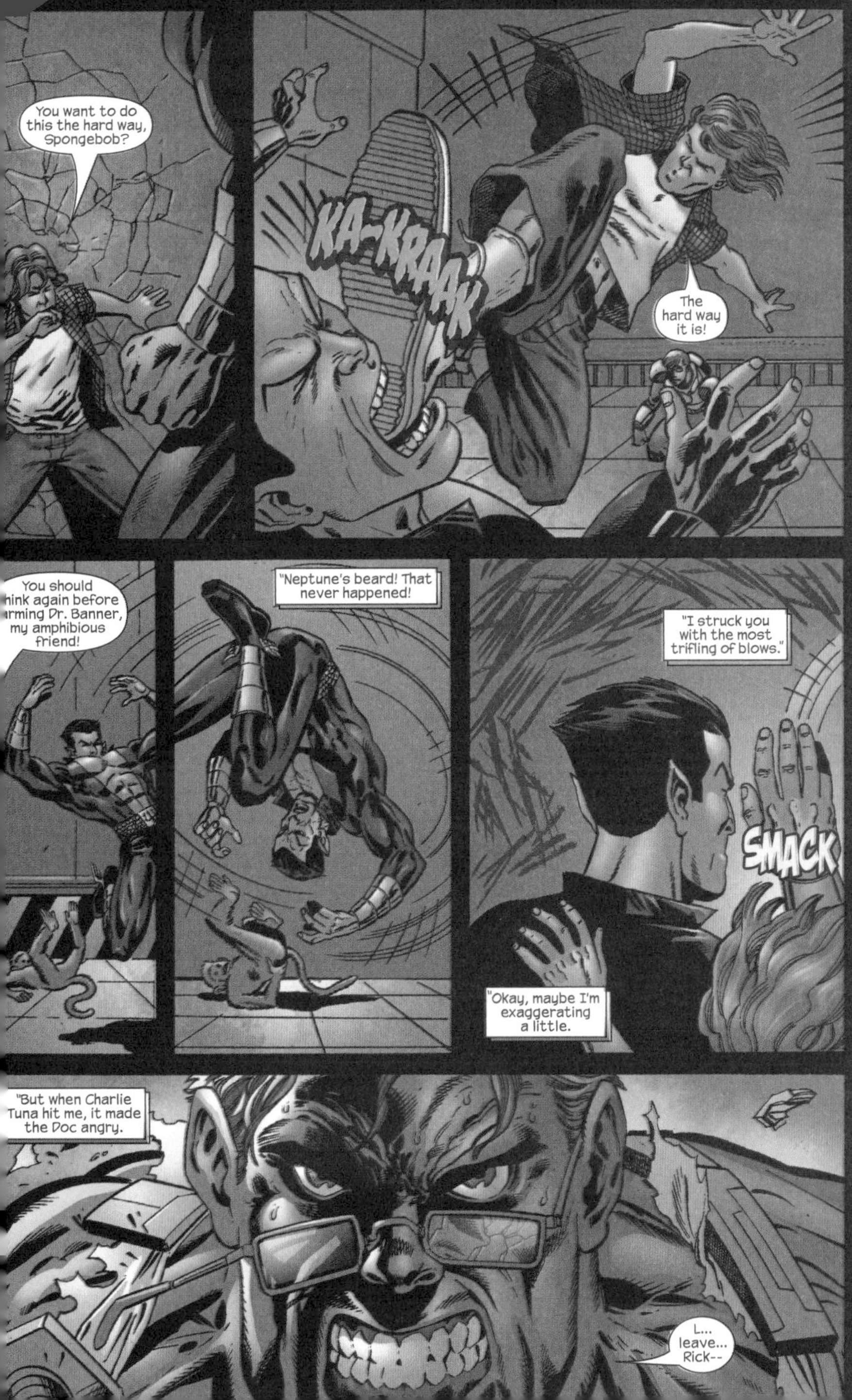
You want to do this the hard way, Spongebob?
KA-KRAAAK
The hard way it is!
You should hink again before arming Dr. Banner, my amphibious friend!
"Neptune's beard! That never happened!
"I struck you with the most trifling of blows."
SMACK
"Okay, maybe I'm exaggerating a little.
"But when Charlie Tuna hit me, it made the Doc angry.
L... leave... Rick--

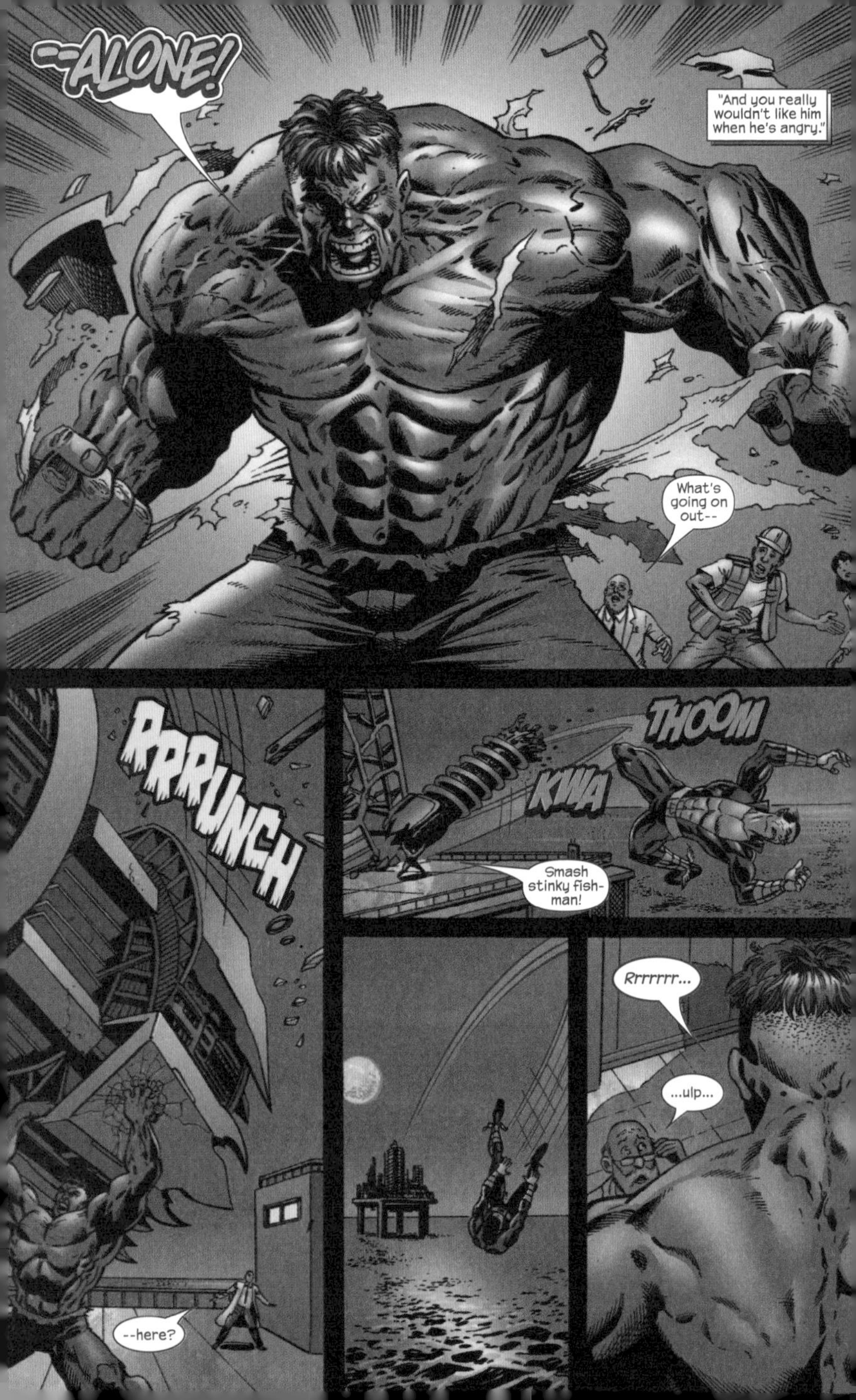
--ALONE!
"And you really wouldn't like him when he's angry."
What's going on out--
RRRUNCH
--here?
THOOM
KWA
Smash stinky fish-man!
Rrrrrrr...
...ulp...

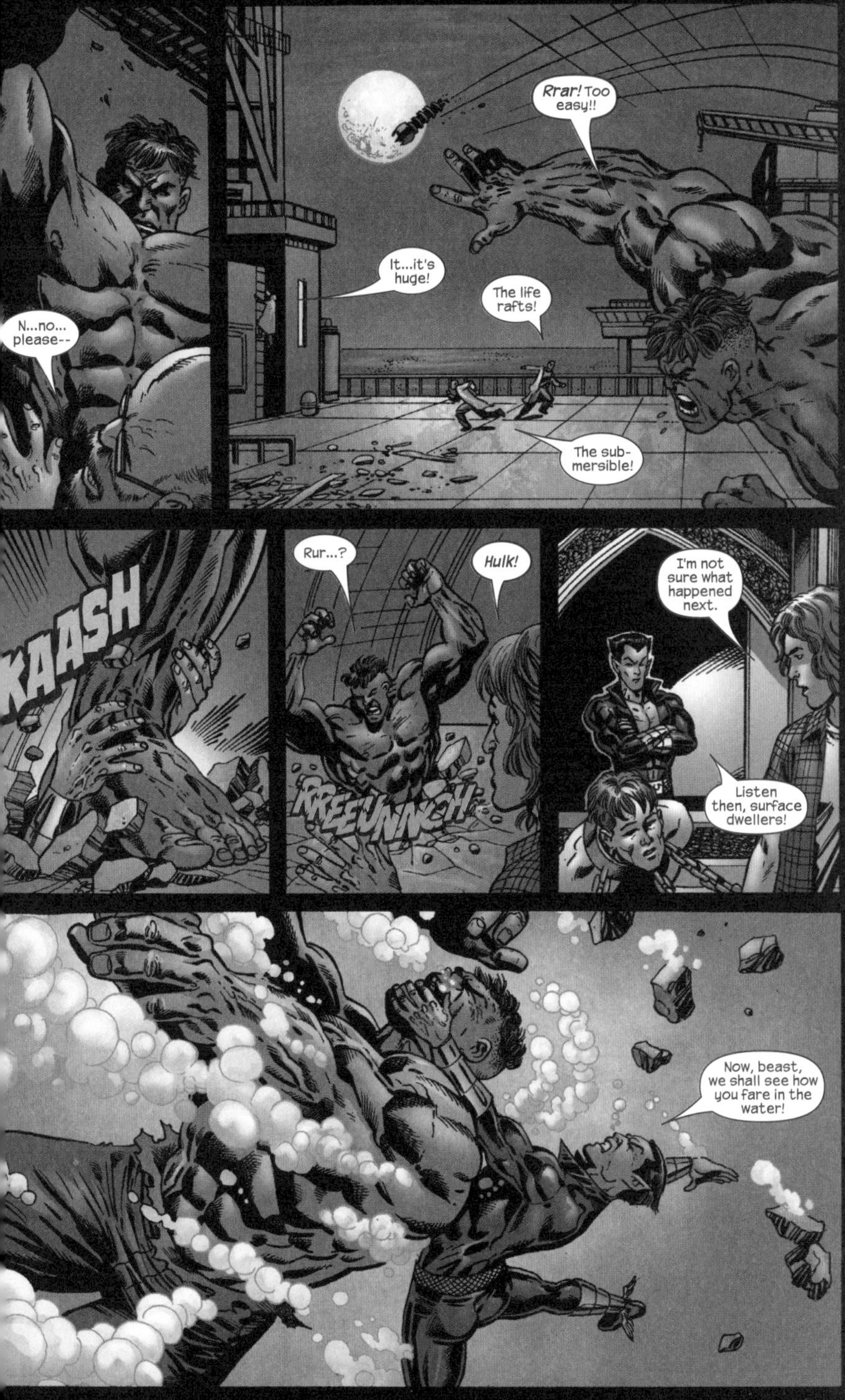

N...no... please--
Rrar! Too easy!!
It...it's huge!
The life rafts!
The sub-mersible!
KAASH
Rur...?
Hulk!
KREEUNNCH
I'm not sure what happened next.
Listen then, surface dwellers!
Now, beast, we shall see how you fare in the water!

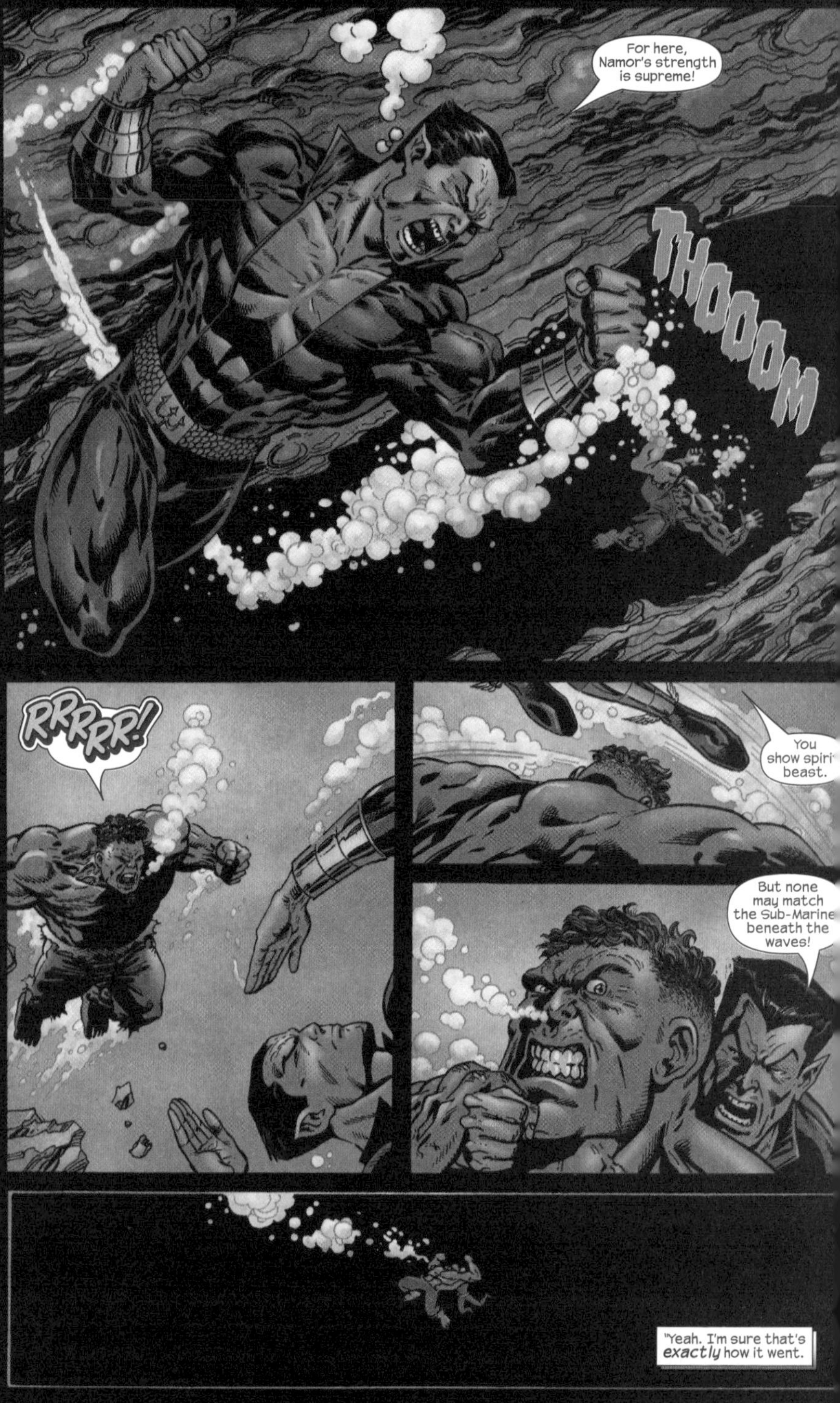
For here, Namor's strength is supreme!
THOOOOM
RRRRR!
You show spiri beast.
But none may match the Sub-Marine beneath the waves!
"Yeah. I'm sure that's *exactly* how it went.

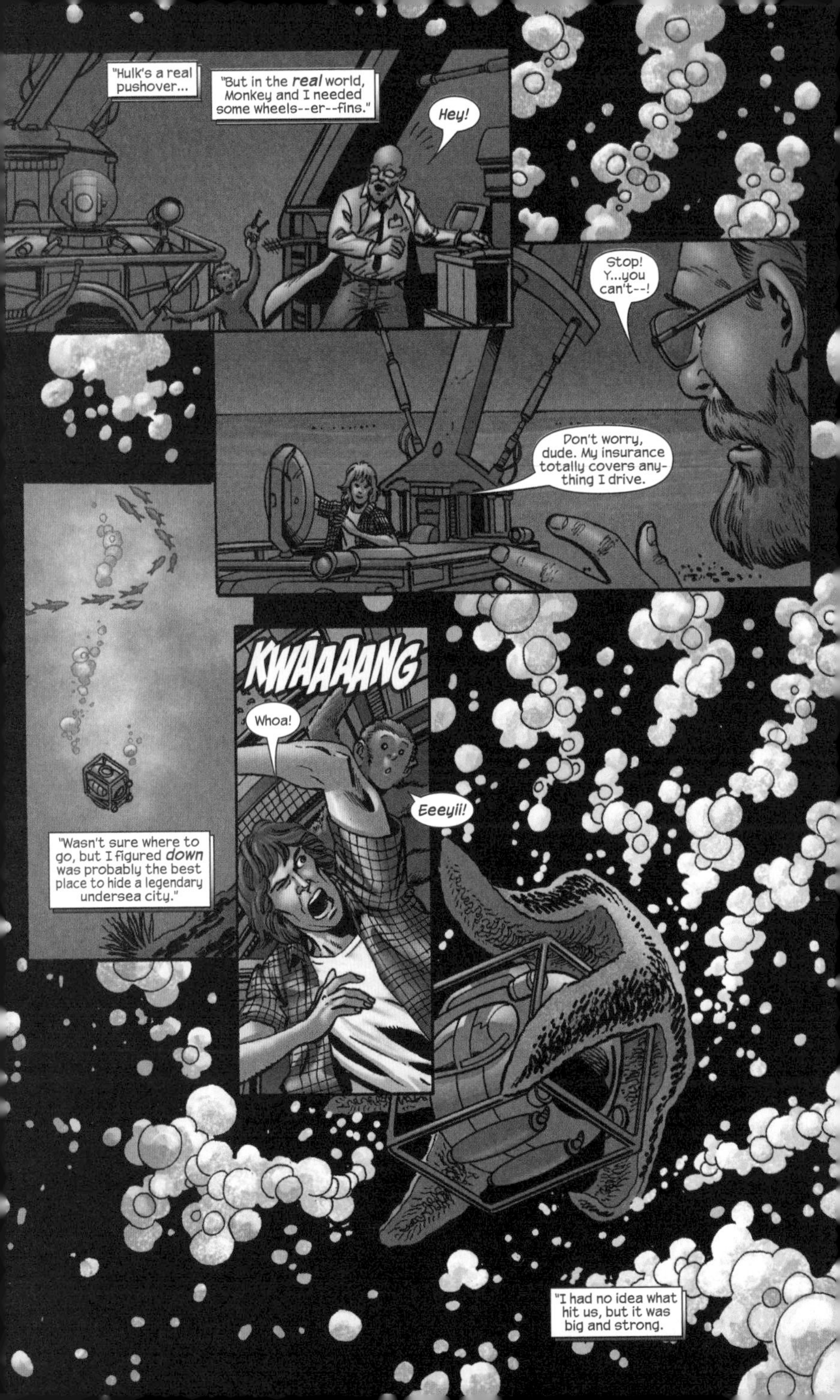

"Hulk's a real pushover...
"But in the real world, Monkey and I needed some wheels--er--fins."
Hey!
Stop! Y...you can't--!
Don't worry, dude. My insurance totally covers anything I drive.
"Wasn't sure where to go, but I figured down was probably the best place to hide a legendary undersea city."
KWAAAAANG
Whoa!
Eeeyii!
"I had no idea what hit us, but it was big and strong.

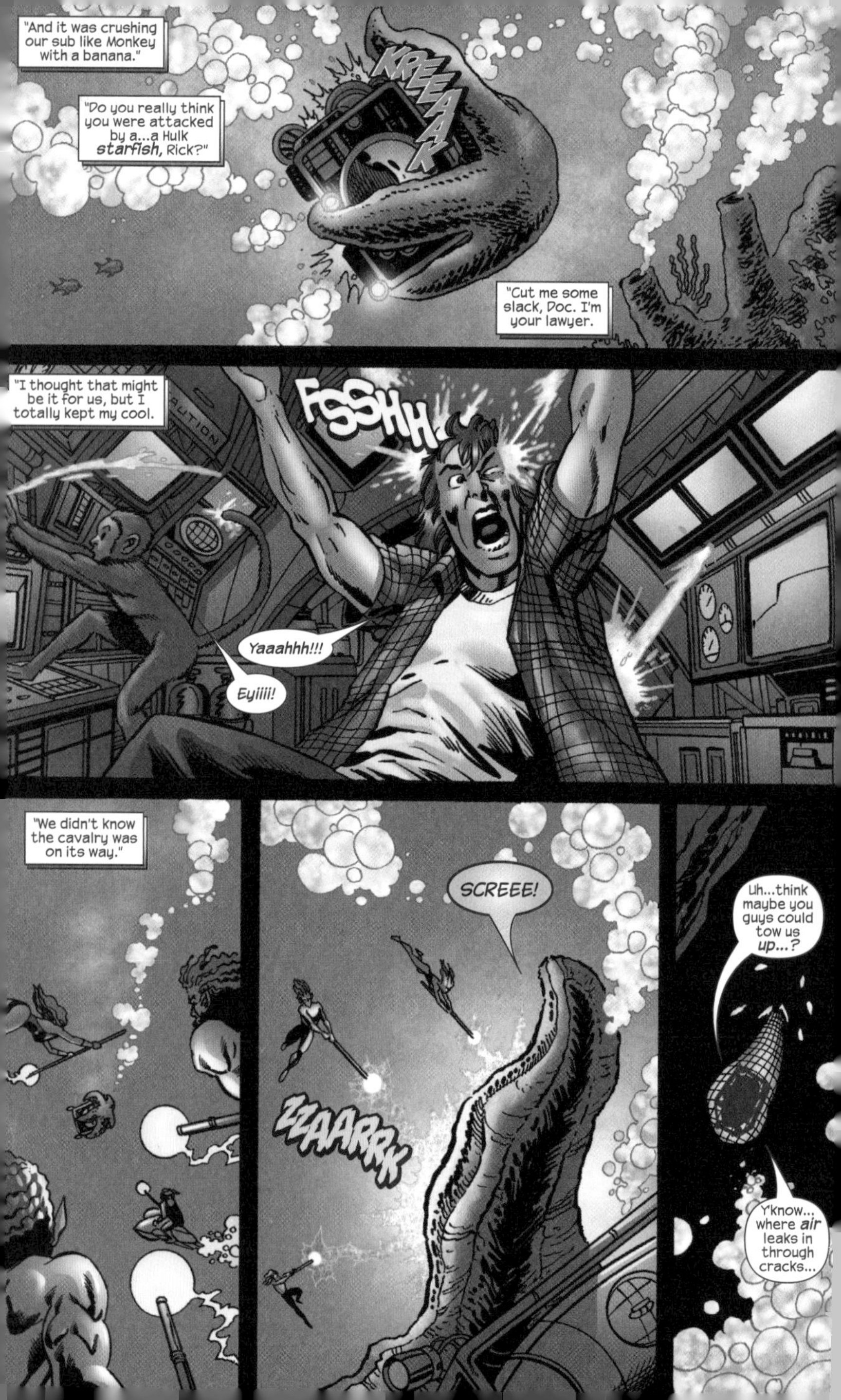
"And it was crushing our sub like Monkey with a banana."
KREEAAK
"Do you really think you were attacked by a...a Hulk starfish, Rick?"
"Cut me some slack, Doc. I'm your lawyer.
"I thought that might be it for us, but I totally kept my cool.
FSSHH
Yaaahhh!!!
Eyiiii!
"We didn't know the cavalry was on its way."
SCREEE!
ZZAARRK
Uh...think maybe you guys could tow us up...?
Y'know... where air leaks in through cracks...

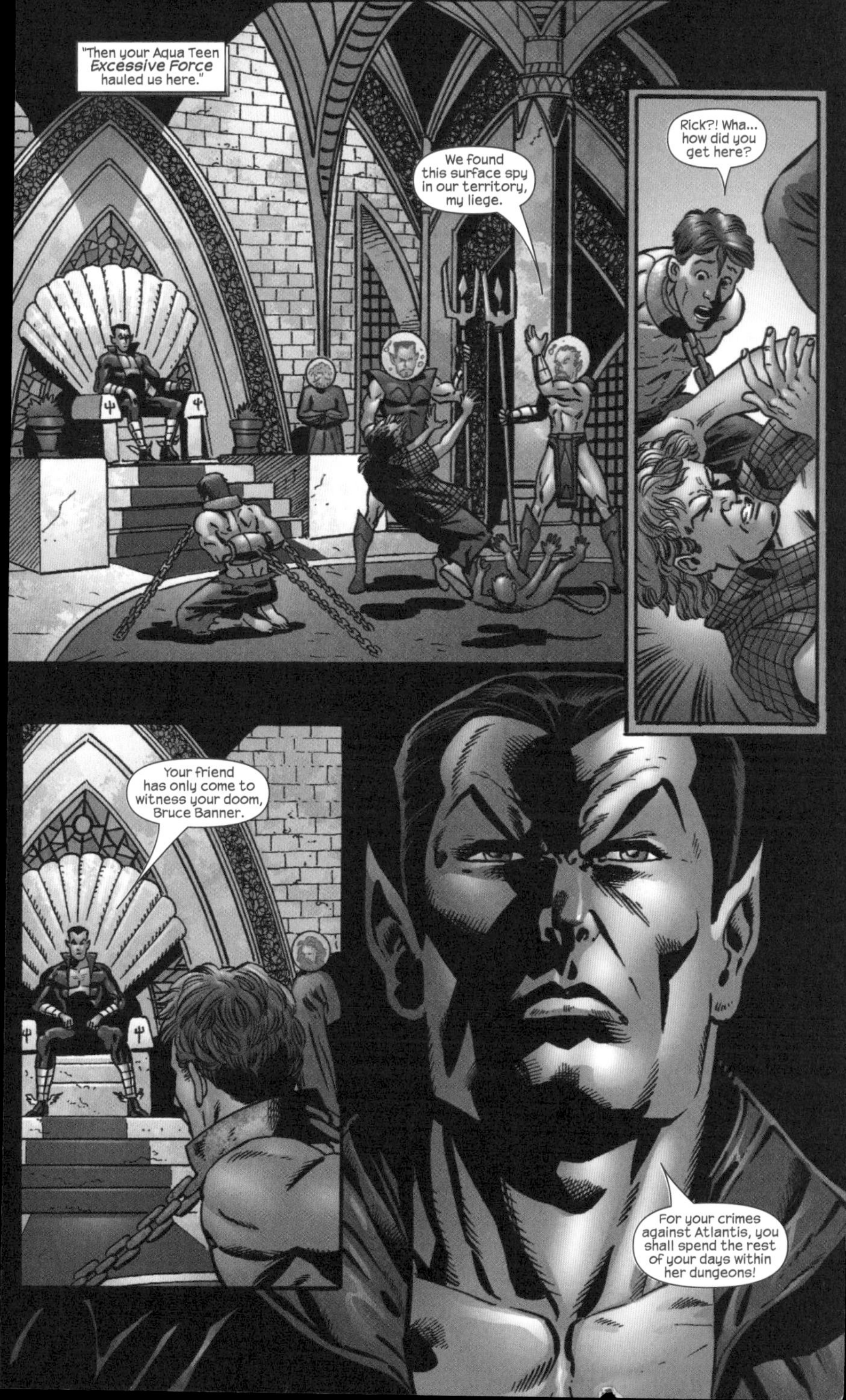
"Then your Aqua Teen *Excessive Force* hauled us here."
We found this surface spy in our territory, my liege.
Rick?! Wha... how did you get here?
Your friend has only come to witness your doom, Bruce Banner.
For your crimes against Atlantis, you shall spend the rest of your days within her dungeons!

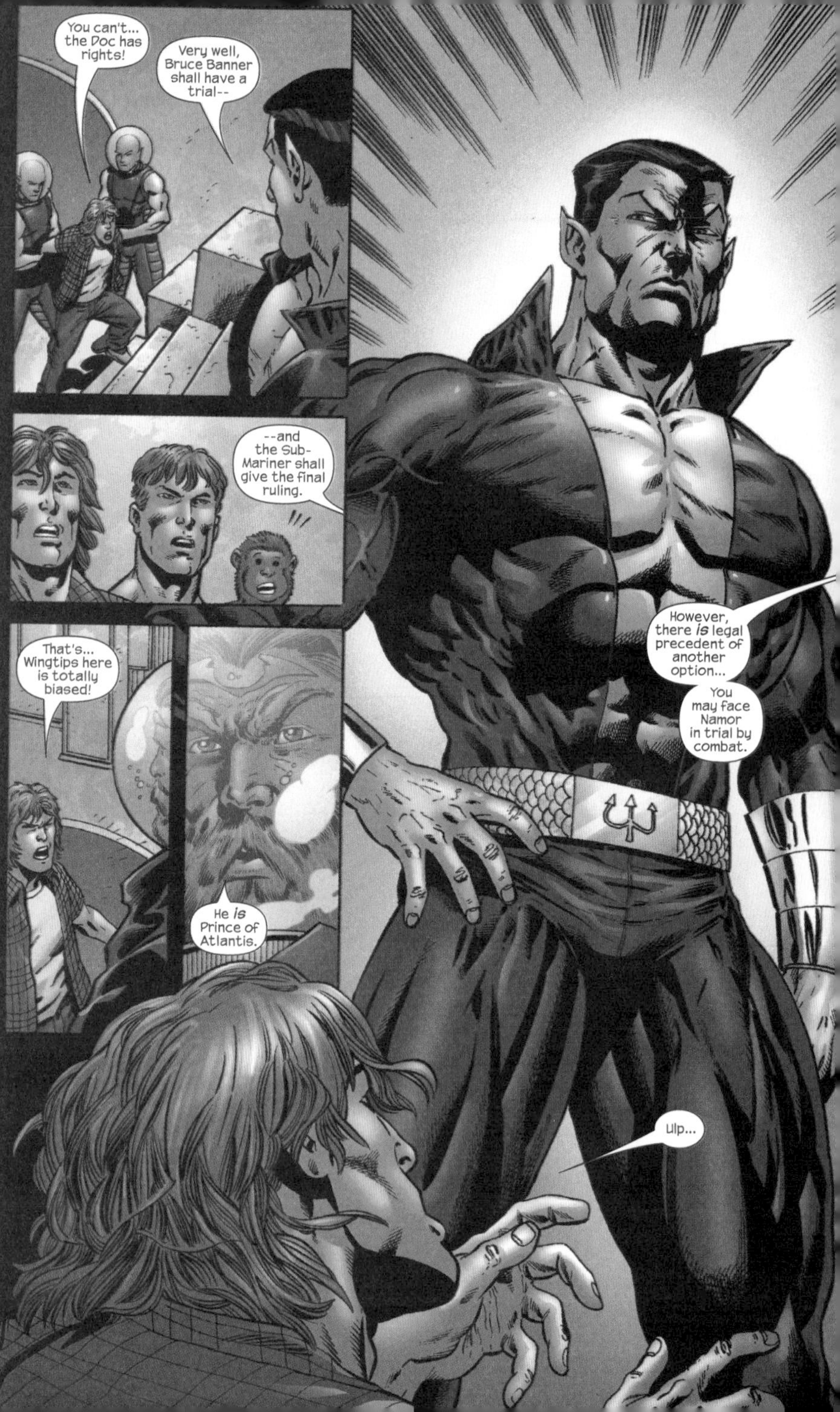

You can't... the Doc has rights!
Very well, Bruce Banner shall have a trial--
--and the Sub-Mariner shall give the final ruling.
That's... Wingtips here is totally biased!
He *is* Prince of Atlantis.
However, there *is* legal precedent of another option...
You may face Namor in trial by combat.
Ulp...

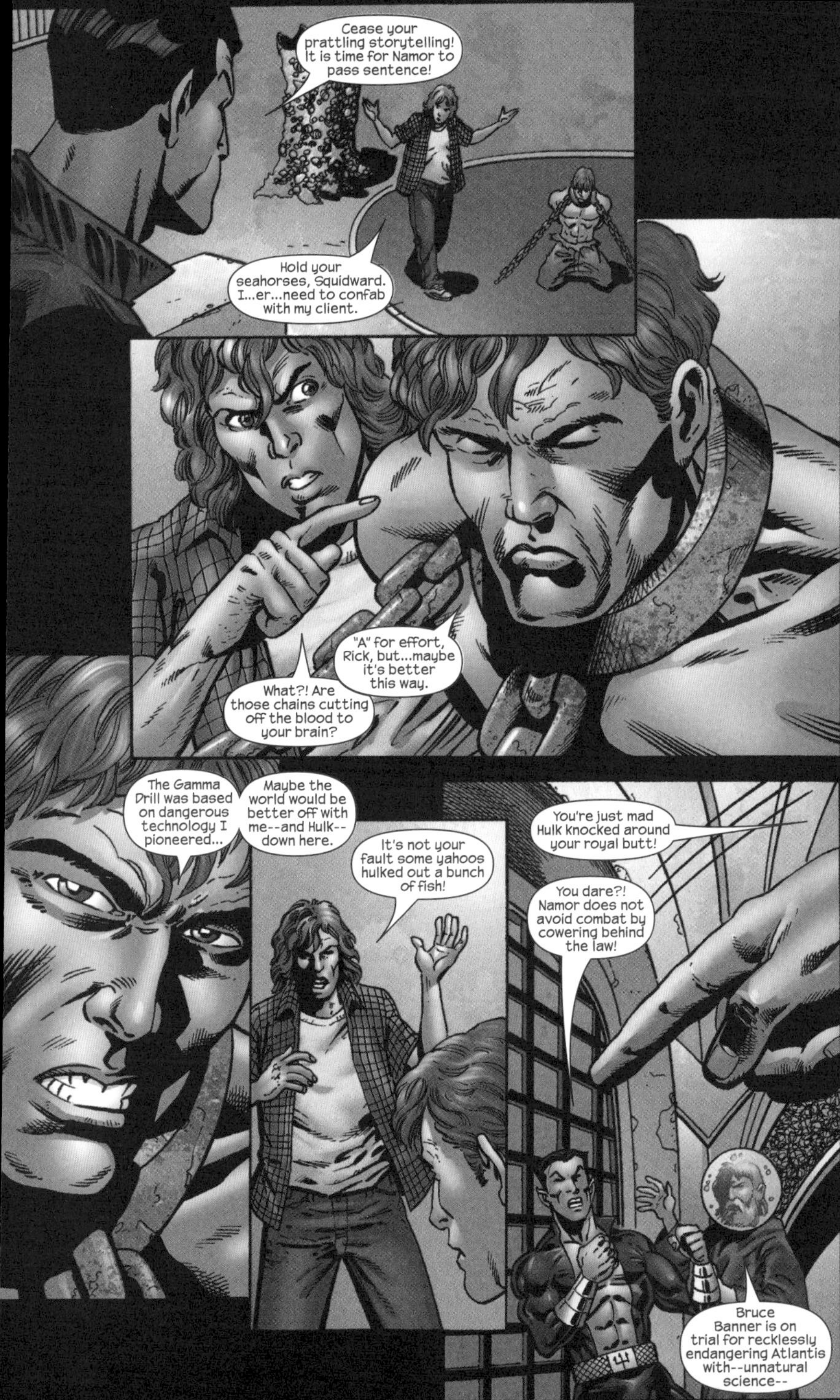
Cease your prattling storytelling! It is time for Namor to pass sentence!
Hold your seahorses, Squidward. I...er...need to confab with my client.
"A" for effort, Rick, but...maybe it's better this way.
What?! Are those chains cutting off the blood to your brain?
The Gamma Drill was based on dangerous technology I pioneered...
Maybe the world would be better off with me--and Hulk--down here.
It's not your fault some yahoos hulked out a bunch of fish!
You're just mad Hulk knocked around your royal butt!
You dare?! Namor does not avoid combat by cowering behind the law!
Bruce Banner is on trial for recklessly endangering Atlantis with--unnatural science--

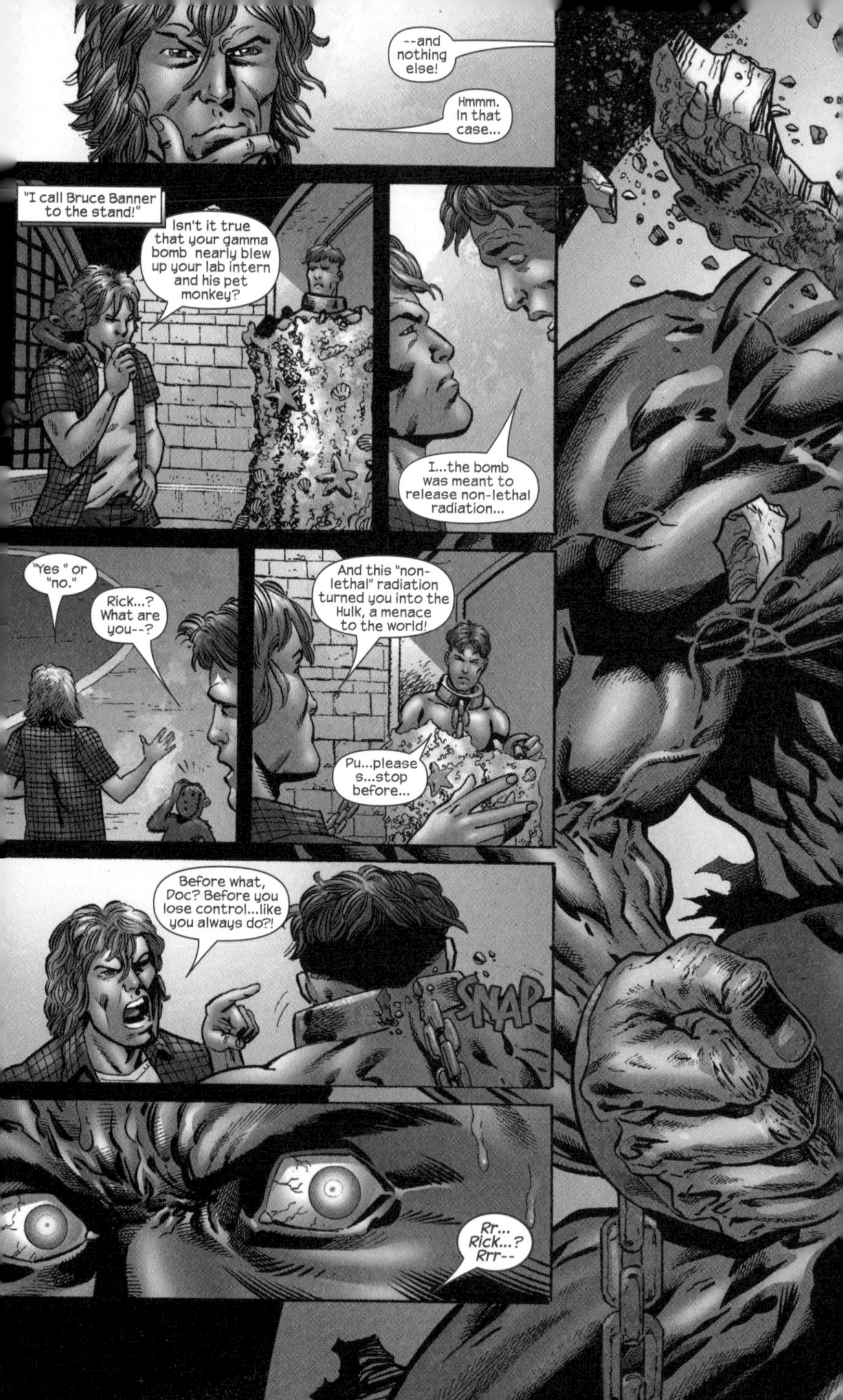
--and nothing else!
Hmmm. In that case...
"I call Bruce Banner to the stand!"
Isn't it true that your gamma bomb nearly blew up your lab intern and his pet monkey?
I...the bomb was meant to release non-lethal radiation...
"Yes " or "no."
Rick...? What are you--?
And this "non-lethal" radiation turned you into the Hulk, a menace to the world!
Pu...please s...stop before...
Before what, Doc? Before you lose control...like you always do?!
SNAP
Rr... Rick...? Rrr--

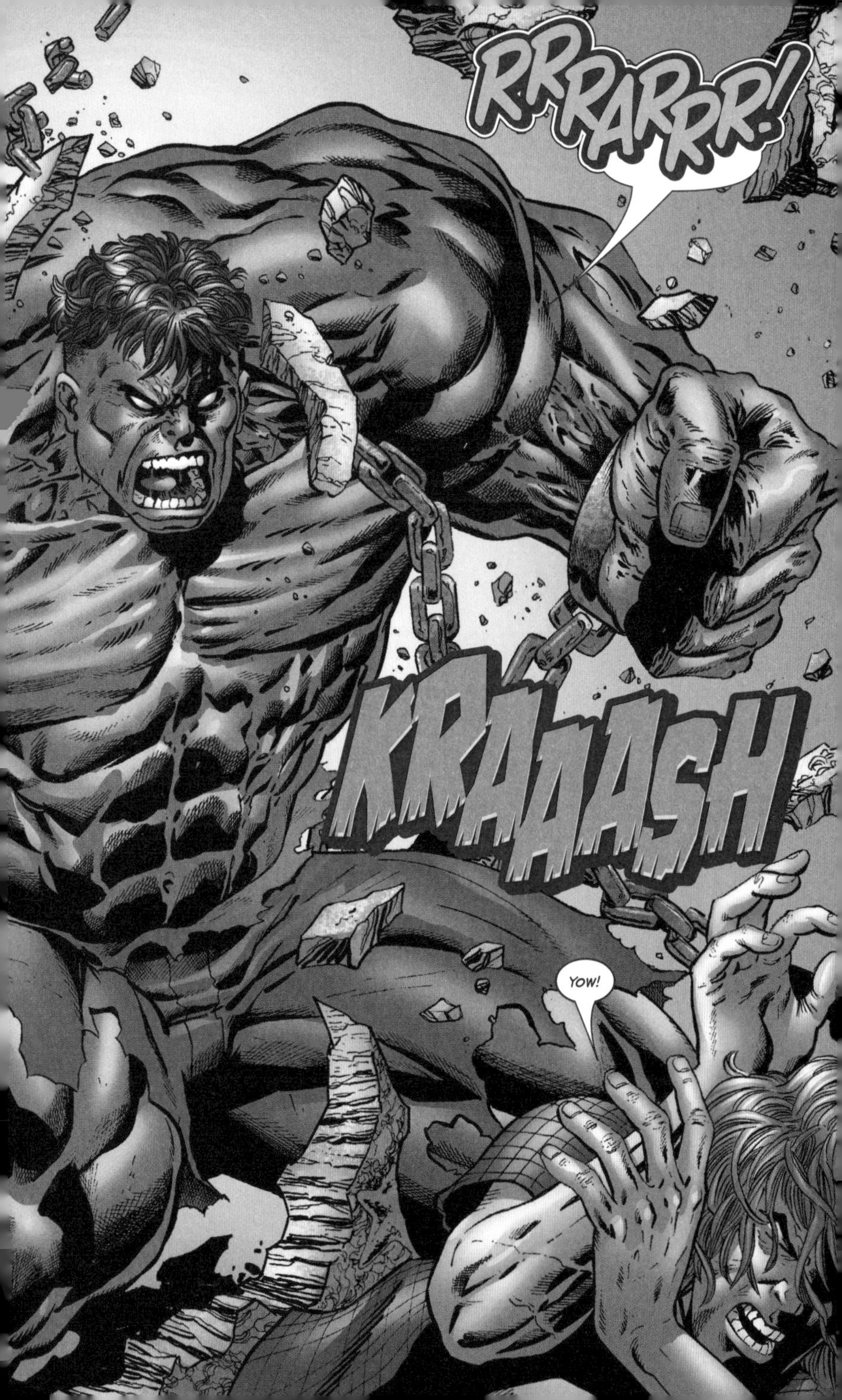
RRRARRR!
KRAAASH
YOW!

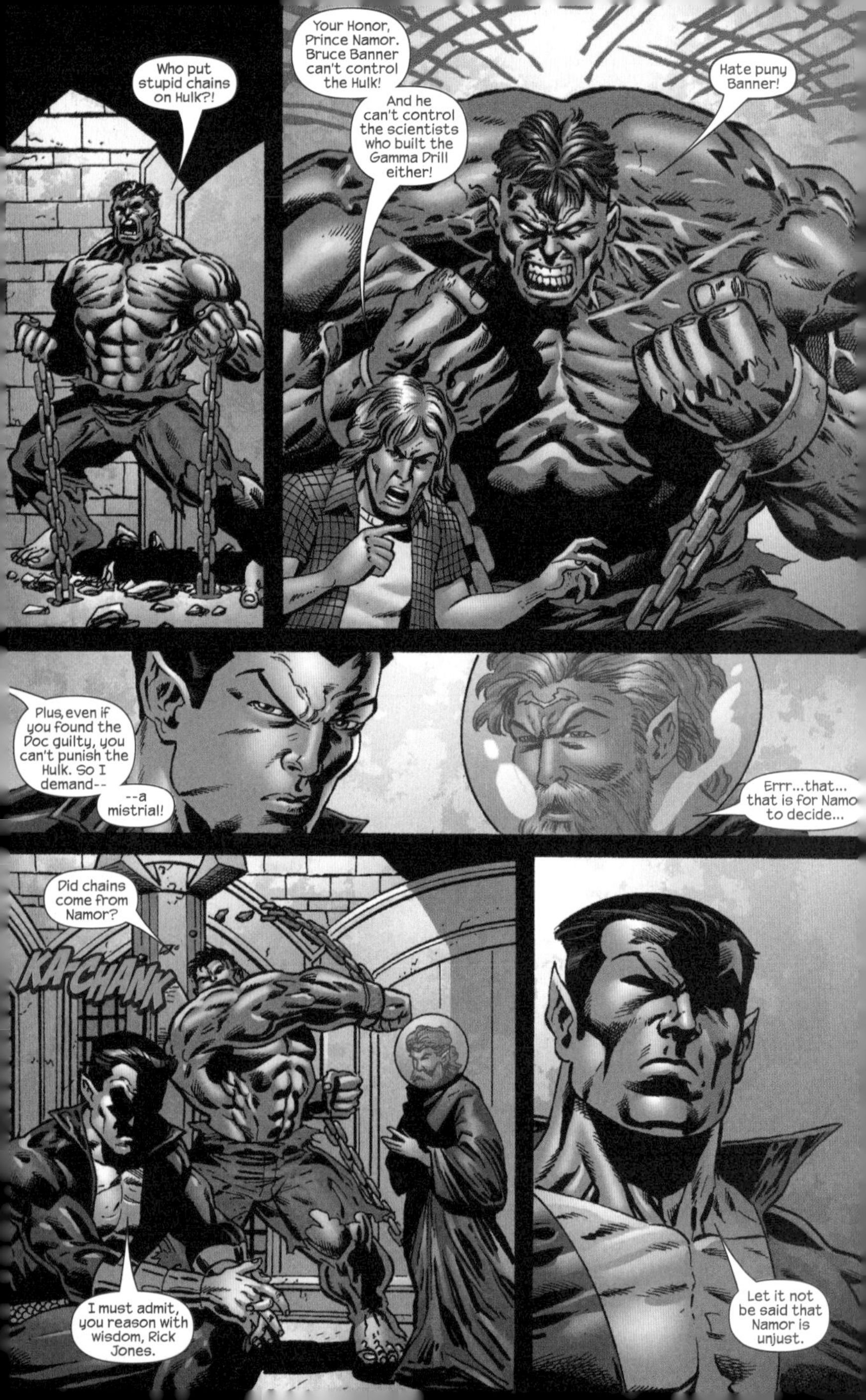
Who put stupid chains on Hulk?!
Your Honor, Prince Namor. Bruce Banner can't control the Hulk!
And he can't control the scientists who built the Gamma Drill either!
Hate puny Banner!
Plus, even if you found the Doc guilty, you can't punish the Hulk. So I demand--
--a mistrial!
Errr...that... that is for Namor to decide...
Did chains come from Namor?
KA-CHANK
I must admit, you reason with wisdom, Rick Jones.
Let it not be said that Namor is unjust.

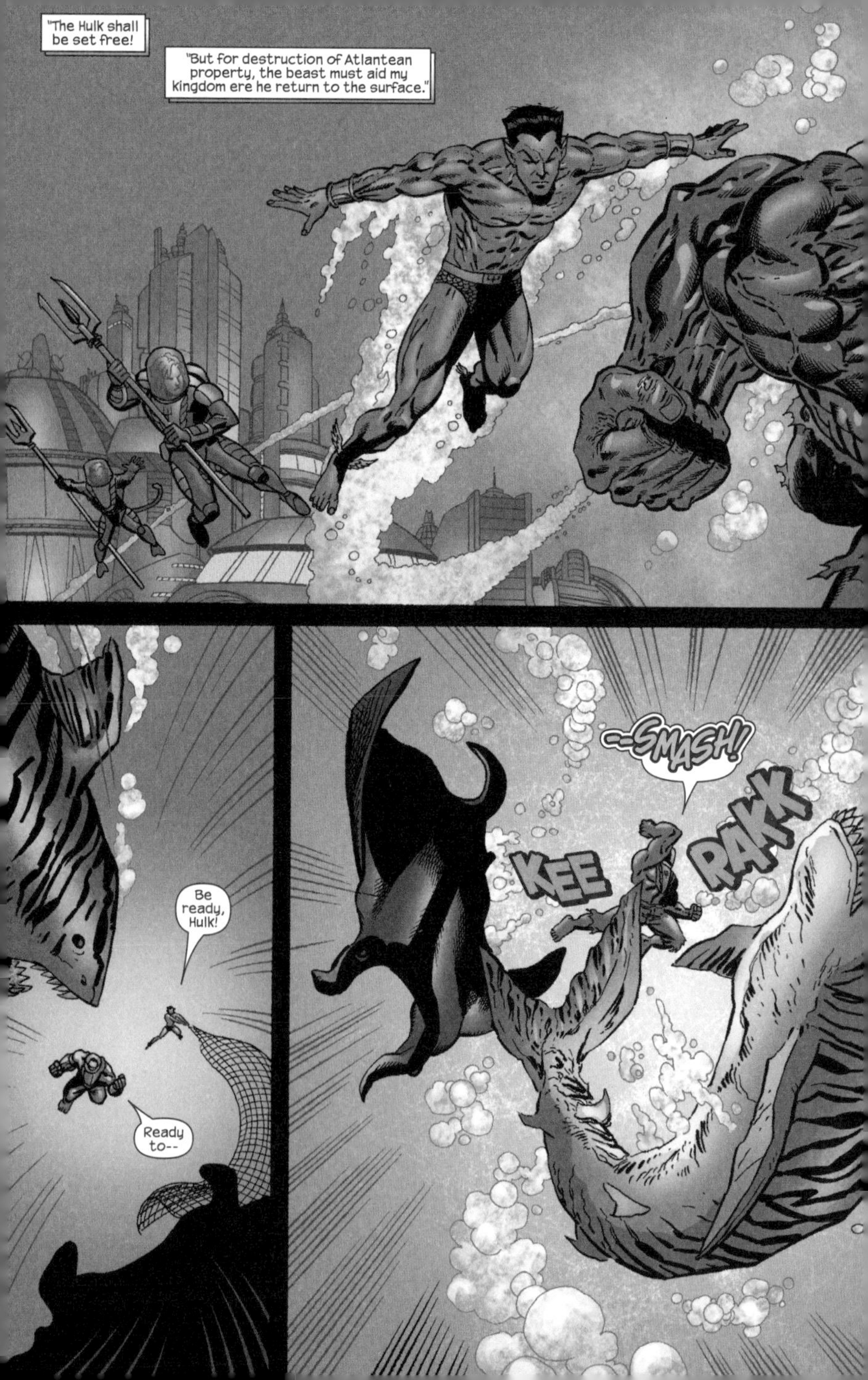
"The Hulk shall be set free!
"But for destruction of Atlantean property, the beast must aid my kingdom ere he return to the surface."
Be ready, Hulk!
Ready to--
--SMASH!
KEE RAKK

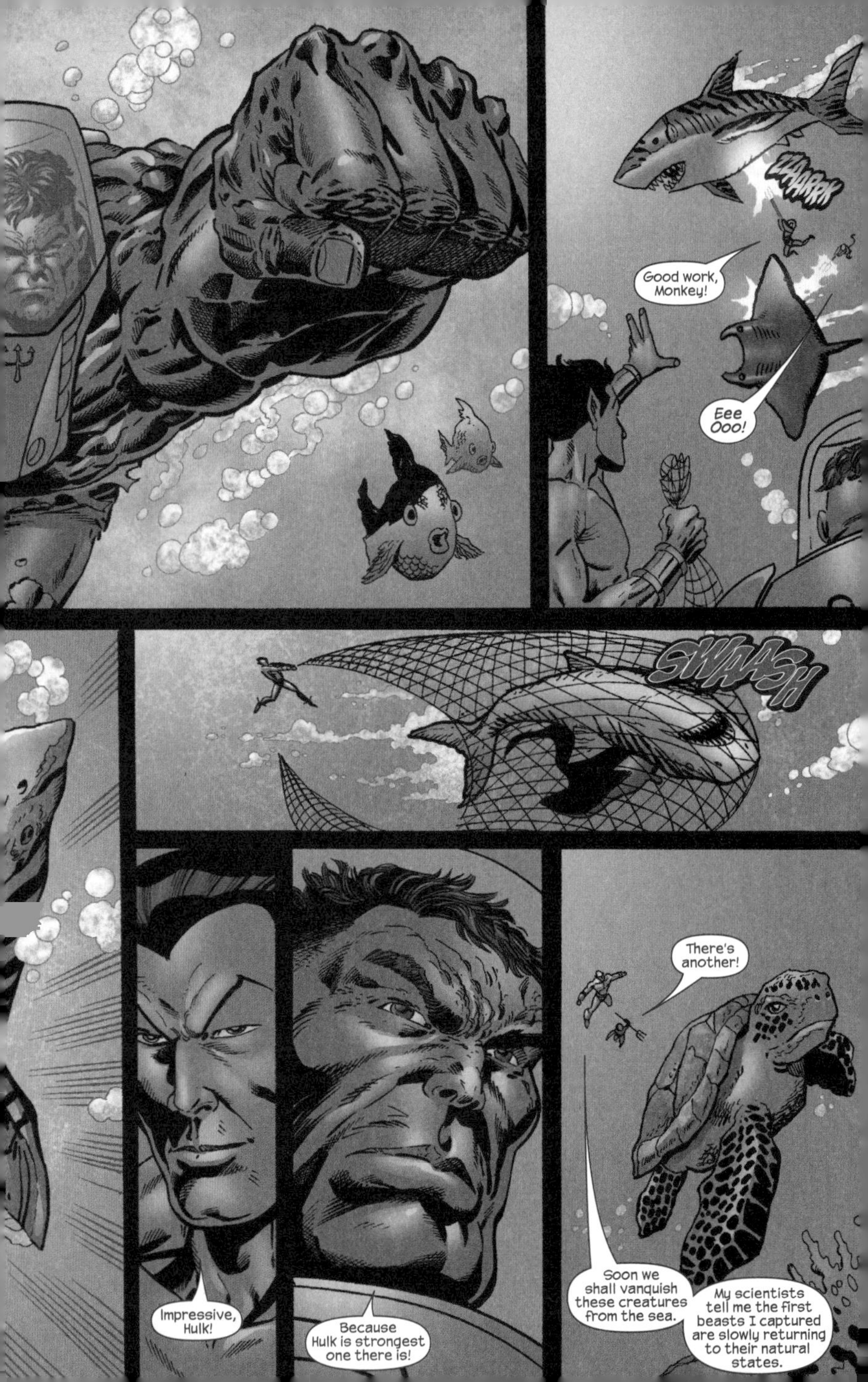
ZZAARK
Good work, Monkey!
Eee Ooo!
SWAASH
Impressive, Hulk!
Because Hulk is strongest one there is!
There's another!
Soon we shall vanquish these creatures from the sea.
My scientists tell me the first beasts I captured are slowly returning to their natural states.

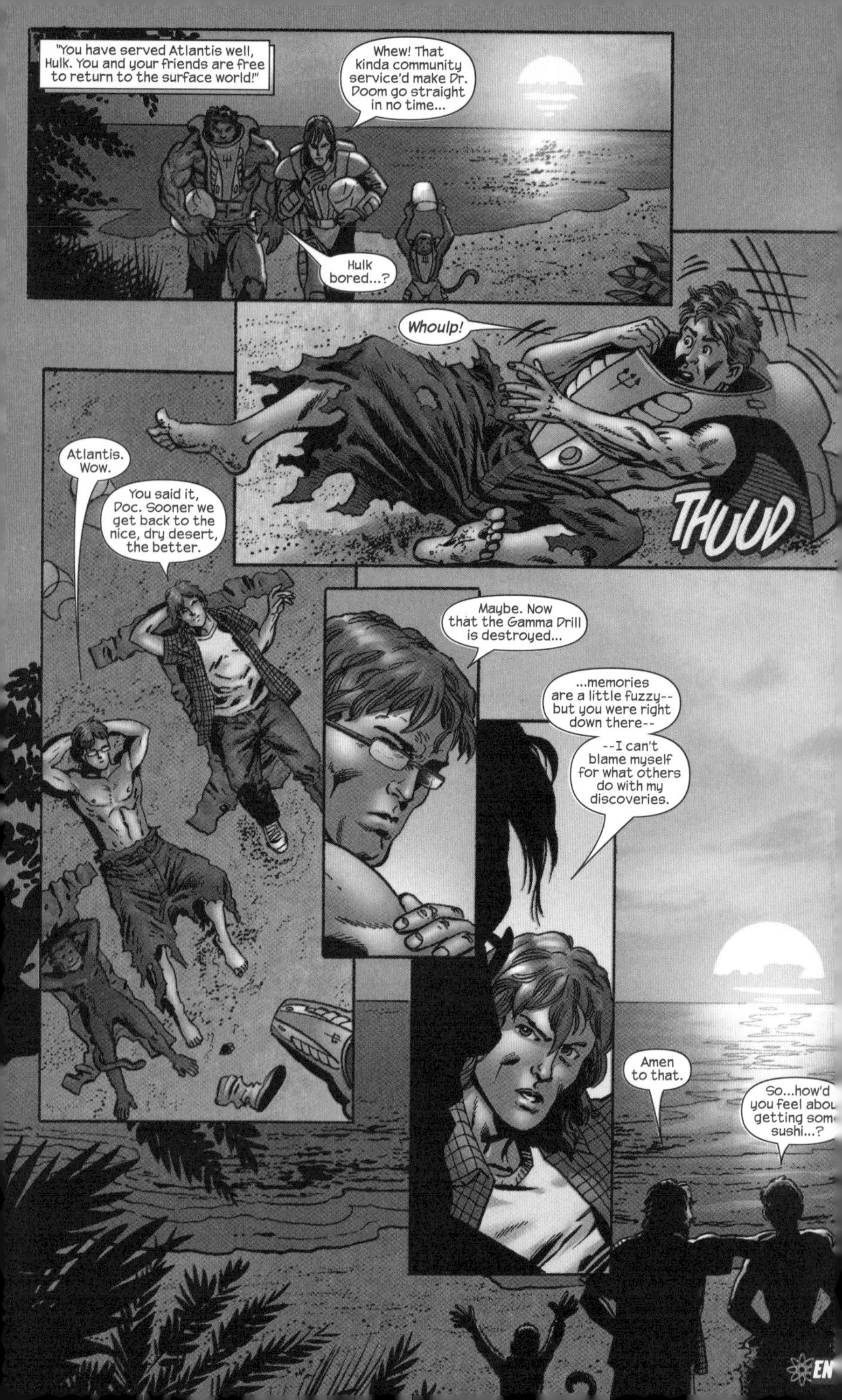

"You have served Atlantis well, Hulk. You and your friends are free to return to the surface world!"
Whew! That kinda community service'd make Dr. Doom go straight in no time...
Hulk bored...?
Whoulp!
THUUD
Atlantis. Wow.
You said it, Doc. Sooner we get back to the nice, dry desert, the better.
Maybe. Now that the Gamma Drill is destroyed...
...memories are a little fuzzy-- but you were right down there--
--I can't blame myself for what others do with my discoveries.
Amen to that.
So...how'd you feel abou getting som sushi...?
EN

SANTACRUZ
18.010107

7

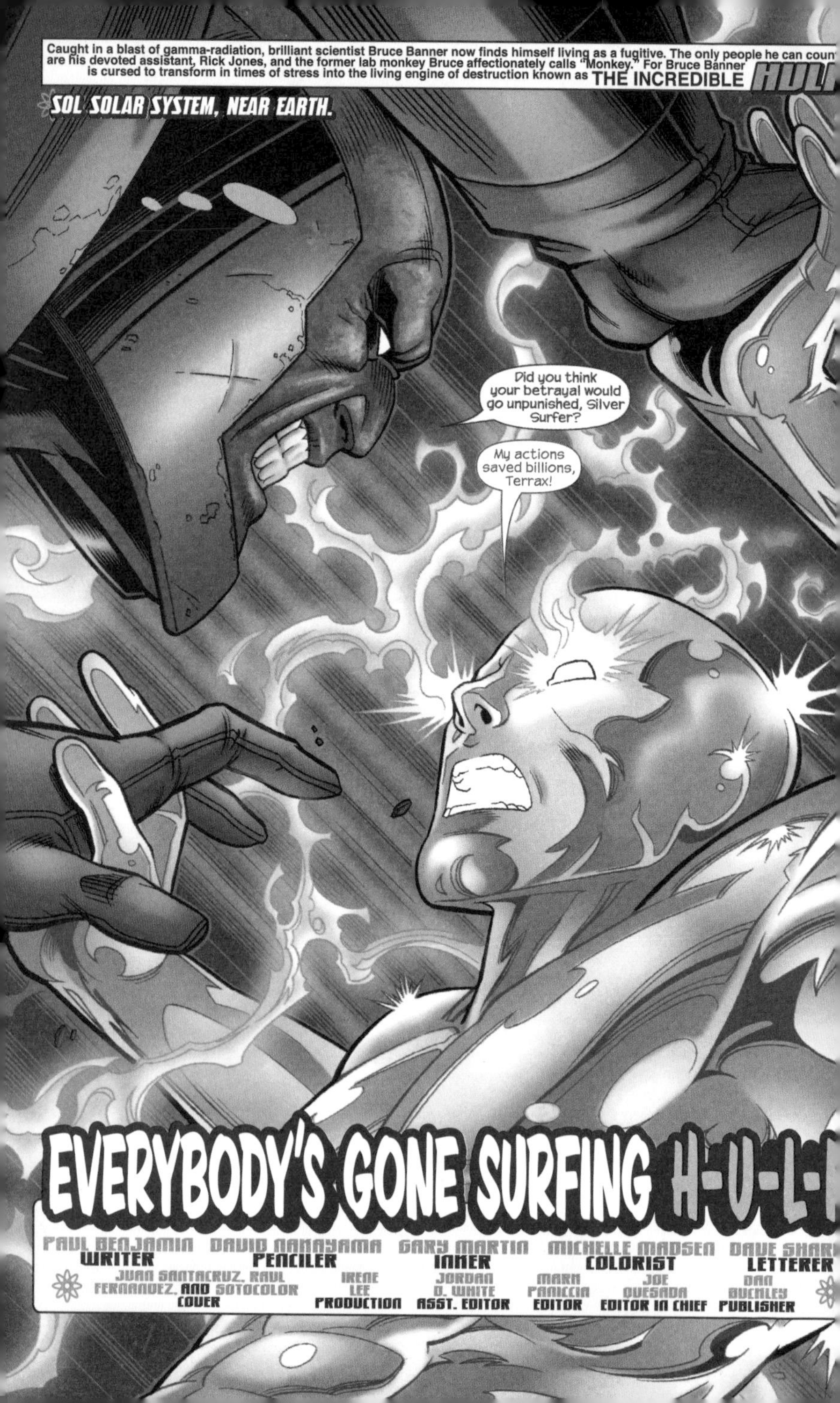

Caught in a blast of gamma-radiation, brilliant scientist Bruce Banner now finds himself living as a fugitive. The only people he can coun are his devoted assistant, Rick Jones, and the former lab monkey Bruce affectionately calls "Monkey." For Bruce Banner is cursed to transform in times of stress into the living engine of destruction known as THE INCREDIBLE HUL
SOL SOLAR SYSTEM, NEAR EARTH.
Did you think your betrayal would go unpunished, Silver Surfer?
My actions saved billions, Terrax!
EVERYBODY'S GONE SURFING H-U-L-
PAUL BENJAMIN WRITER
DAVID NAKAYAMA PENCILER
GARY MARTIN INKER
MICHELLE MADSEN COLORIST
DAVE SHAR LETTERER
JUAN SANTACRUZ, RAUL FERNANDEZ, AND SOTOCOLOR COVER
IRENE LEE PRODUCTION
JORDAN D. WHITE ASST. EDITOR
MARK PANICCIA EDITOR
JOE QUESADA EDITOR IN CHIEF
DAN BUCKLEY PUBLISHER

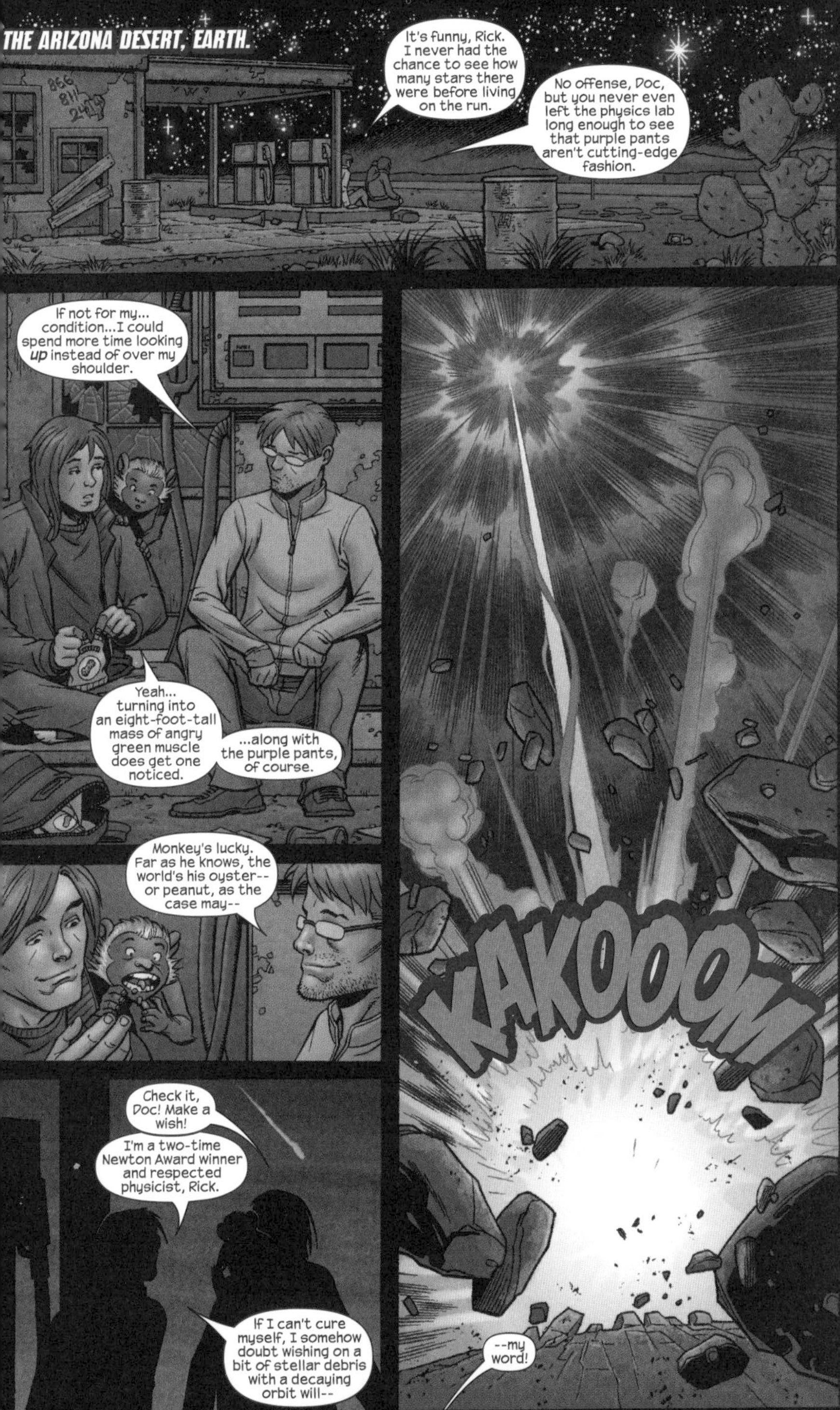
THE ARIZONA DESERT, EARTH.
It's funny, Rick. I never had the chance to see how many stars there were before living on the run.
No offense, Doc, but you never even left the physics lab long enough to see that purple pants aren't cutting-edge fashion.
If not for my... condition...I could spend more time looking *up* instead of over my shoulder.
Yeah... turning into an eight-foot-tall mass of angry green muscle does get one noticed.
...along with the purple pants, of course.
Monkey's lucky. Far as he knows, the world's his oyster-- or peanut, as the case may--
Check it, Doc! Make a wish!
I'm a two-time Newton Award winner and respected physicist, Rick.
If I can't cure myself, I somehow doubt wishing on a bit of stellar debris with a decaying orbit will--
KAKOOOM
--my word!

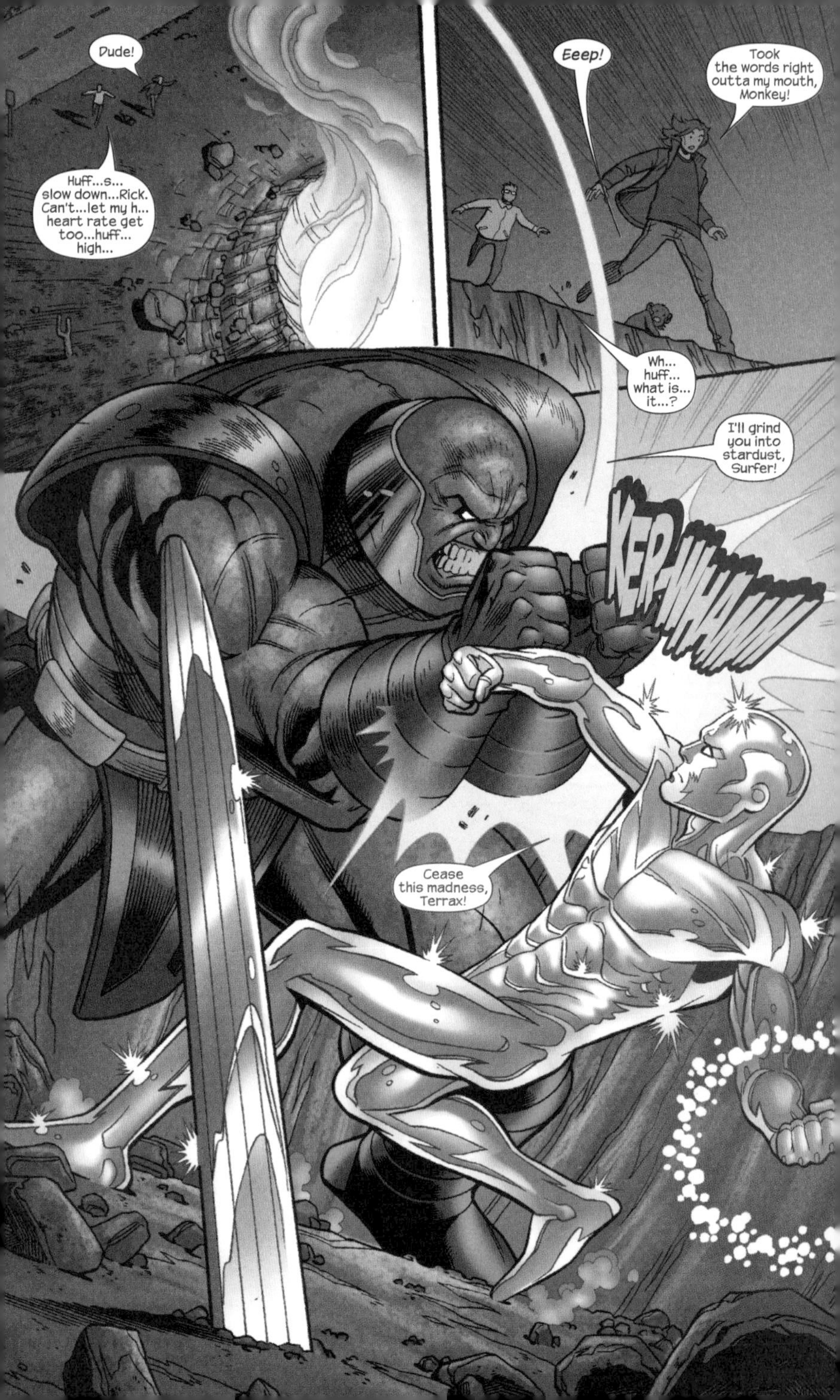
Dude!
Huff...s... slow down...Rick. Can't...let my h... heart rate get too...huff... high...
Eeep!
Took the words right outta my mouth, Monkey!
Wh... huff... what is... it...?
I'll grind you into stardust, Surfer!
KER-WHAMM
Cease this madness, Terrax!

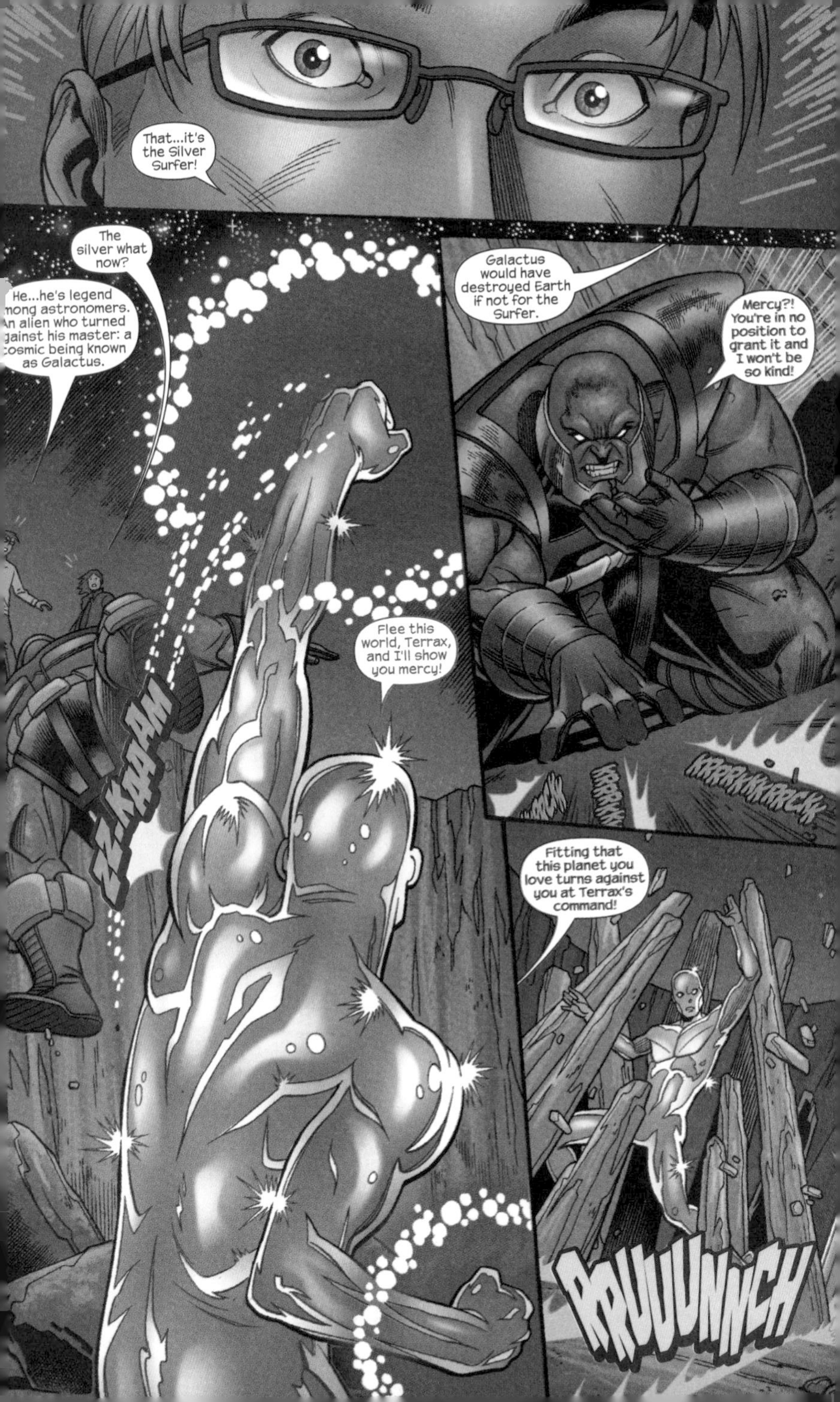

That...it's the Silver Surfer!
The silver what now?
He...he's legend mong astronomers. An alien who turned gainst his master: a cosmic being known as Galactus.
Galactus would have destroyed Earth if not for the Surfer.
Flee this world, Terrax, and I'll show you mercy!
Mercy?! You're in no position to grant it and I won't be so kind!
ZZ-KRAKAM
KRRRKKRRCK
Fitting that this planet you love turns against you at Terrax's command!
KRUUUNNCH

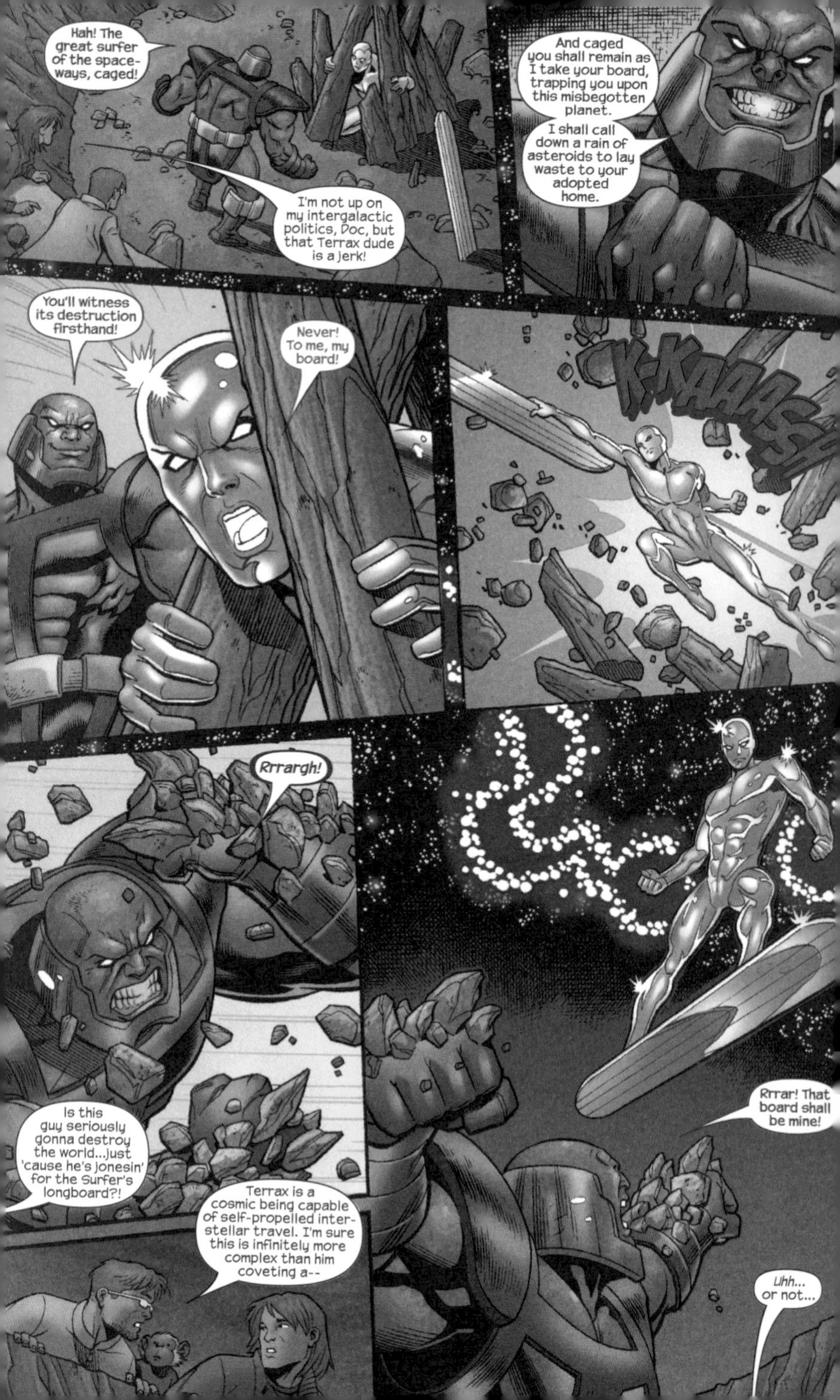
Hah! The great surfer of the space-ways, caged!
I'm not up on my intergalactic politics, Doc, but that Terrax dude is a jerk!
And caged you shall remain as I take your board, trapping you upon this misbegotten planet.
I shall call down a rain of asteroids to lay waste to your adopted home.
You'll witness its destruction firsthand!
Never! To me, my board!
K-KAAASH
Rrrargh!
Is this guy seriously gonna destroy the world...just 'cause he's jonesin' for the Surfer's longboard?!
Terrax is a cosmic being capable of self-propelled inter-stellar travel. I'm sure this is infinitely more complex than him coveting a--
Rrrar! That board shall be mine!
Uhh... or not...

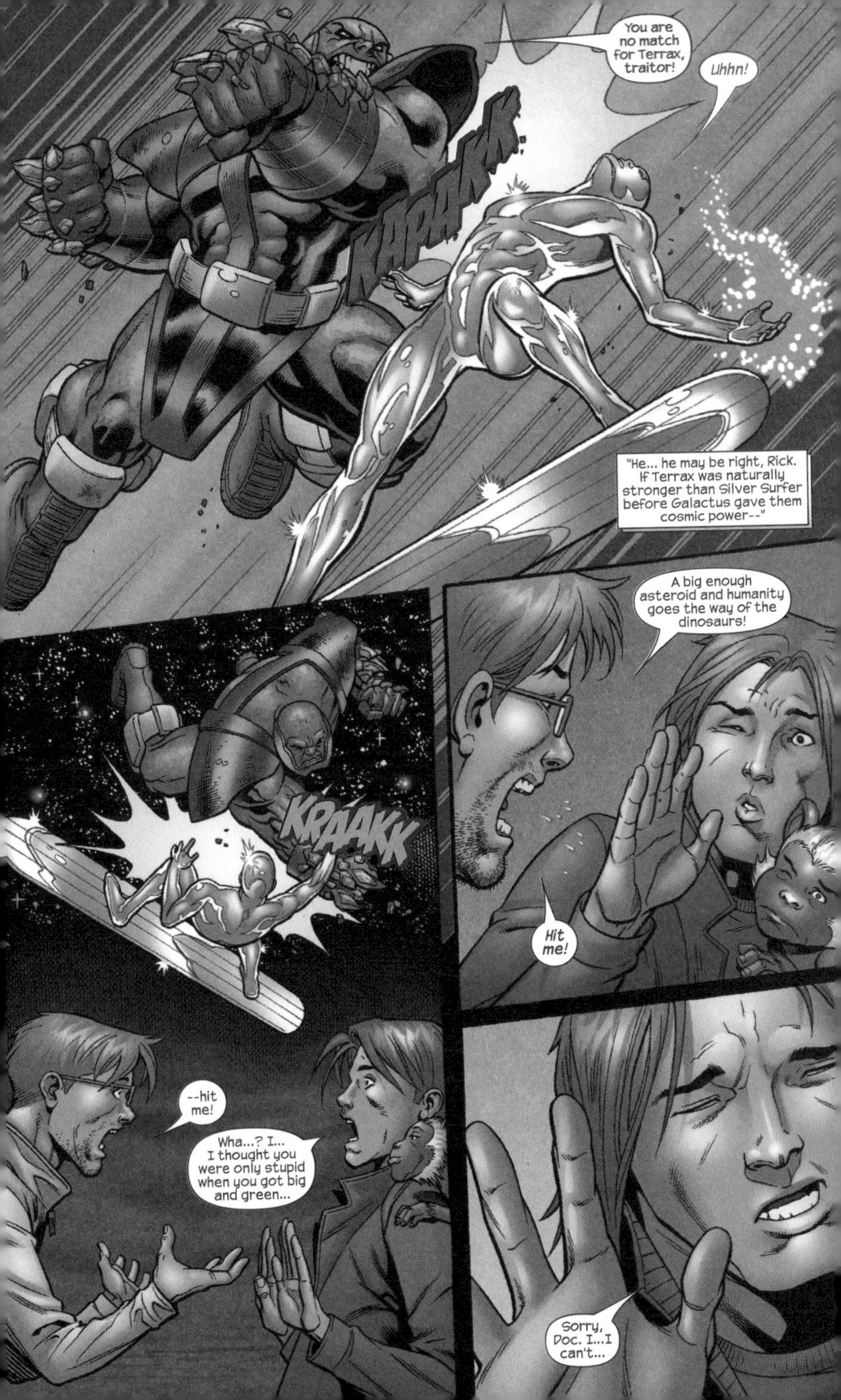
You are no match for Terrax, traitor!
Uhhn!
KAPAKK
"He... he may be right, Rick. If Terrax was naturally stronger than Silver Surfer before Galactus gave them cosmic power--"
A big enough asteroid and humanity goes the way of the dinosaurs!
Hit me!
KRAAKK
--hit me!
Wha...? I... I thought you were only stupid when you got big and green...
Sorry, Doc. I...I can't...

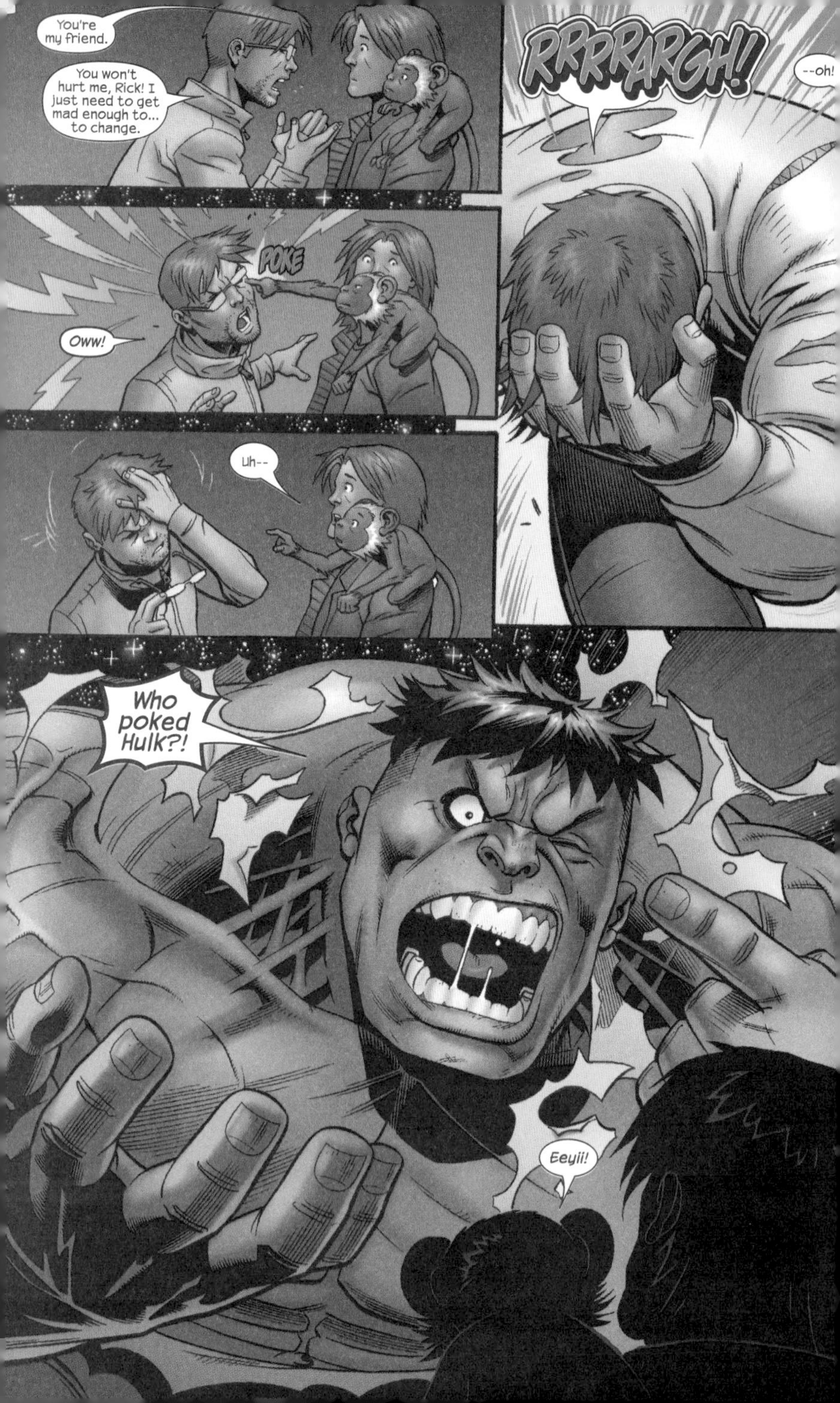
You're my friend.
You won't hurt me, Rick! I just need to get mad enough to... to change.
RRRRARGH!
--oh!
POKE
Oww!
Uh--
Who poked Hulk?!
Eeyii!

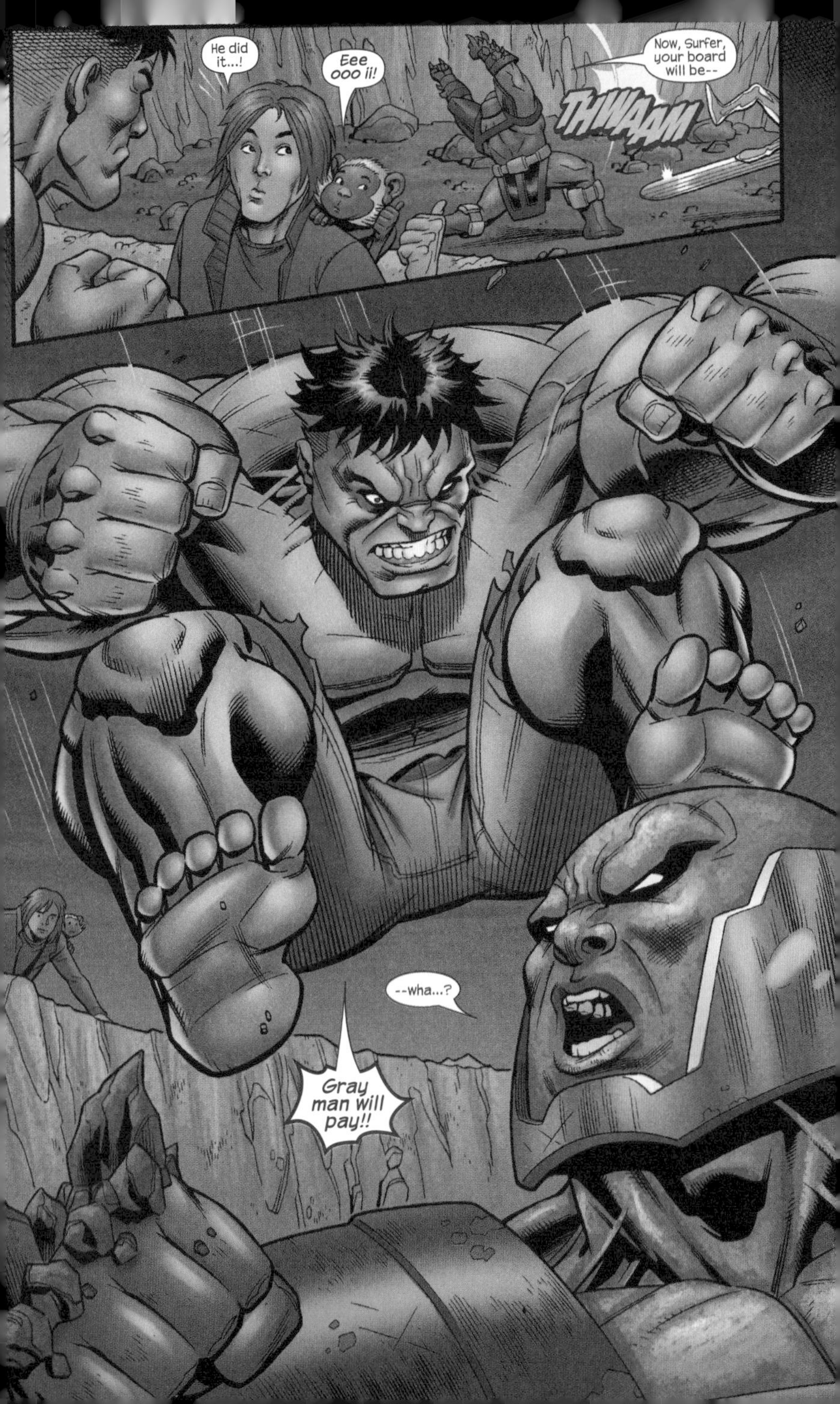
He did it...!
Eee ooo ii!
Now, Surfer, your board will be--
THWAAM
--wha...?
Gray man will pay!!

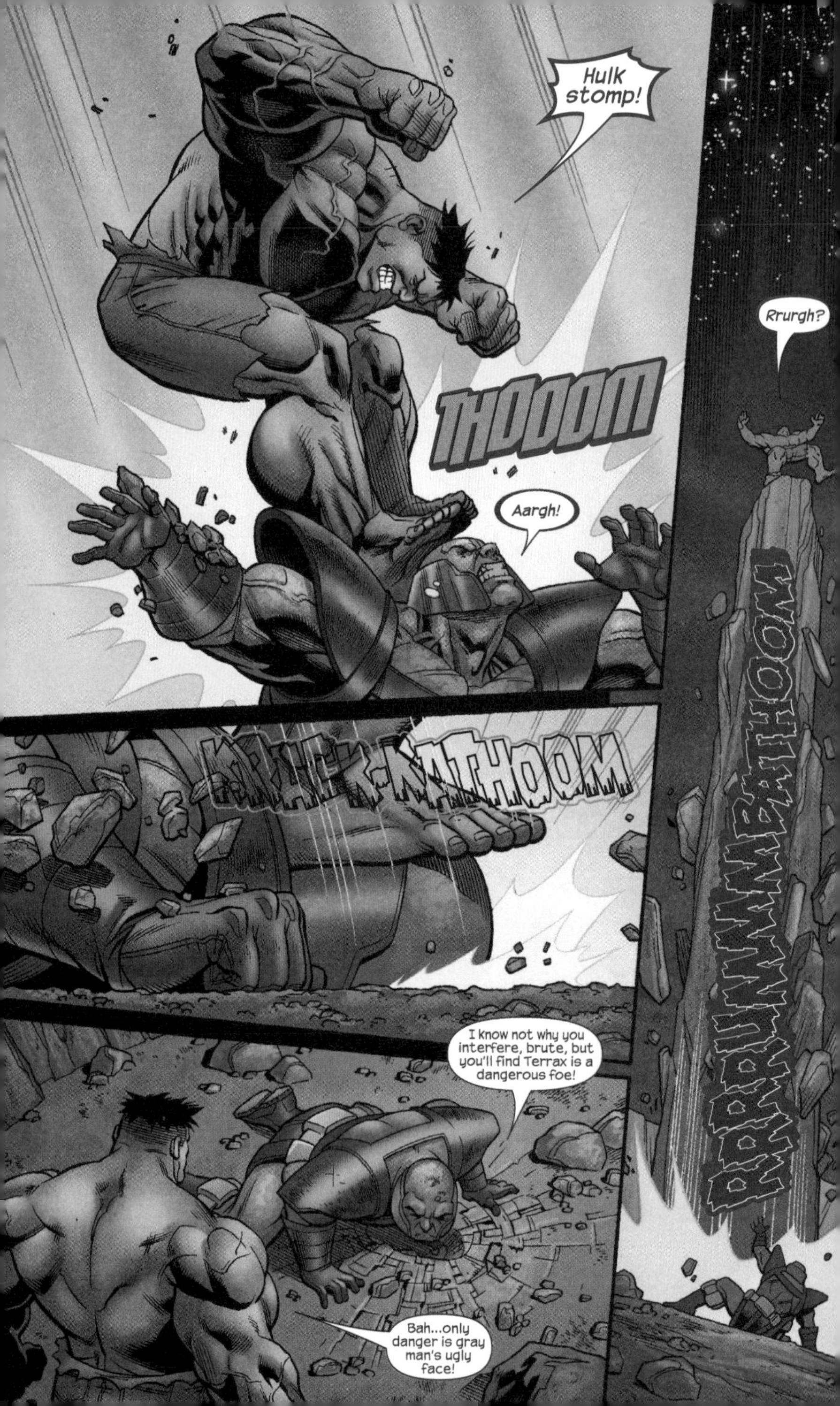
Hulk stomp!
THOOOM
Aargh!
KATHOOM
Rrurgh?
BRRRUMMMBATHOOM
I know not why you interfere, brute, but you'll find Terrax is a dangerous foe!
Bah...only danger is gray man's ugly face!

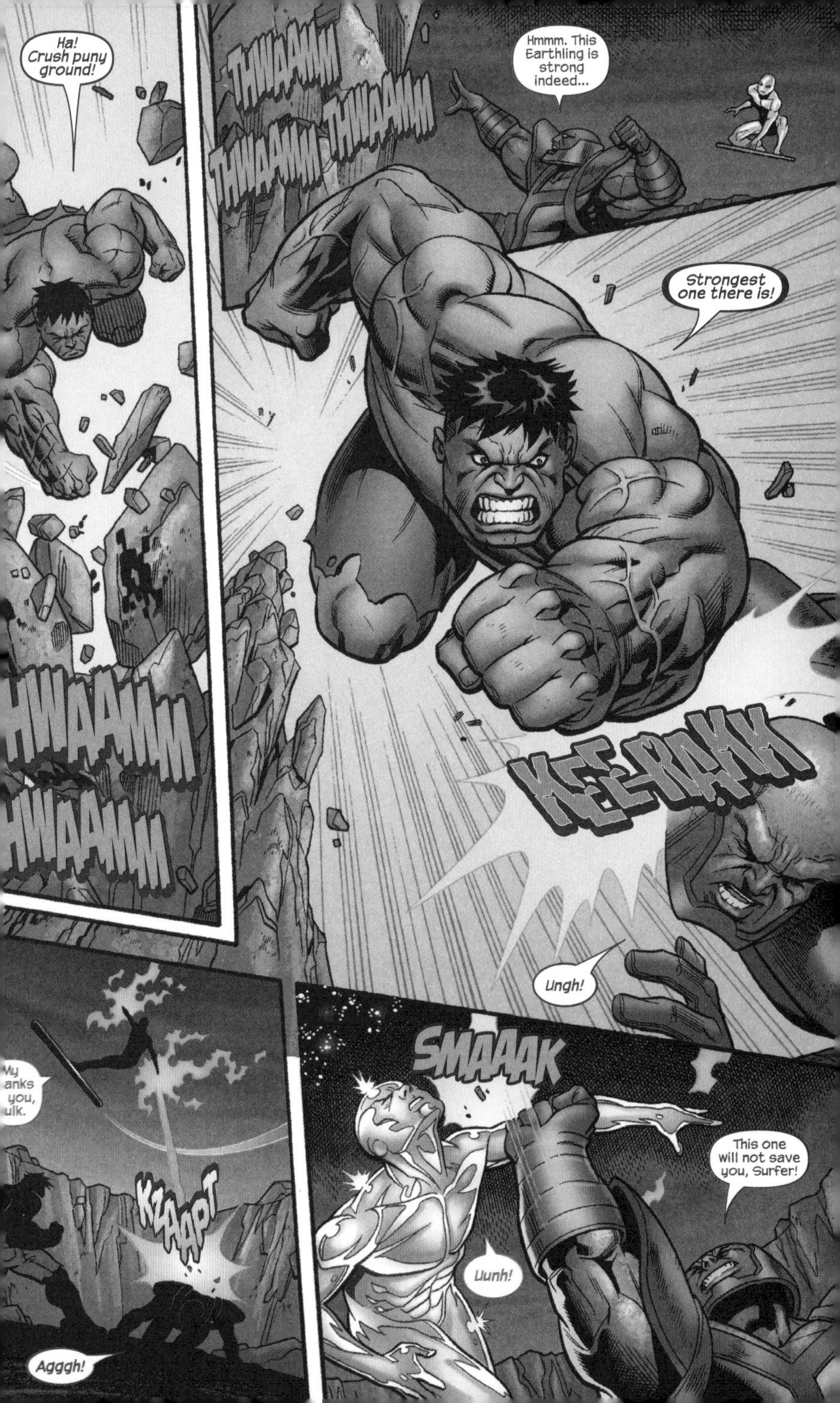
Ha! Crush puny ground!
THWAAMM THWAAMM
THWAAMM
THWAAMM THWAAMM THWAAMM
Hmmm. This Earthling is strong indeed...
Strongest one there is!
KEE-RAKK
Ungh!
My ...anks ...you, ...ulk.
KZAAPT
Agggh!
SMAAAK
This one will not save you, Surfer!
Uunh!

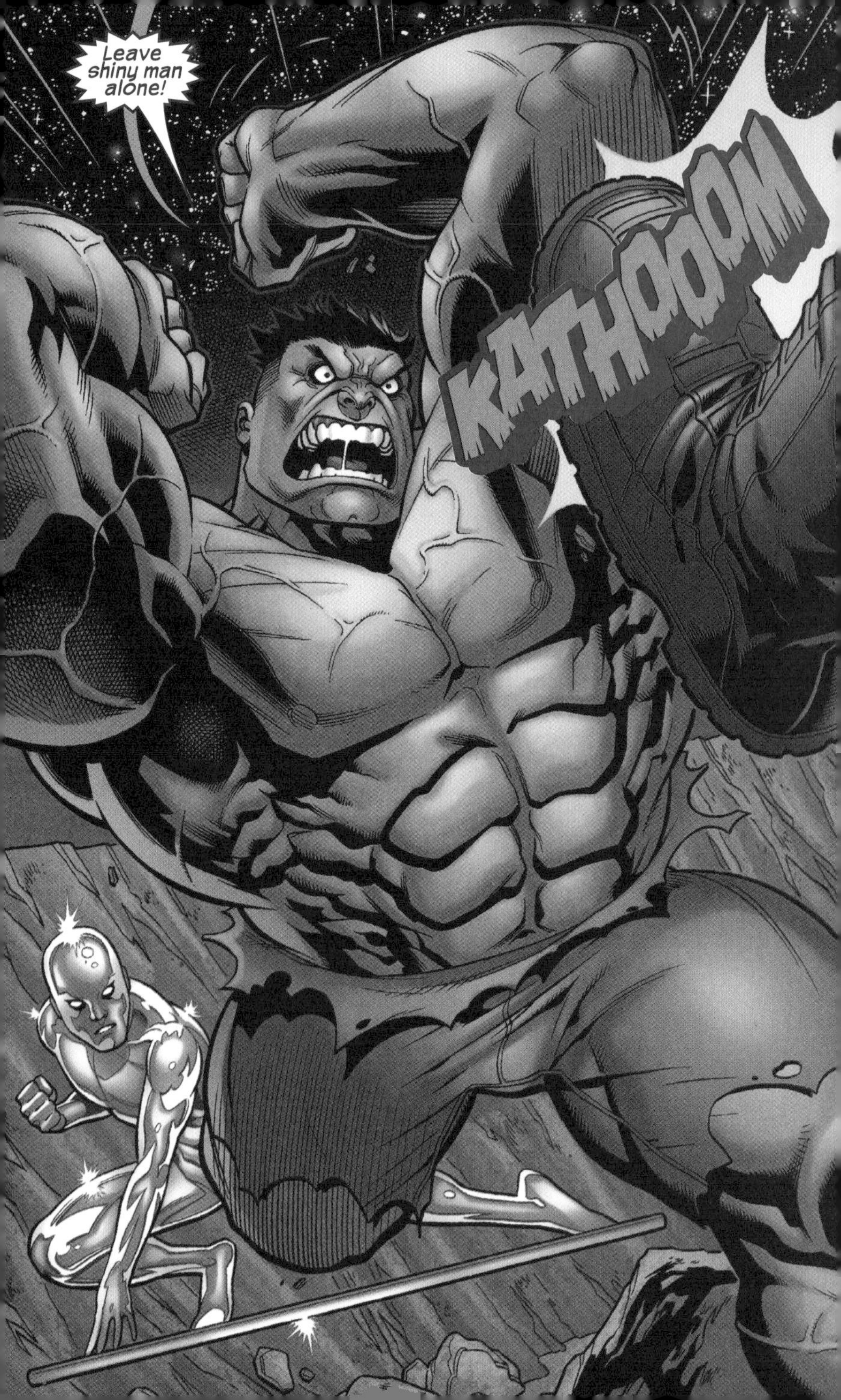
Leave shiny man alone!
KATHOOOM

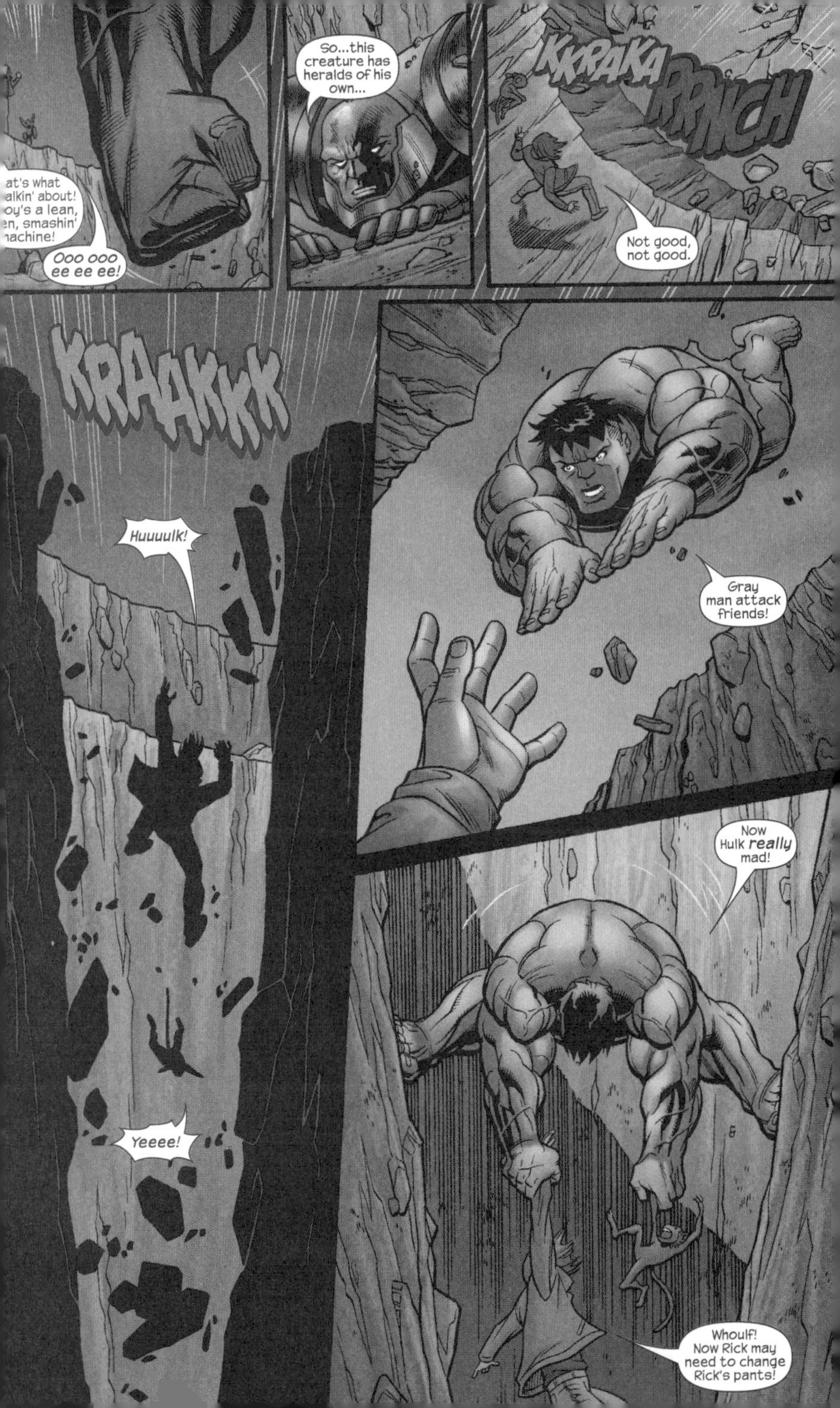
at's what
alkin' about!
oy's a lean,
en, smashin'
achine!
Ooo ooo ee ee ee!
So...this creature has heralds of his own...
KKRAKA RRNCH
Not good, not good.
KRAAKKK
Huuuulk!
Yeeee!
Gray man attack friends!
Now Hulk really mad!
Whoulf! Now Rick may need to change Rick's pants!

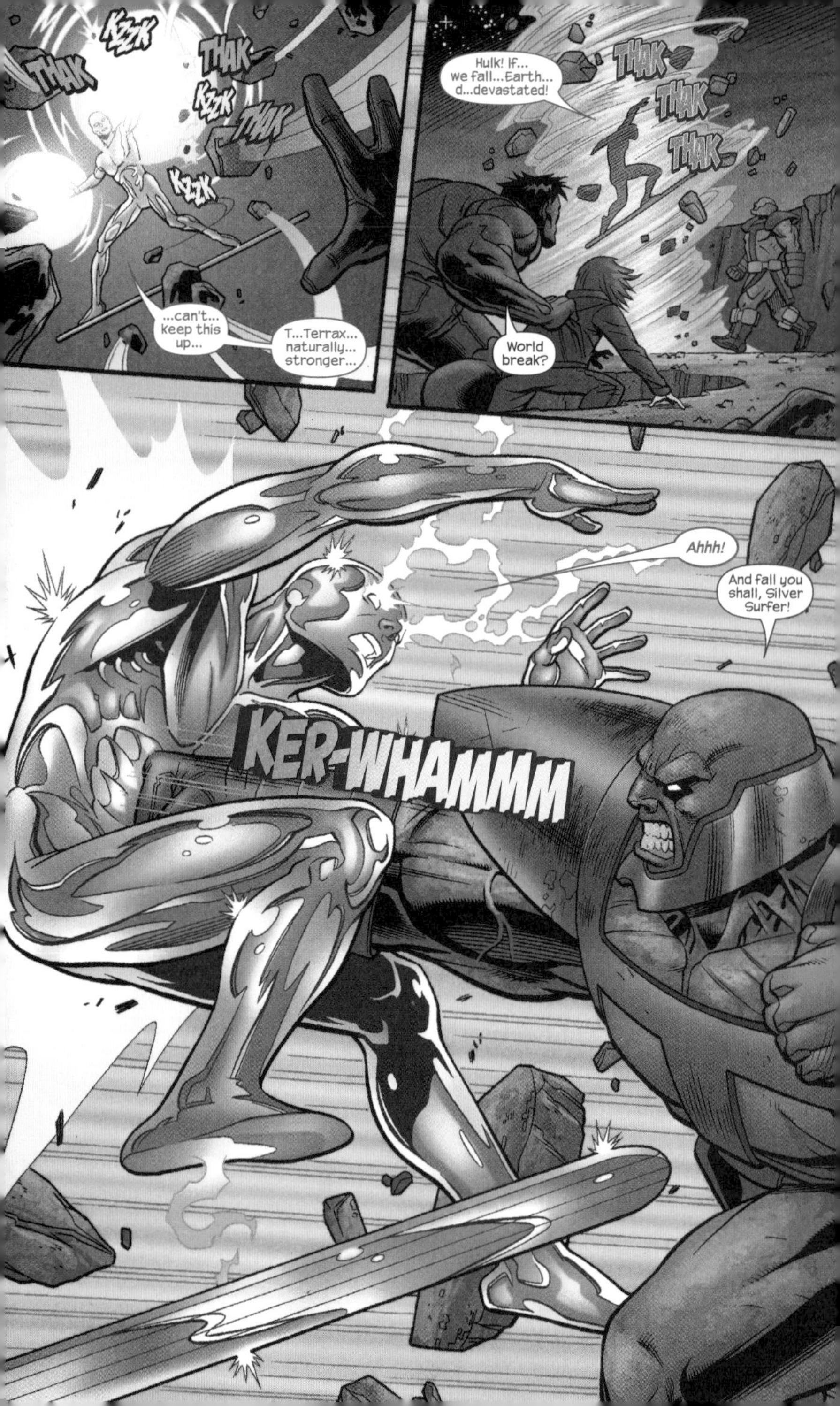
KZZK
THAK
THAK
KZZK
THAK
KZZK
...can't... keep this up...
T...Terrax... naturally... stronger...
Hulk! If... we fall...Earth... d...devastated!
THAK
THAK
THAK
World break?
Ahhh!
And fall you shall, Silver Surfer!
KER-WHAMMM

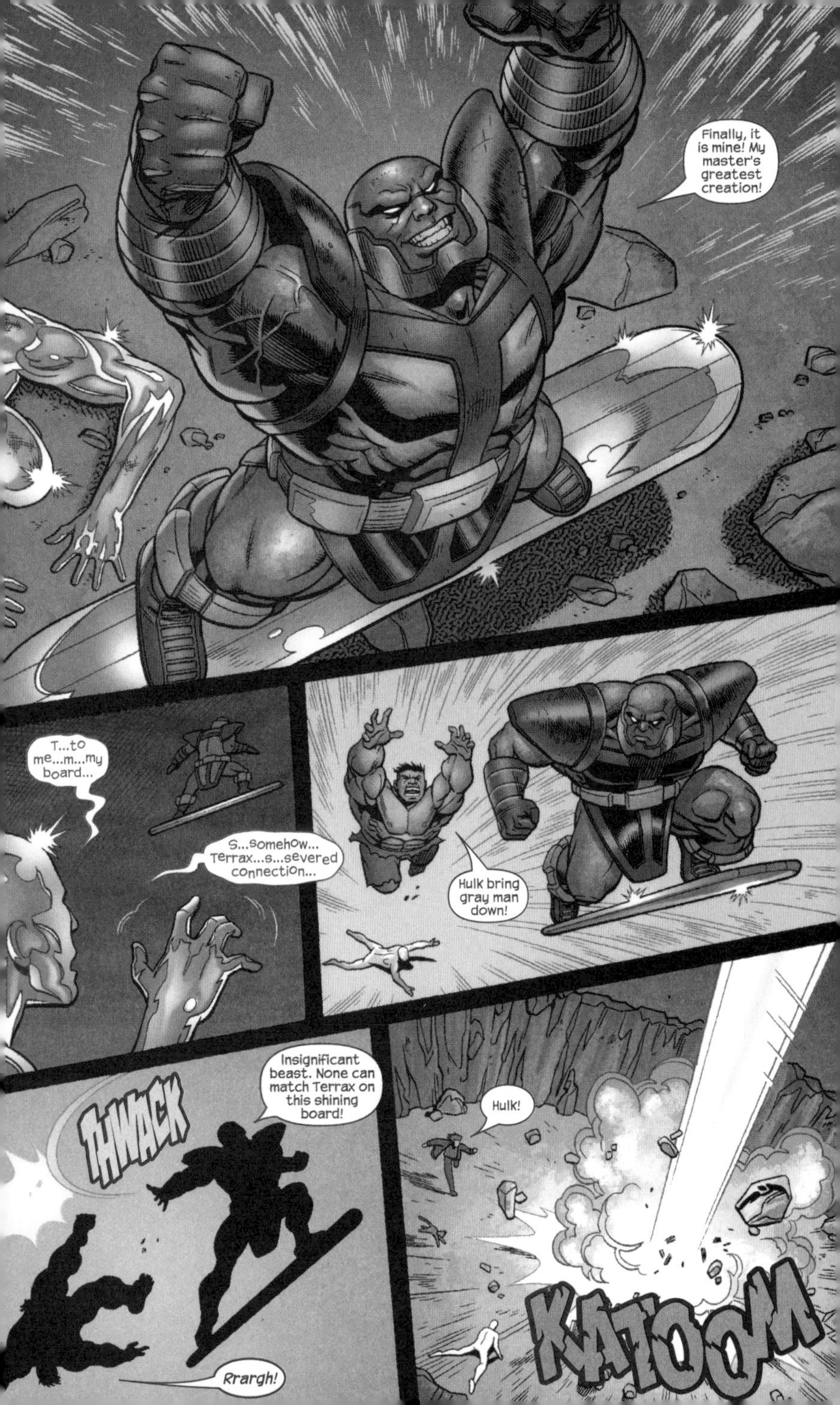
Finally, it is mine! My master's greatest creation!
T...to me...m...my board...
S...somehow... Terrax...s...severed connection...
Hulk bring gray man down!
Insignificant beast. None can match Terrax on this shining board!
THWACK
Rrargh!
Hulk!
KATOOM

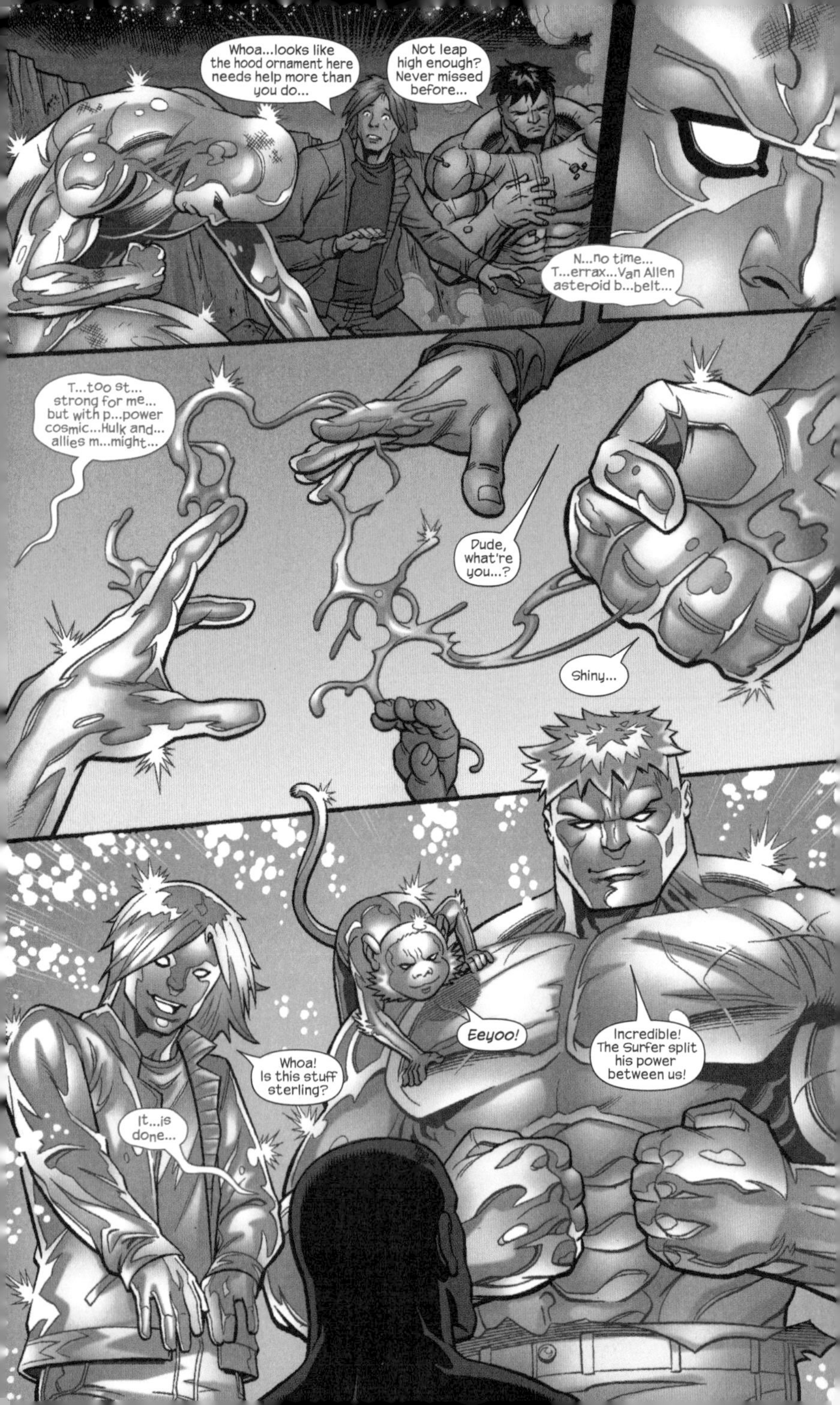
Whoa...looks like the hood ornament here needs help more than you do...
Not leap high enough? Never missed before...
N...no time... T...errax...Van Allen asteroid b...belt...
T...too st... strong for me... but with p...power cosmic...Hulk and... allies m...might...
Dude, what're you...?
Shiny...
Whoa! Is this stuff sterling?
Eeyoo!
Incredible! The Surfer split his power between us!
It...is done...

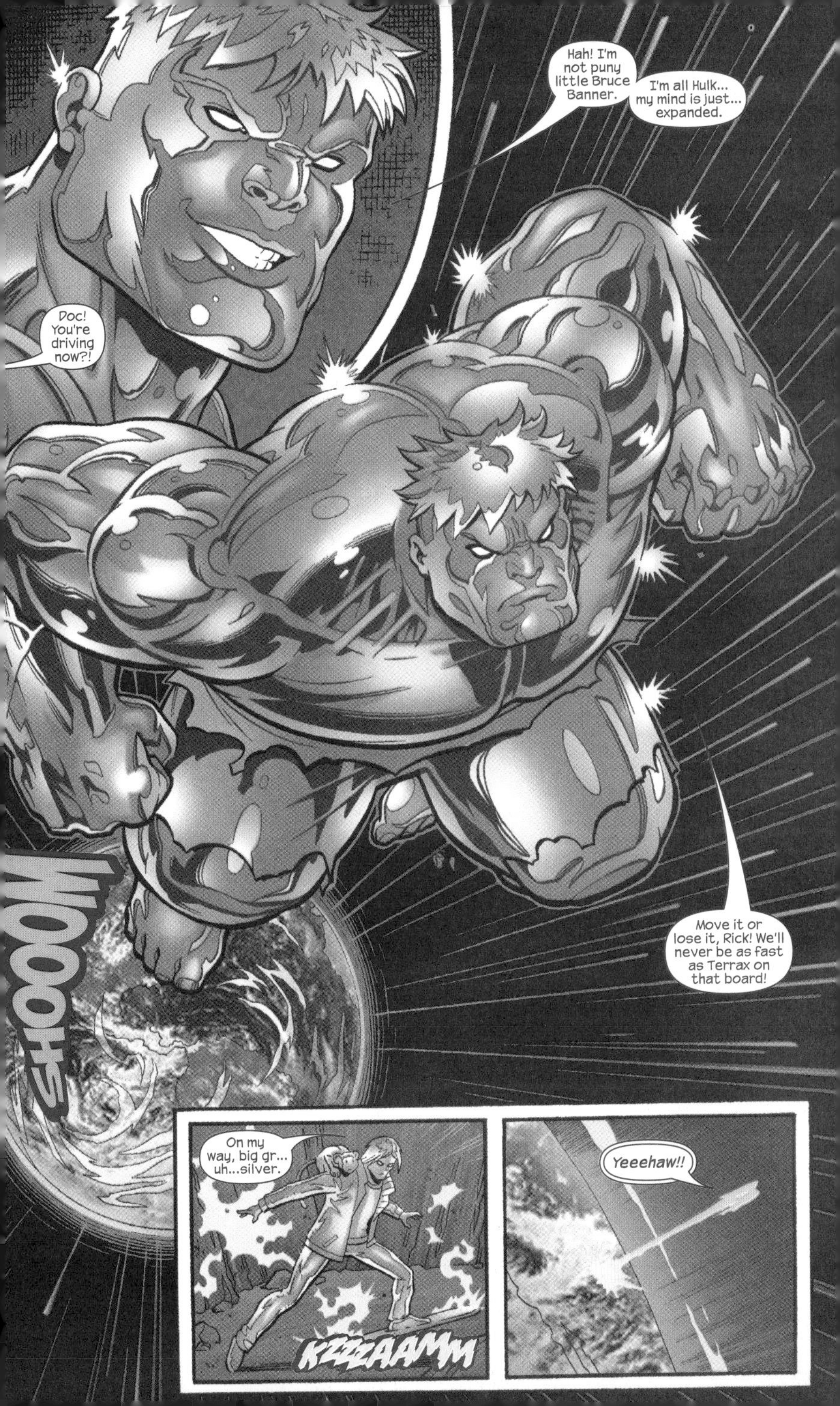
Hah! I'm not puny little Bruce Banner.
I'm all Hulk... my mind is just... expanded.
Doc! You're driving now?!
Move it or lose it, Rick! We'll never be as fast as Terrax on that board!
SHOOOOM
On my way, big gr... uh...silver.
KZZZAAMM
Yeeehaw!!

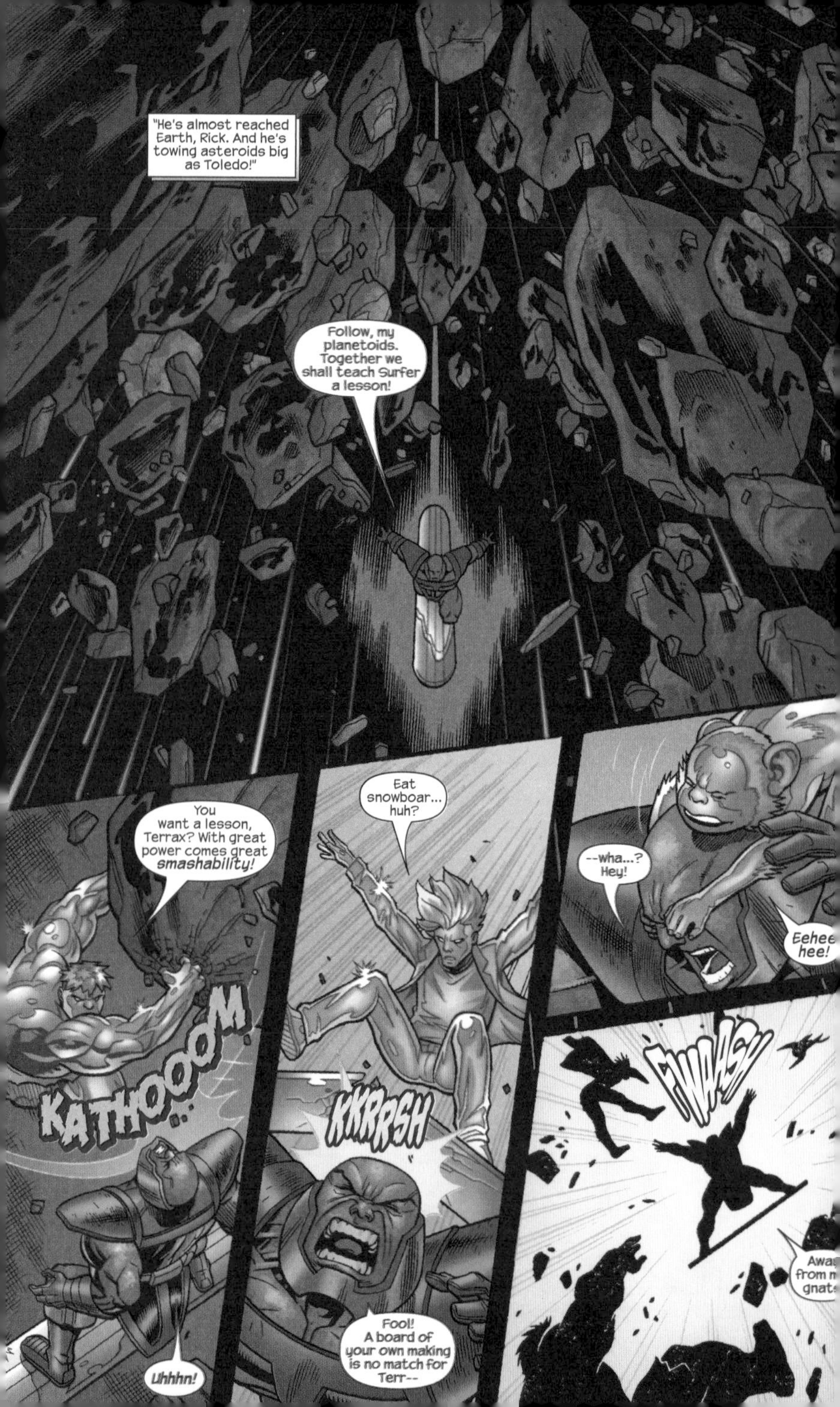
"He's almost reached Earth, Rick. And he's towing asteroids big as Toledo!"
Follow, my planetoids. Together we shall teach Surfer a lesson!
You want a lesson, Terrax? With great power comes great *smashability!*
KATHOOOM
Uhhhn!
Eat snowboar... huh?
KKRRSH
Fool! A board of your own making is no match for Terr--
--wha...? Hey!
Eehee hee!
FWOOSH
Awa from m gnat

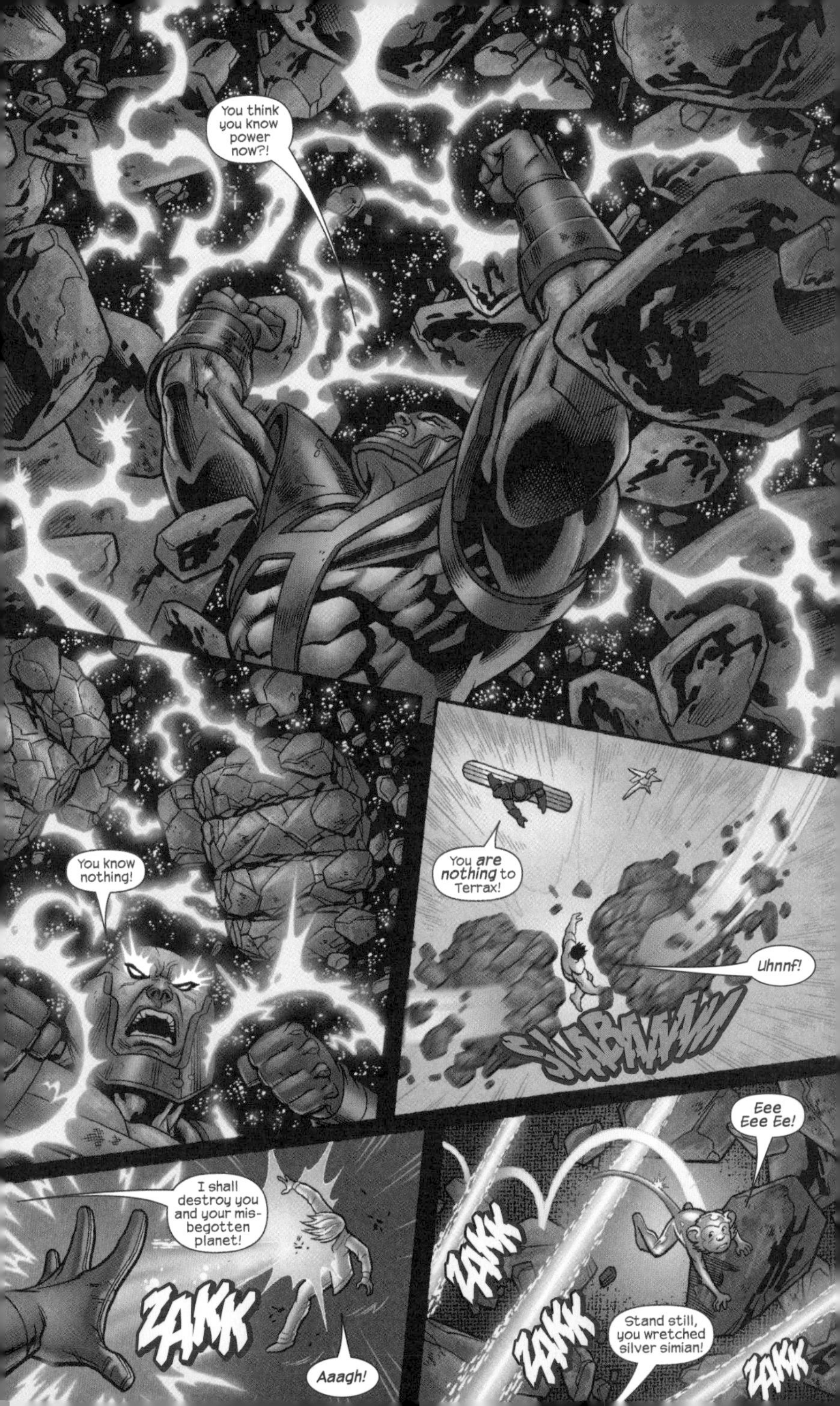

You think you know power now?!
You know nothing!
You are nothing to Terrax!
Uhnnf!
I shall destroy you and your mis-begotten planet!
ZAKK
Aaagh!
Eee Eee Ee!
ZAKK
ZAKK
Stand still, you wretched silver simian!
ZAKK

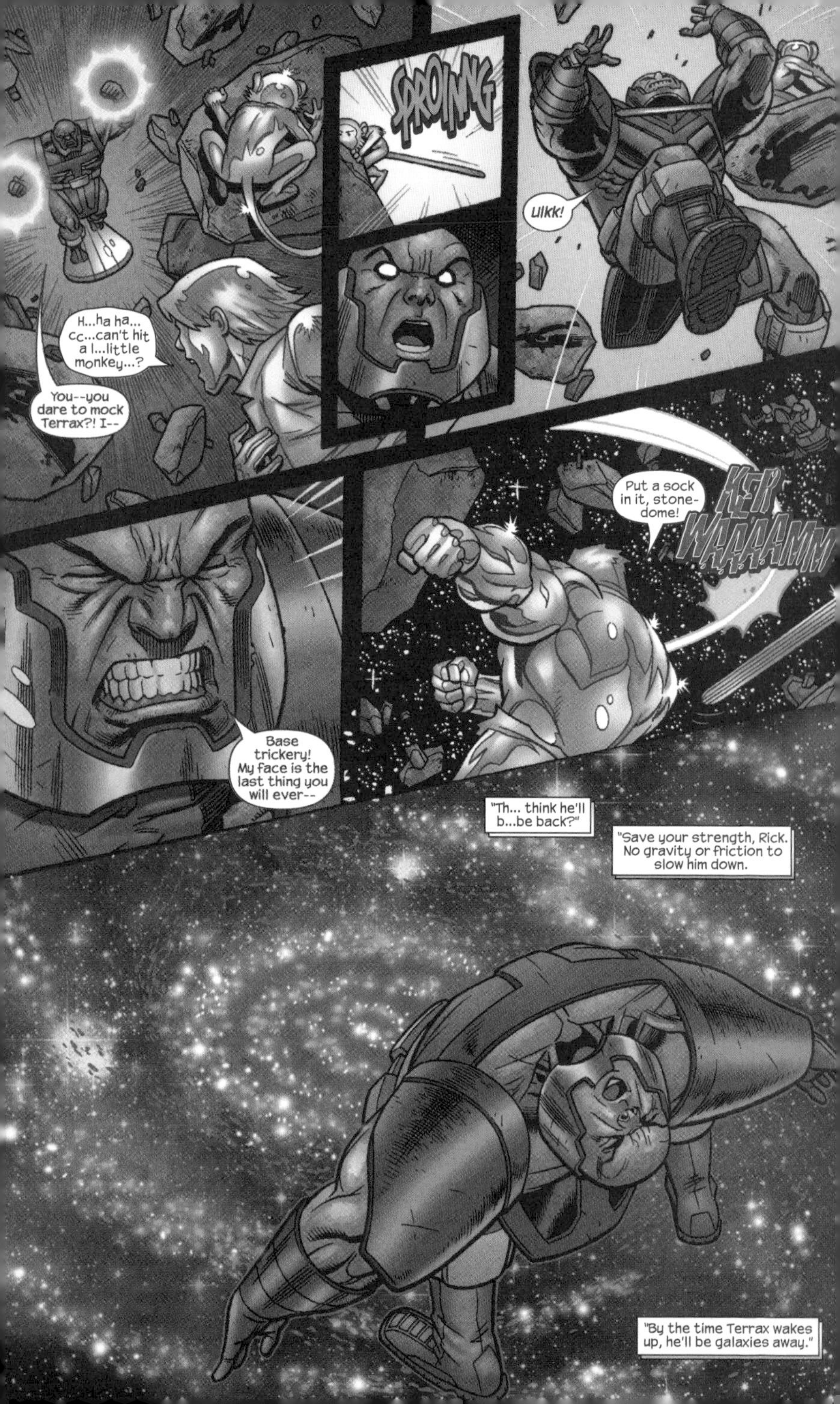
SPROING
UIKK!
H...ha ha... cc...can't hit a l...little monkey...?
You--you dare to mock Terrax?! I--
Put a sock in it, stone-dome!
KER WAAAAMM
Base trickery! My face is the last thing you will ever--
"Th... think he'll b...be back?"
"Save your strength, Rick. No gravity or friction to slow him down.
"By the time Terrax wakes up, he'll be galaxies away."

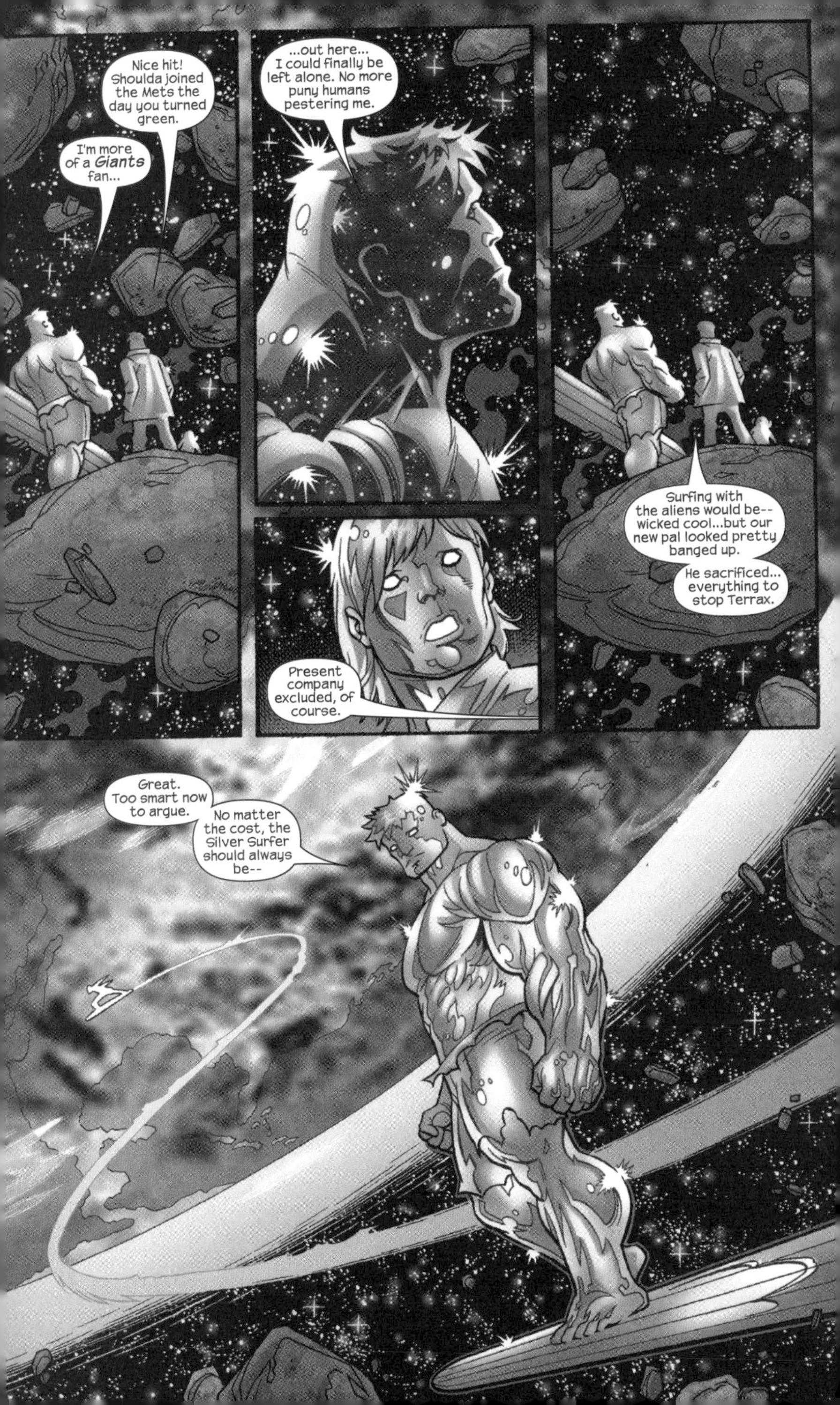

Nice hit! Shoulda joined the Mets the day you turned green.
I'm more of a *Giants* fan...
...out here... I could finally be left alone. No more puny humans pestering me.
Present company excluded, of course.
Surfing with the aliens would be--wicked cool...but our new pal looked pretty banged up.
He sacrificed... everything to stop Terrax.
Great. Too smart now to argue.
No matter the cost, the Silver Surfer should always be--

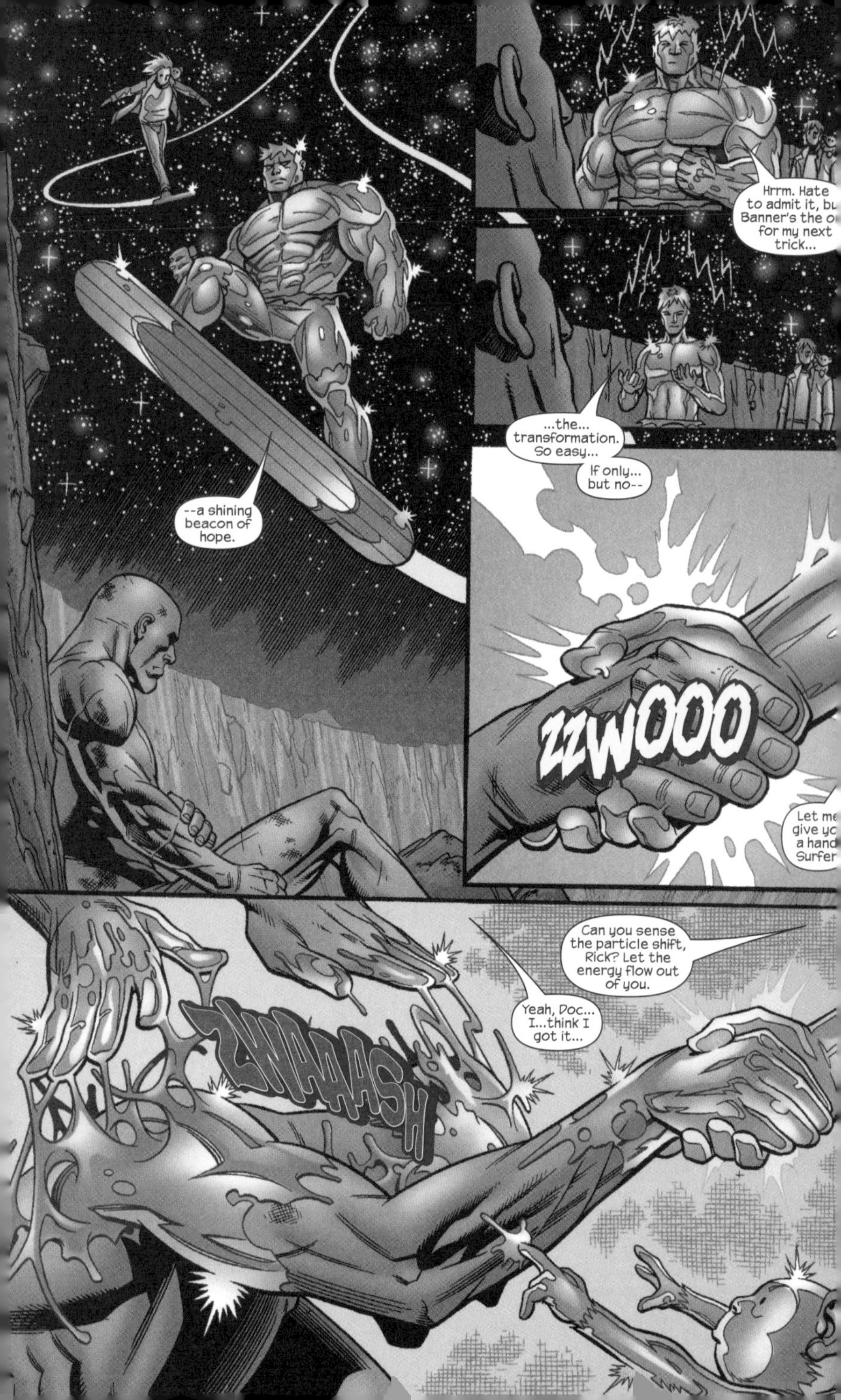
--a shining beacon of hope.
Hrrm. Hate to admit it, bu Banner's the o for my next trick...
...the... transformation. So easy...
If only... but no--
ZZWOOO
Let me give yo a hand Surfer
Can you sense the particle shift, Rick? Let the energy flow out of you.
Yeah, Doc... I...think I got it...
ZWAAASH

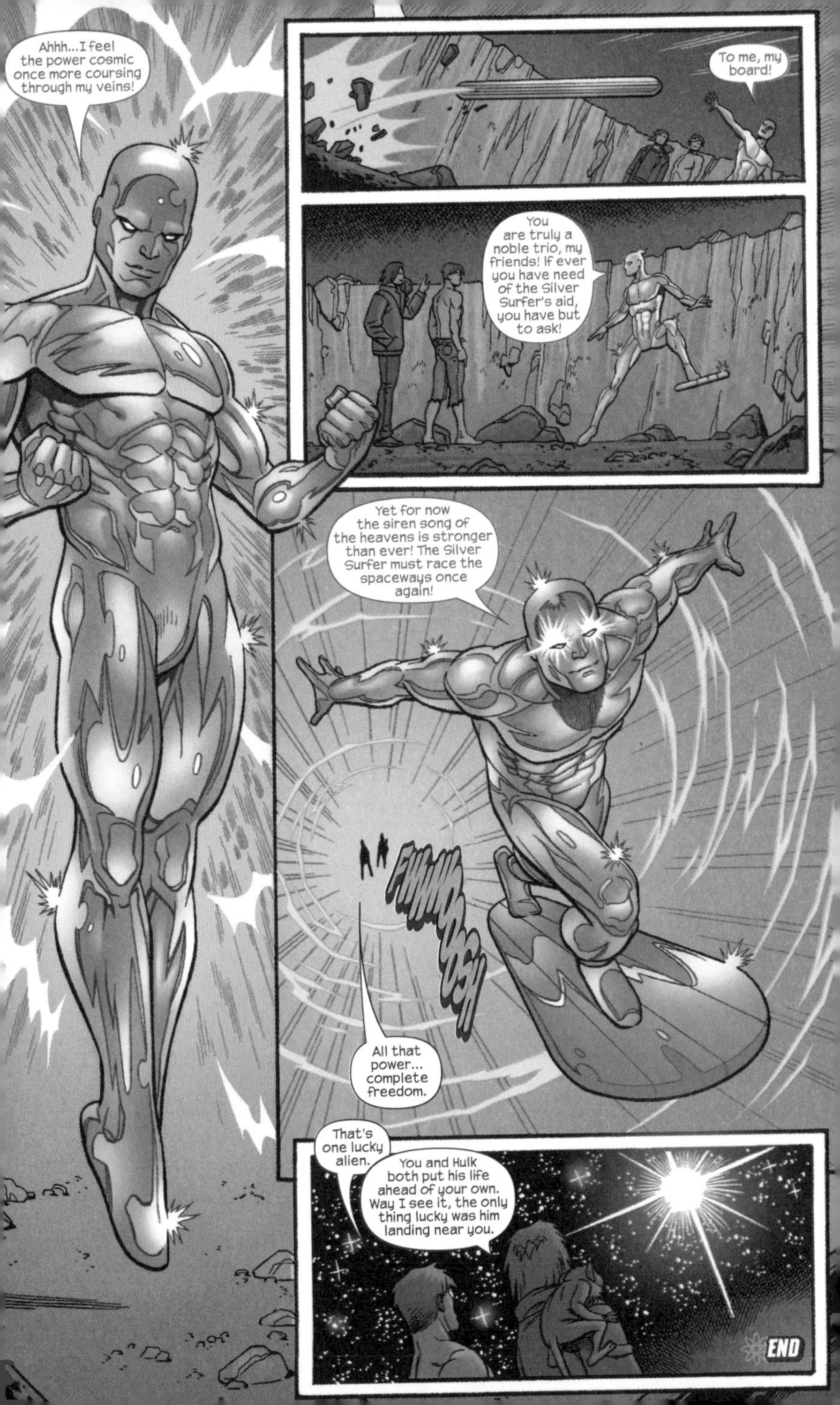
Ahhh...I feel the power cosmic once more coursing through my veins!
To me, my board!
You are truly a noble trio, my friends! If ever you have need of the Silver Surfer's aid, you have but to ask!
Yet for now the siren song of the heavens is stronger than ever! The Silver Surfer must race the spaceways once again!
FWHOOOSH
All that power... complete freedom.
That's one lucky alien.
You and Hulk both put his life ahead of your own. Way I see it, the only thing lucky was him landing near you.
END

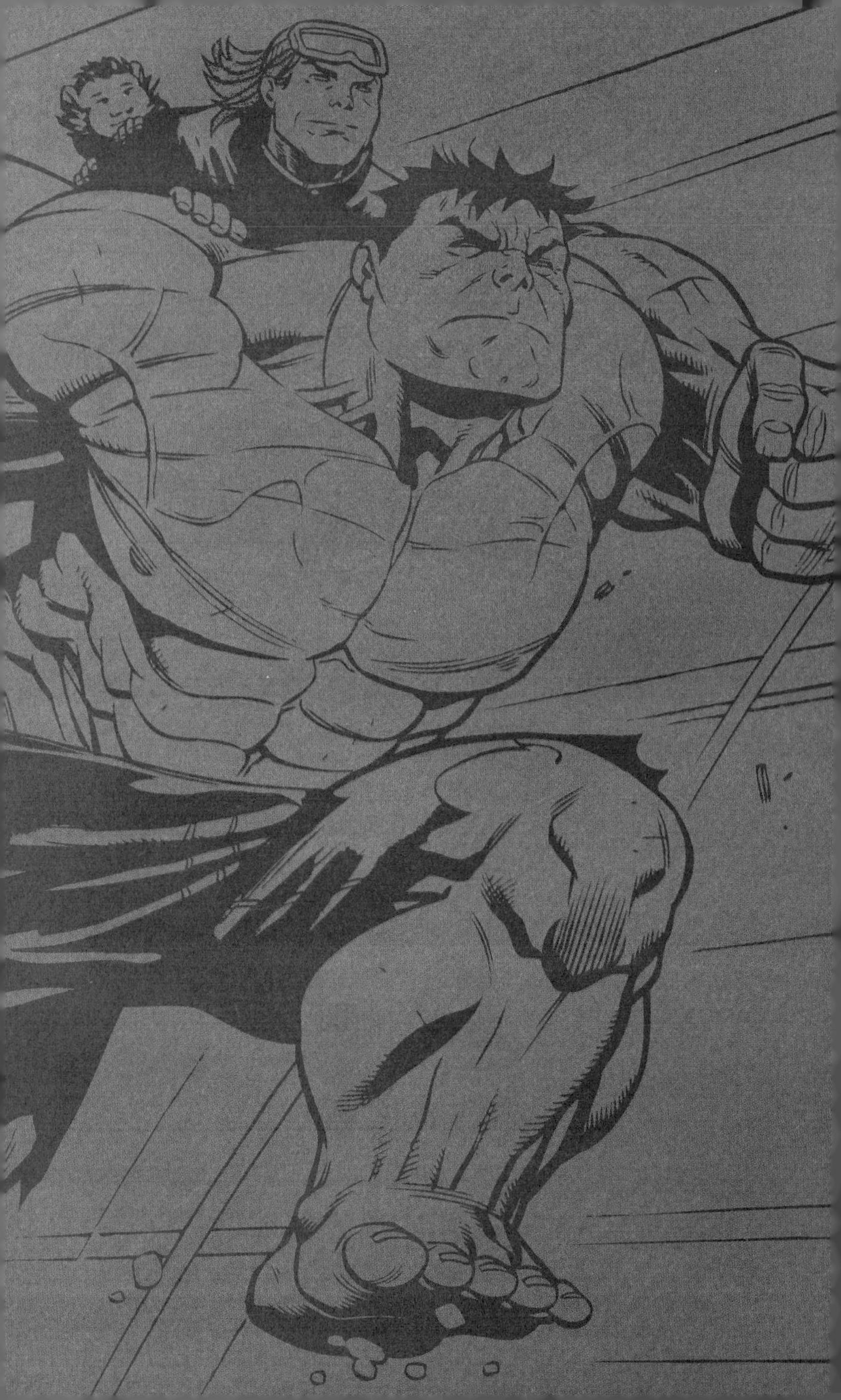

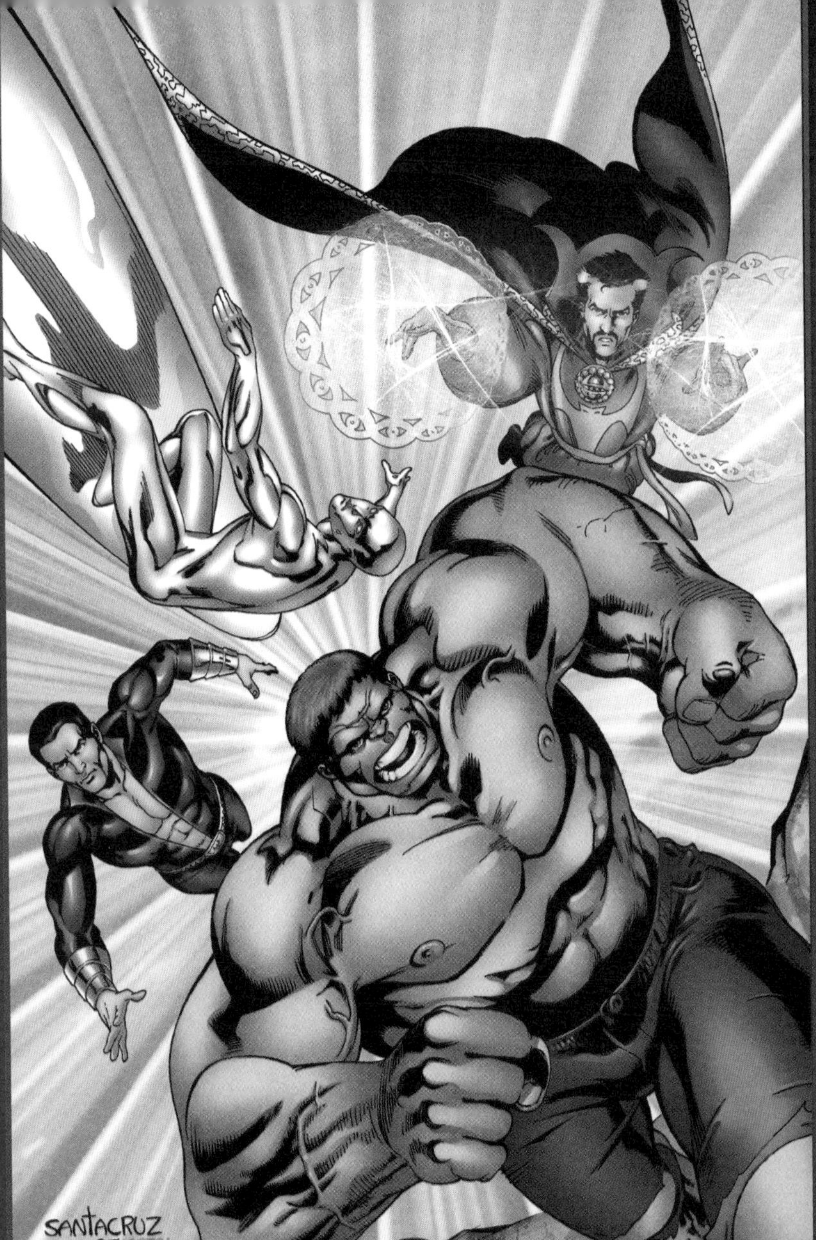
SANTACRUZ
07 ISOTO!

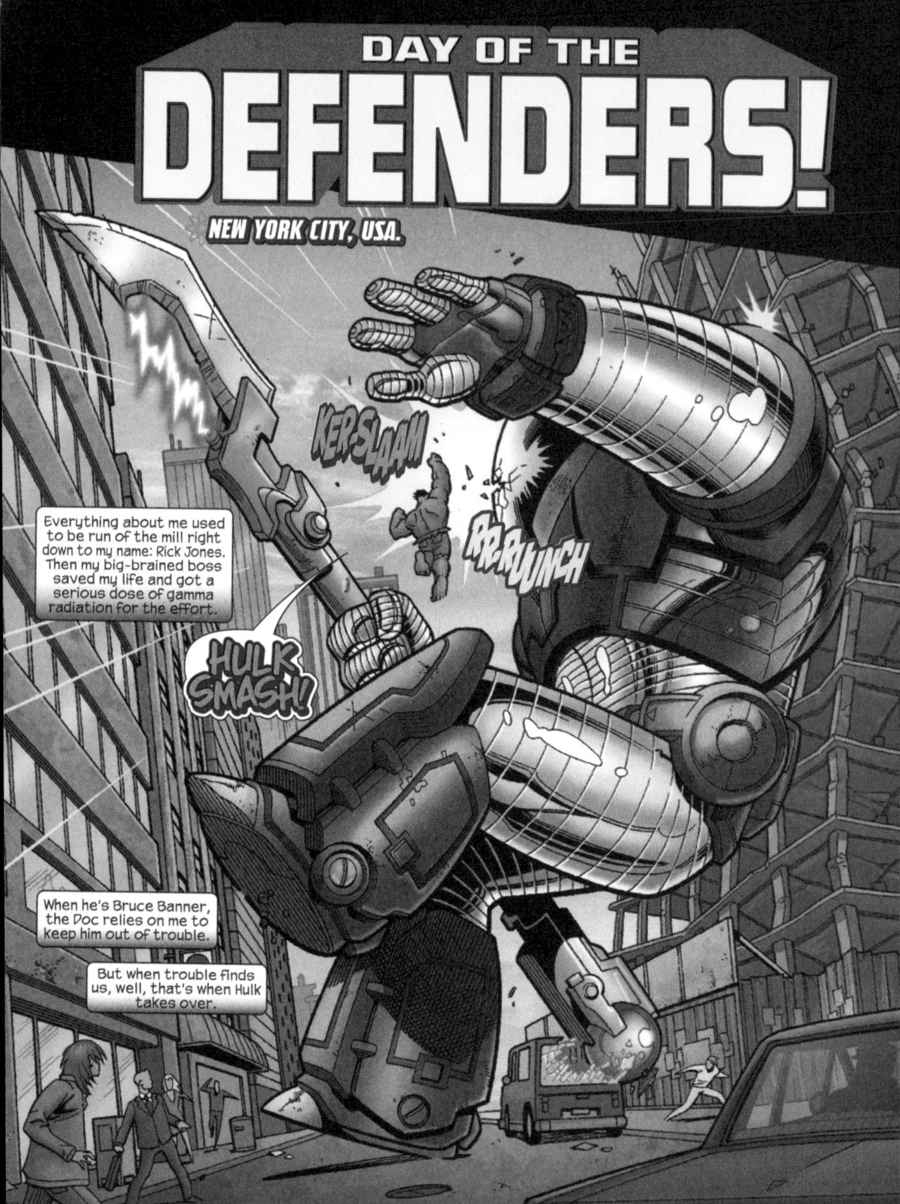
DAY OF THE
DEFENDERS!
NEW YORK CITY, USA.
KER-SLAAM
Everything about me used to be run of the mill right down to my name: Rick Jones. Then my big-brained boss saved my life and got a serious dose of gamma radiation for the effort.
RR-RUUNCH
HULK SMASH!
When he's Bruce Banner, the Doc relies on me to keep him out of trouble.
But when trouble finds us, well, that's when Hulk takes over.

Caught in a blast of gamma radiation, brilliant scientist Bruce Banner now finds himself living as a fugitive. The only people he can coun on are his devoted assistant, Rick Jones, and the former lab monkey Bruce affectionately calls "Monkey." For Bruce Banner is cursed to transform in times of stress into the living engine of destruction known as THE INCREDIBLE HULK

PAUL BENJAMIN WRITER
DAVID NAKAYAMA PENCILER
GARY MARTIN INKER
MICHELLE MADSEN COLORIST
DAVE SHARPE LETTERER
SANTACRUZ, FERNANDEZ AND SOTOCOLOR COVER ARTISTS
RICH GINTER PRODUCTION
JORDAN D. WHITE ASST. EDITOR
MARK PANICCIA EDITOR
JOE QUESADA EDITOR IN CHIEF
DAN BUCKLEY PUBLISHER

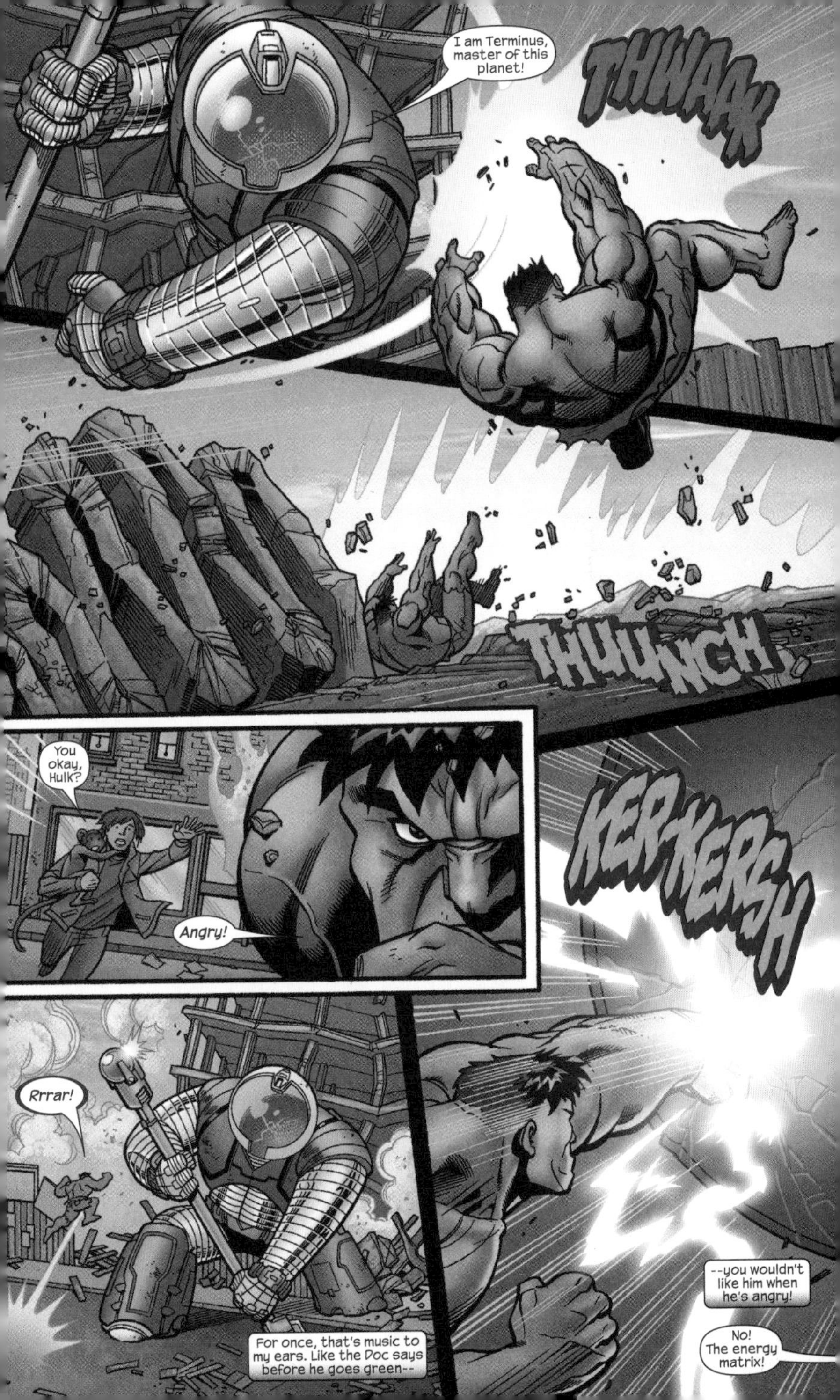
I am Terminus, master of this planet!
THWAAK
THUUNCH
You okay, Hulk?
Angry!
KER-KERSH
Rrrar!
For once, that's music to my ears. Like the Doc says before he goes green--
--you wouldn't like him when he's angry!
No! The energy matrix!

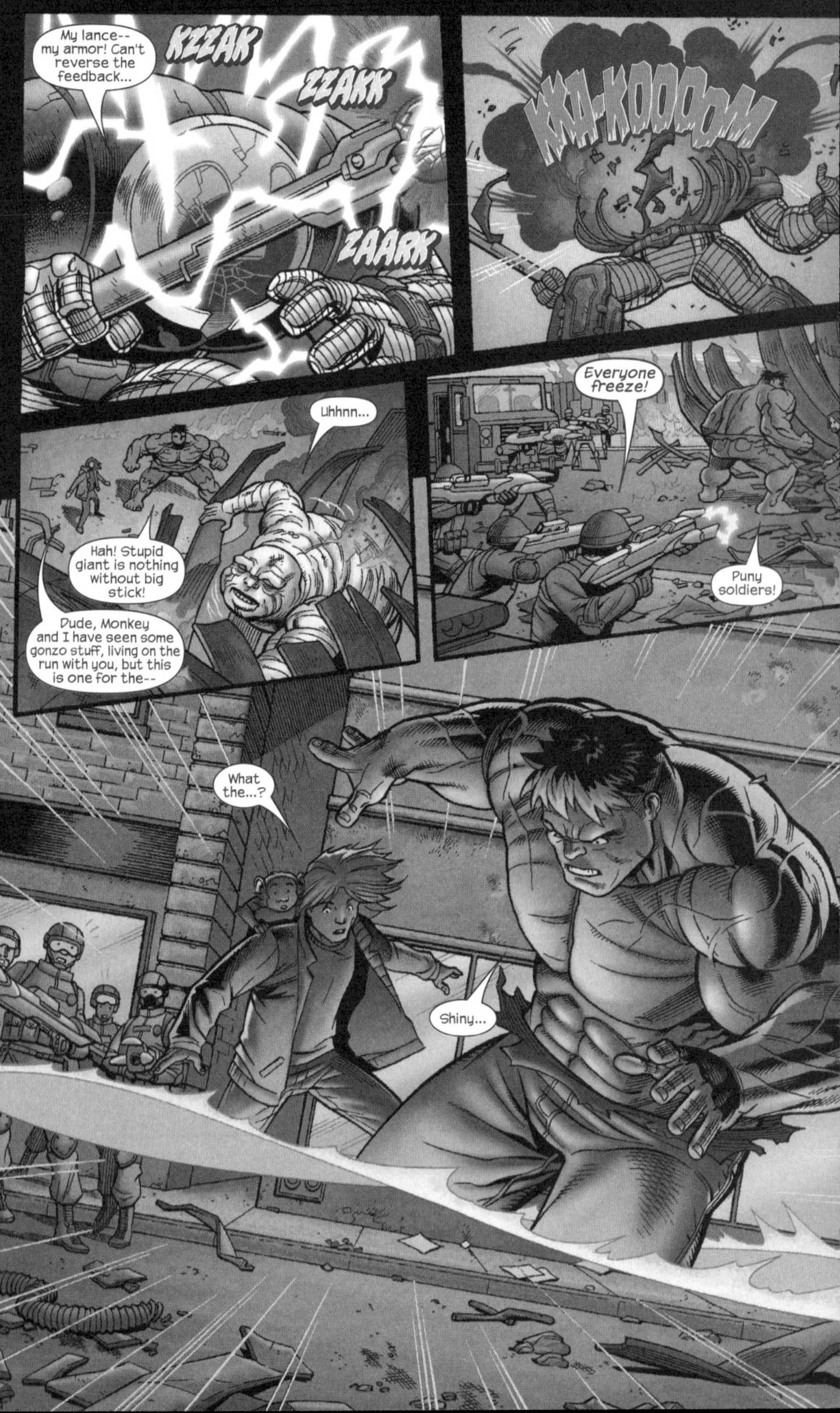
My lance-- my armor! Can't reverse the feedback...
KZZAK
ZZAKK
ZAARK
KKA-KOOOOM
Uhhnn...
Hah! Stupid giant is nothing without big stick!
Dude, Monkey and I have seen some gonzo stuff, living on the run with you, but this is one for the--
Everyone freeze!
Puny soldiers!
What the...?
Shiny...

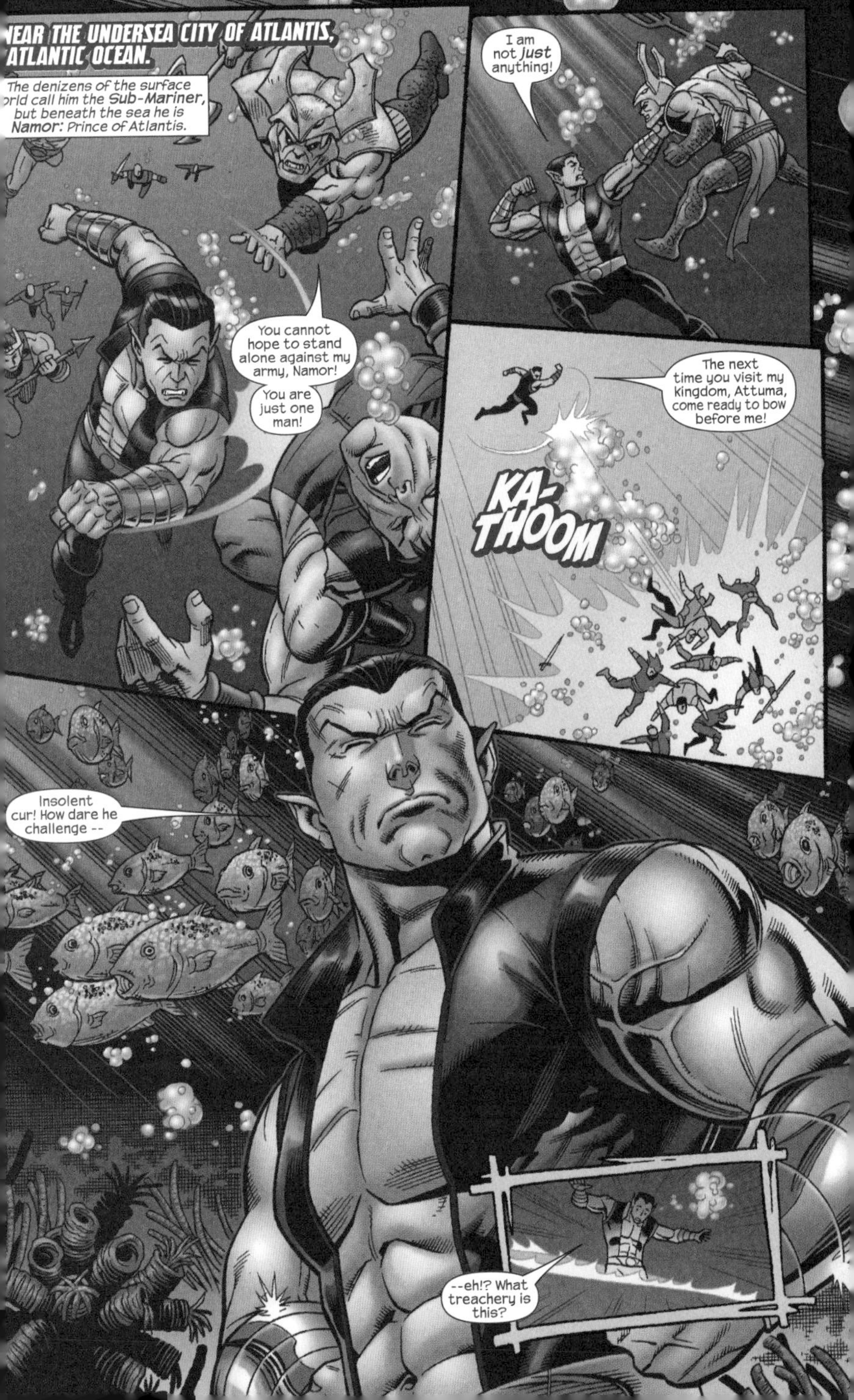
NEAR THE UNDERSEA CITY OF ATLANTIS, ATLANTIC OCEAN.
The denizens of the surface world call him the Sub-Mariner, but beneath the sea he is Namor: Prince of Atlantis.
You cannot hope to stand alone against my army, Namor!
You are just one man!
I am not just anything!
The next time you visit my kingdom, Attuma, come ready to bow before me!
KA-THOOM
Insolent cur! How dare he challenge --
--eh!? What treachery is this?

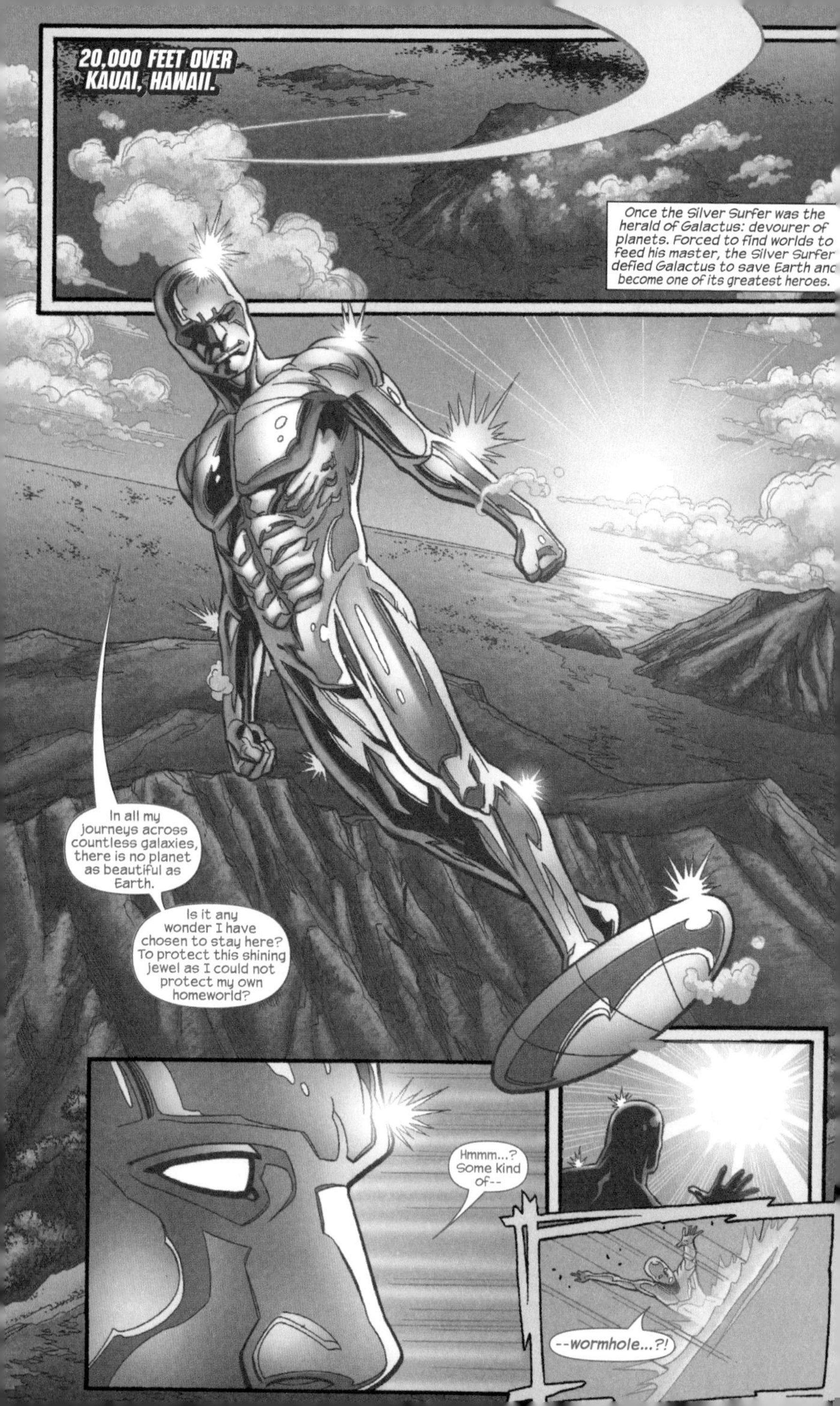
20,000 FEET OVER KAUAI, HAWAII.
Once the Silver Surfer was the herald of Galactus: devourer of planets. Forced to find worlds to feed his master, the Silver Surfer defied Galactus to save Earth and become one of its greatest heroes.
In all my journeys across countless galaxies, there is no planet as beautiful as Earth.
Is it any wonder I have chosen to stay here? To protect this shining jewel as I could not protect my own homeworld?
Hmmm...? Some kind of--
--wormhole...?!

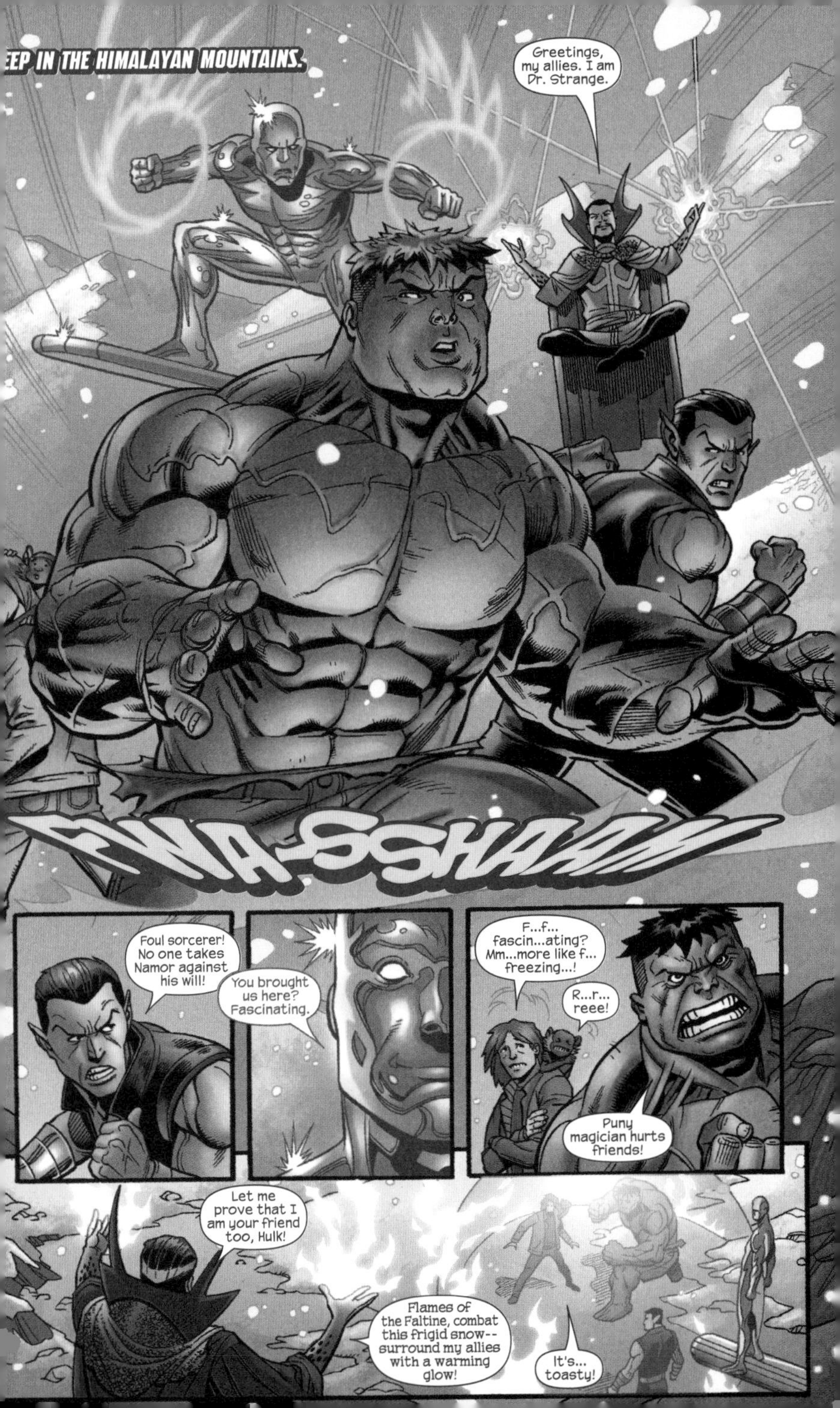
EEP IN THE HIMALAYAN MOUNTAINS.
Greetings, my allies. I am Dr. Strange.
Foul sorcerer! No one takes Namor against his will!
You brought us here? Fascinating.
F...f... fascin...ating? Mm...more like f... freezing...!
R...r... reee!
Puny magician hurts friends!
Let me prove that I am your friend too, Hulk!
Flames of the Faltine, combat this frigid snow-- surround my allies with a warming glow!
It's... toasty!

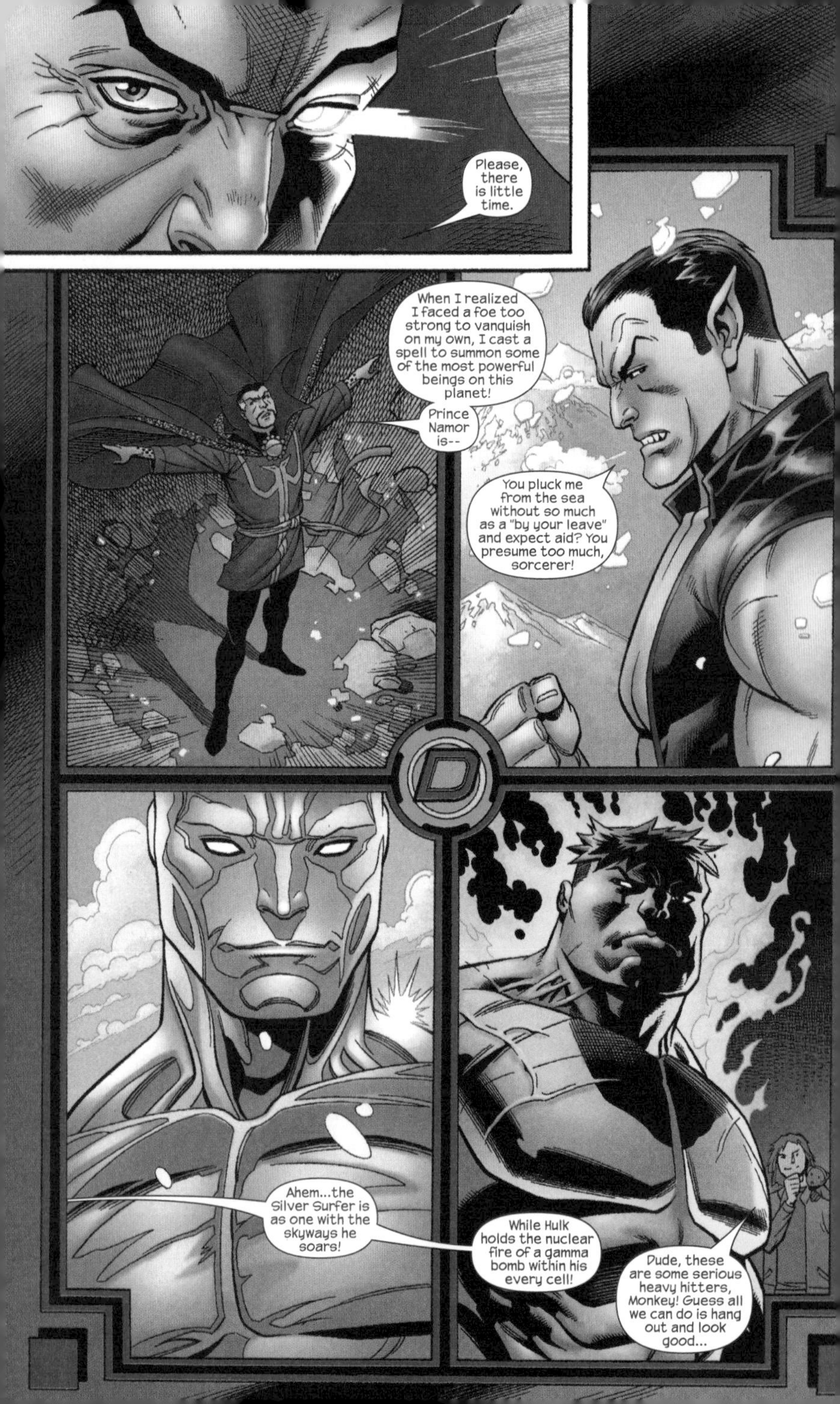

Please, there is little time.
When I realized I faced a foe too strong to vanquish on my own, I cast a spell to summon some of the most powerful beings on this planet!
Prince Namor is--
You pluck me from the sea without so much as a "by your leave" and expect aid? You presume too much, sorcerer!
Ahem...the Silver Surfer is as one with the skyways he soars!
While Hulk holds the nuclear fire of a gamma bomb within his every cell!
Dude, these are some serious heavy hitters, Monkey! Guess all we can do is hang out and look good...

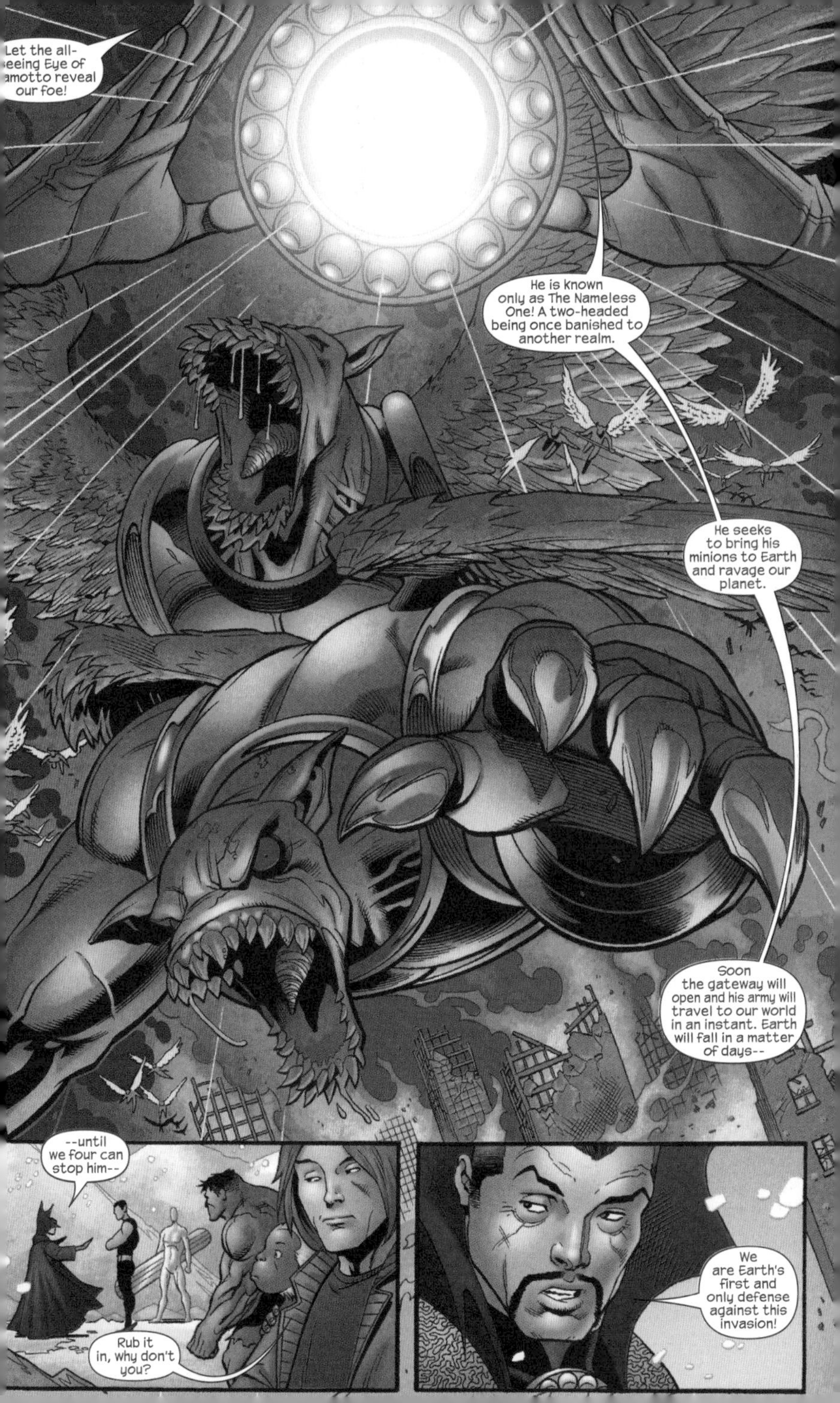
Let the all-seeing Eye of Agamotto reveal our foe!
He is known only as The Nameless One! A two-headed being once banished to another realm.
He seeks to bring his minions to Earth and ravage our planet.
Soon the gateway will open and his army will travel to our world in an instant. Earth will fall in a matter of days--
--until we four can stop him--
Rub it in, why don't you?
We are Earth's first and only defense against this invasion!

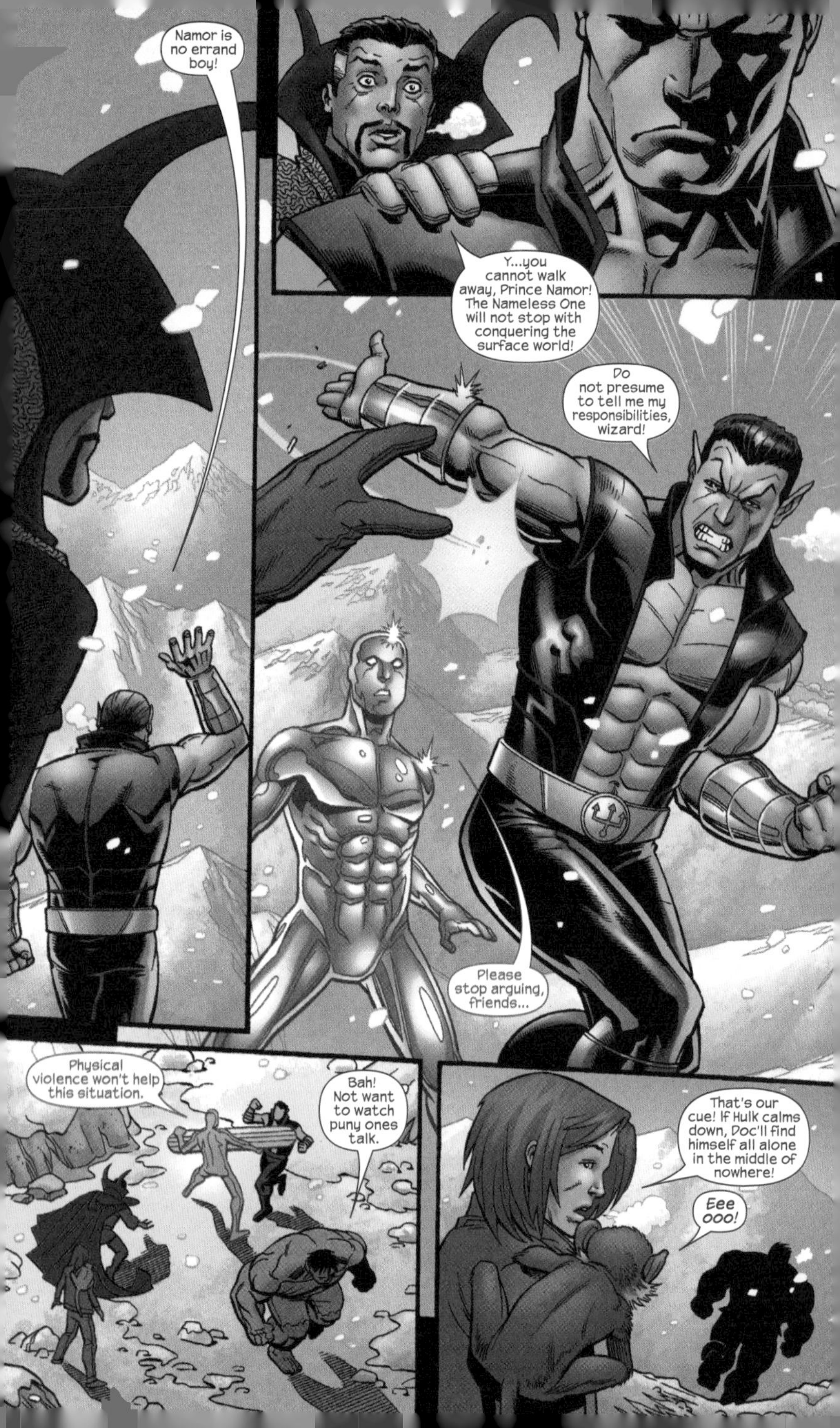
Namor is no errand boy!
Y...you cannot walk away, Prince Namor! The Nameless One will not stop with conquering the surface world!
Do not presume to tell me my responsibilities, wizard!
Please stop arguing, friends...
Physical violence won't help this situation.
Bah! Not want to watch puny ones talk.
That's our cue! If Hulk calms down, Doc'll find himself all alone in the middle of nowhere!
Eee ooo!

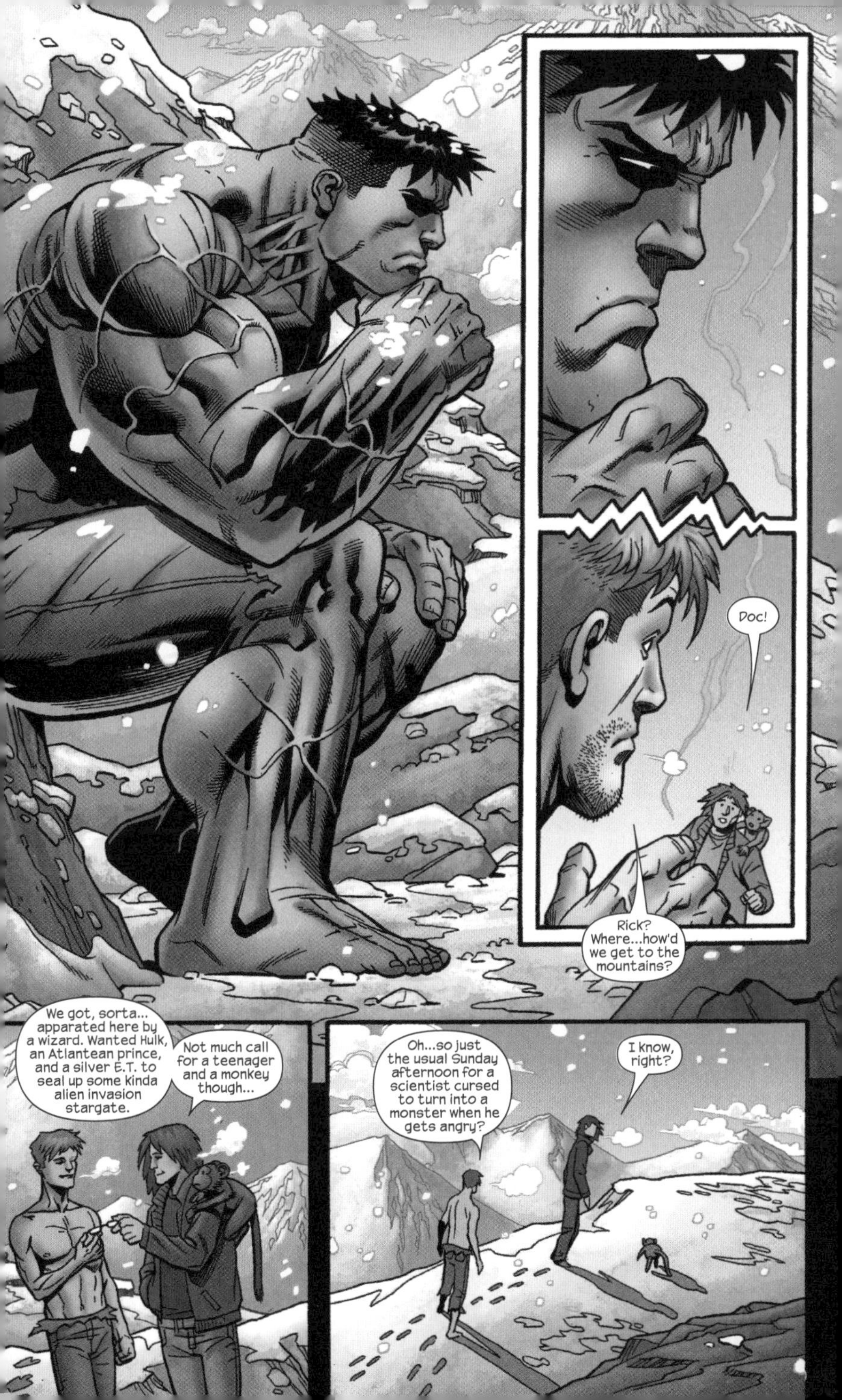
Doc!
Rick? Where...how'd we get to the mountains?
We got, sorta... apparated here by a wizard. Wanted Hulk, an Atlantean prince, and a silver E.T. to seal up some kinda alien invasion stargate.
Not much call for a teenager and a monkey though...
Oh...so just the usual Sunday afternoon for a scientist cursed to turn into a monster when he gets angry?
I know, right?

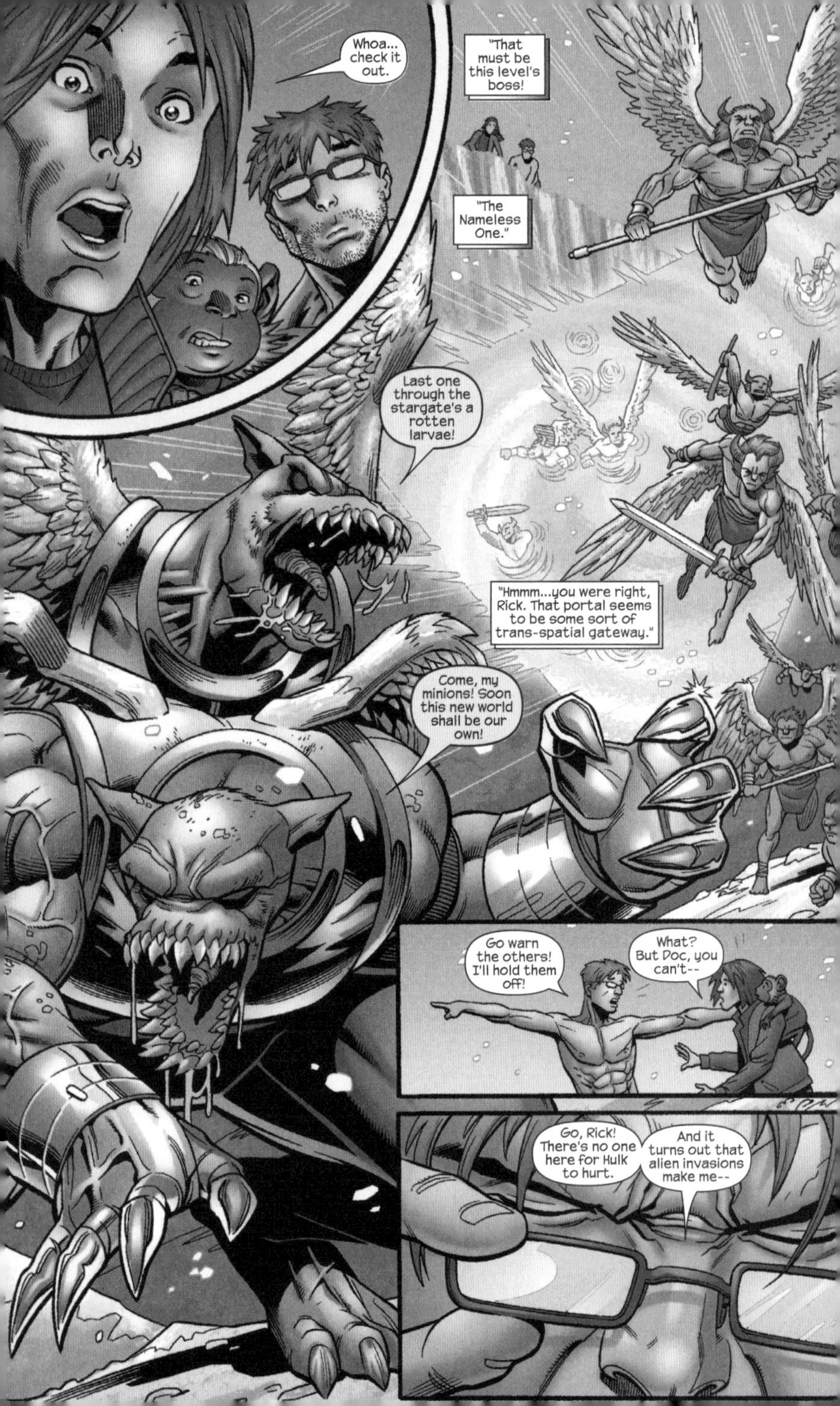
Whoa... check it out.
"That must be this level's boss!
"The Nameless One."
Last one through the stargate's a rotten larvae!
"Hmmm...you were right, Rick. That portal seems to be some sort of trans-spatial gateway."
Come, my minions! Soon this new world shall be our own!
Go warn the others! I'll hold them off!
What? But Doc, you can't--
Go, Rick! There's no one here for Hulk to hurt.
And it turns out that alien invasions make me--

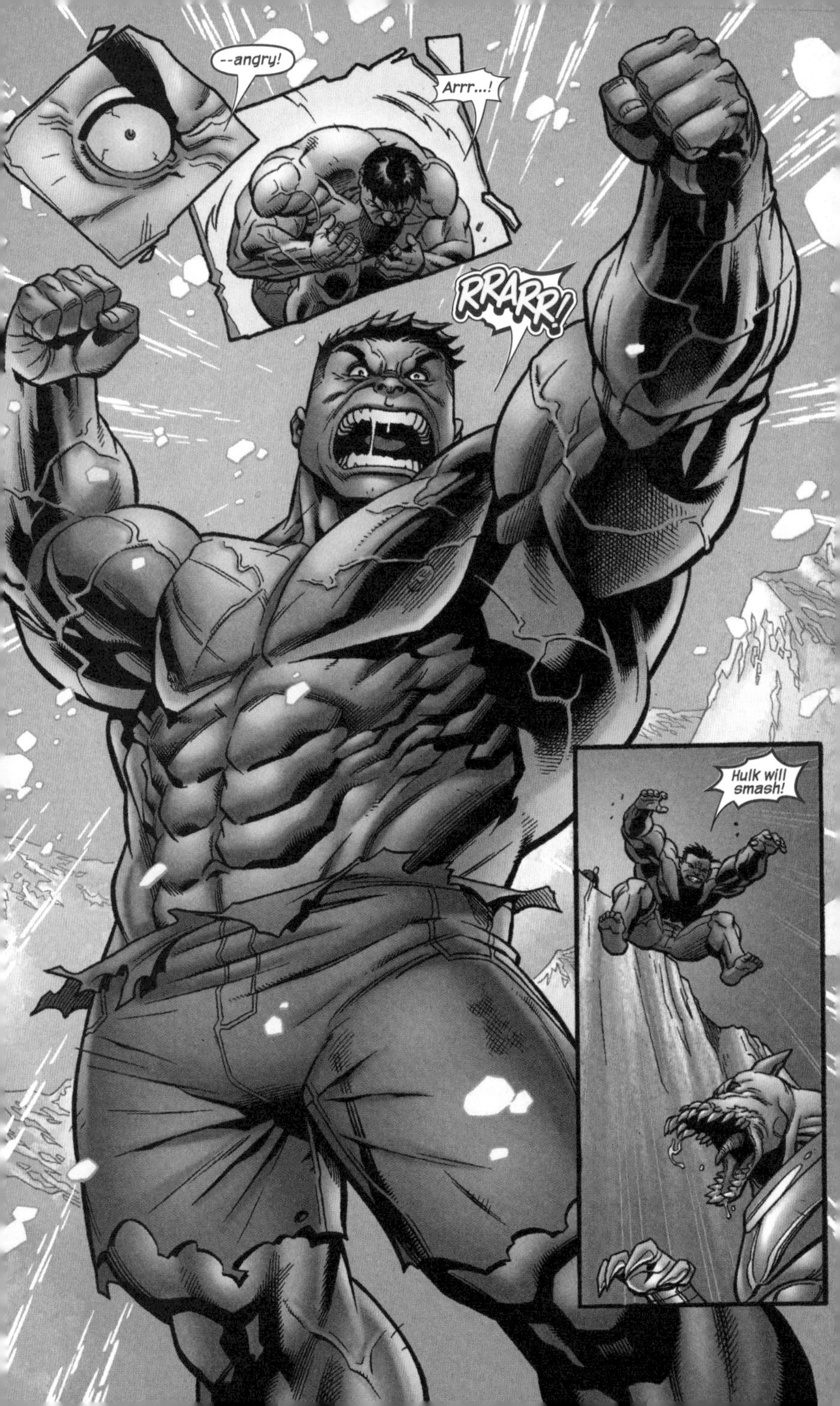
--angry!
Arrr...!
RRARR!
Hulk will smash!

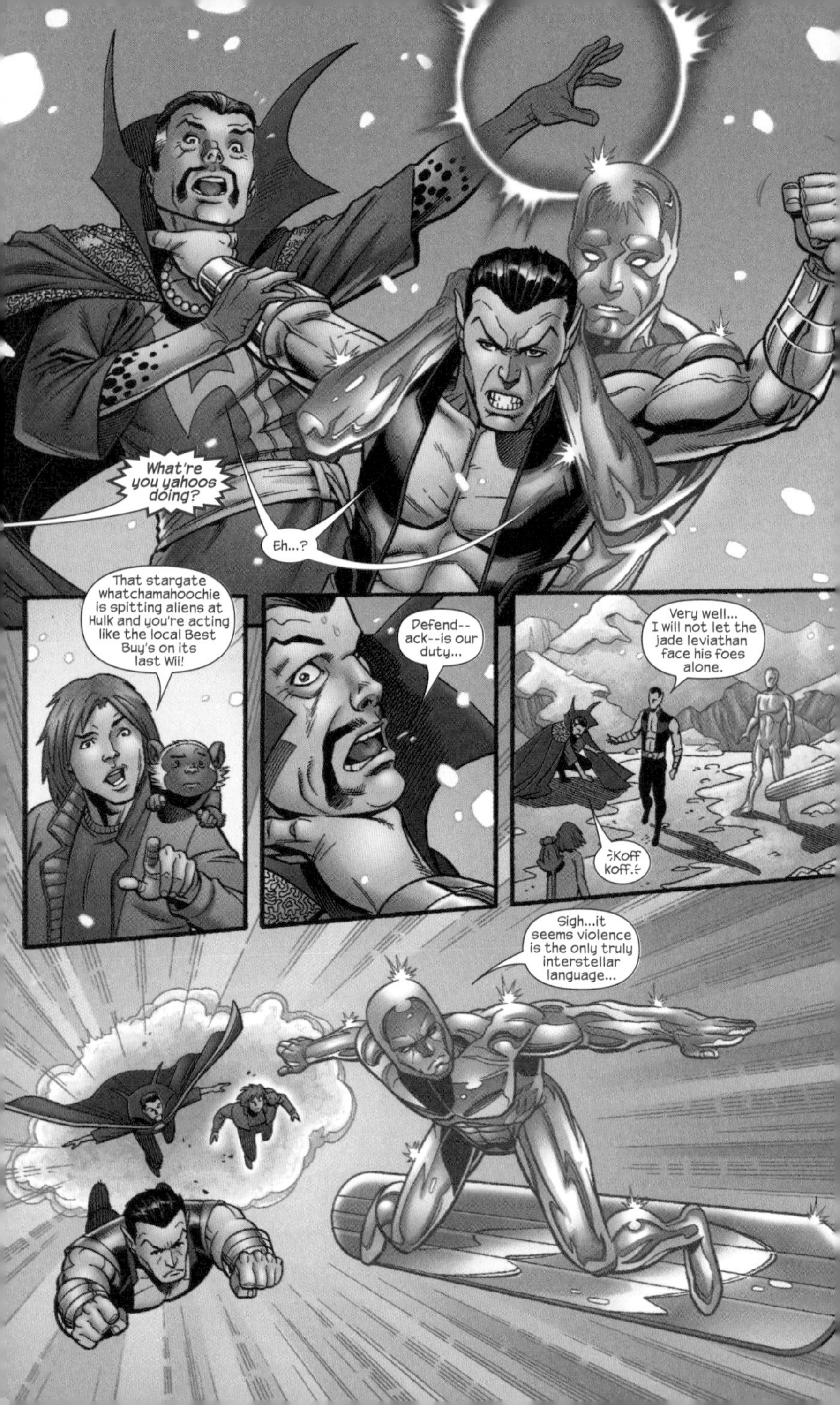

What're you yahoos doing?
Eh...?
That stargate whatchamahoochie is spitting aliens at Hulk and you're acting like the local Best Buy's on its last Wii!
Defend--ack--is our duty...
Very well... I will not let the jade leviathan face his foes alone.
Koff koff.
Sigh...it seems violence is the only truly interstellar language...

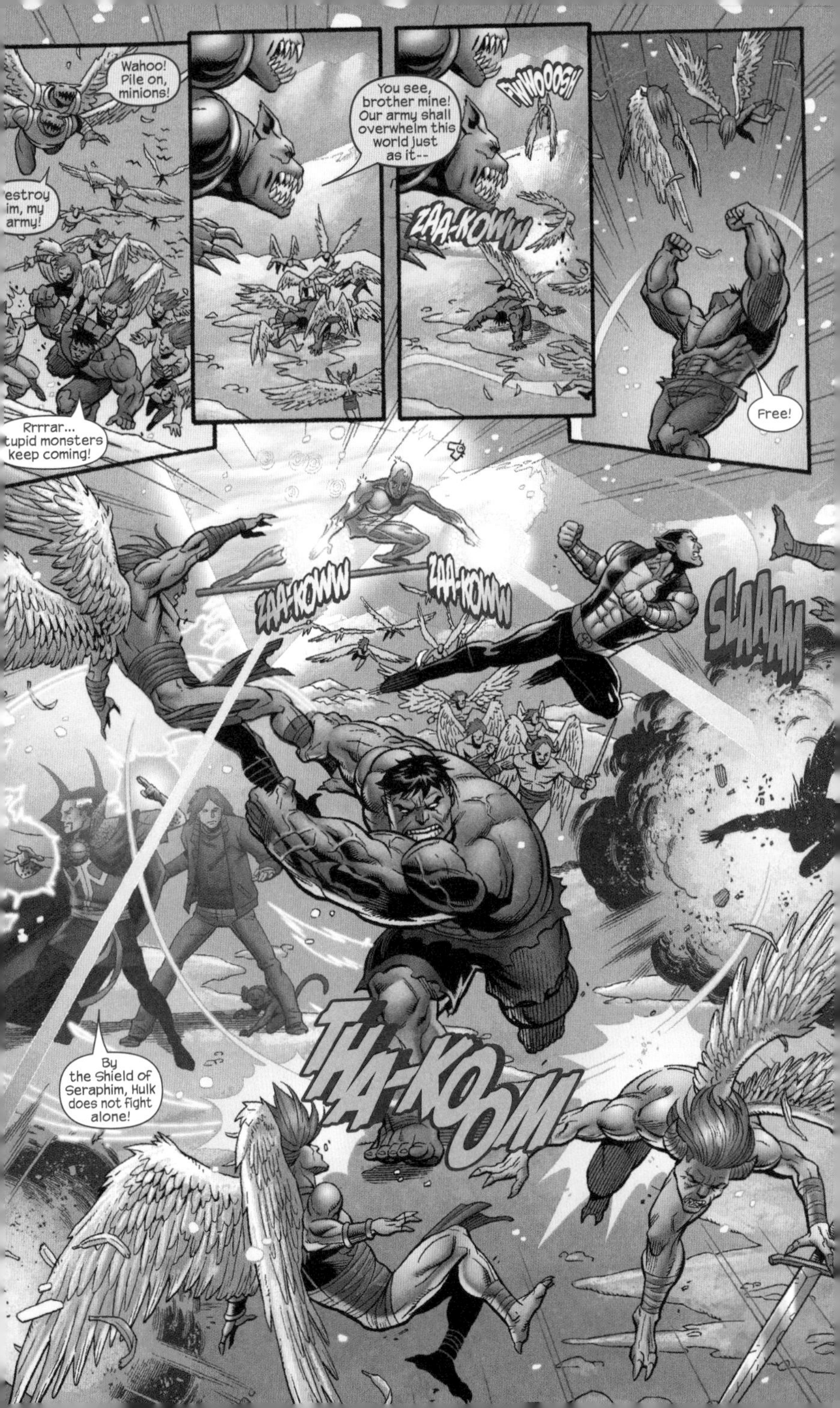

Wahoo! Pile on, minions!
estroy im, my army!
Rrrrar... tupid monsters keep coming!
You see, brother mine! Our army shall overwhelm this world just as it--
FWWOOOSH
ZAA-KOWW
Free!
ZAA-KOWW
ZAA-KOWW
SLAAAM
By the Shield of Seraphim, Hulk does not fight alone!
THA-KOOM

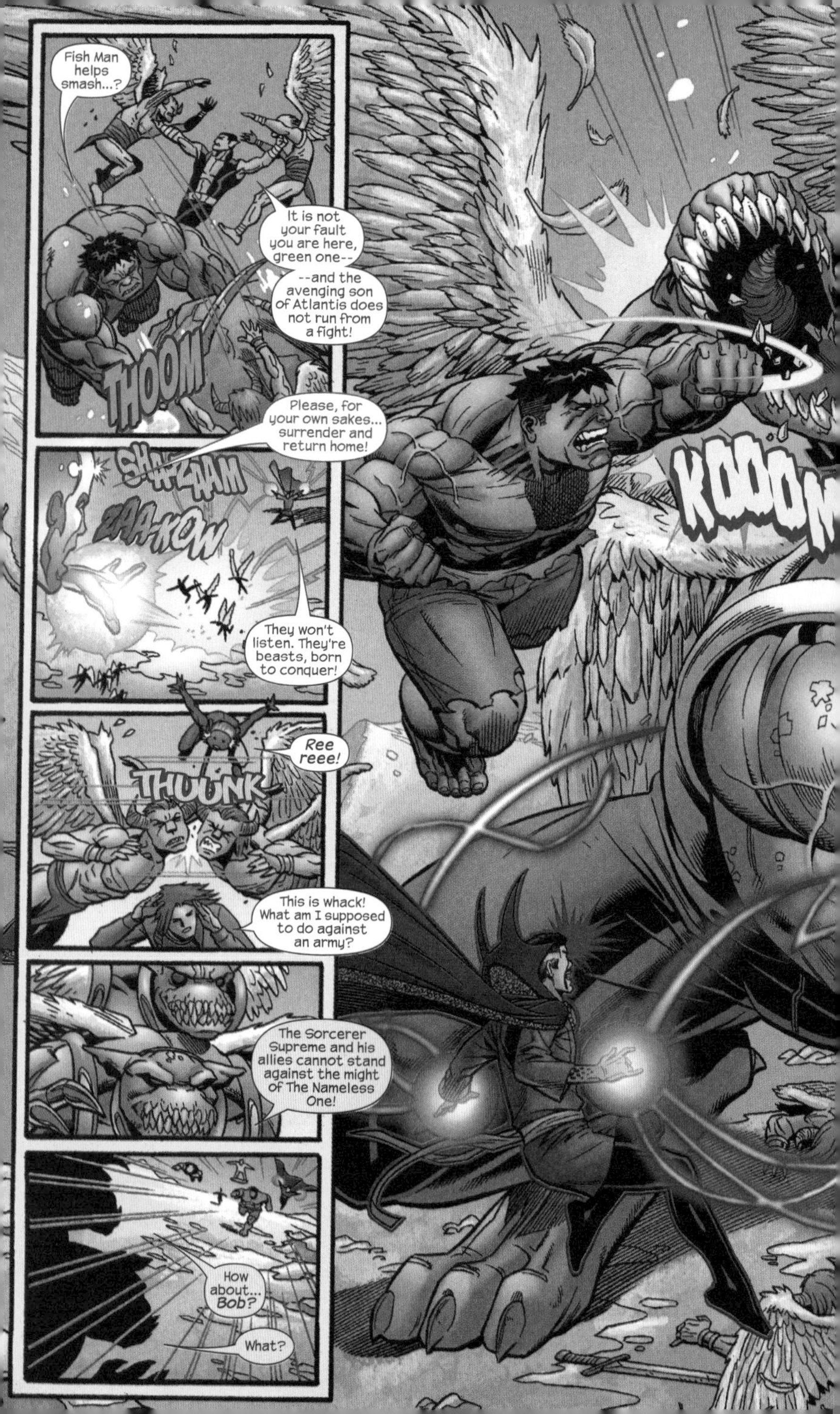

Fish Man helps smash...?
It is not your fault you are here, green one--
--and the avenging son of Atlantis does not run from a fight!
THOOM
Please, for your own sakes... surrender and return home!
SHAZAAM
ZAA-KOW
They won't listen. They're beasts, born to conquer!
Ree reee!
THUUNK
This is whack! What am I supposed to do against an army?
The Sorcerer Supreme and his allies cannot stand against the might of The Nameless One!
How about... Bob?
What?
KOOOOM

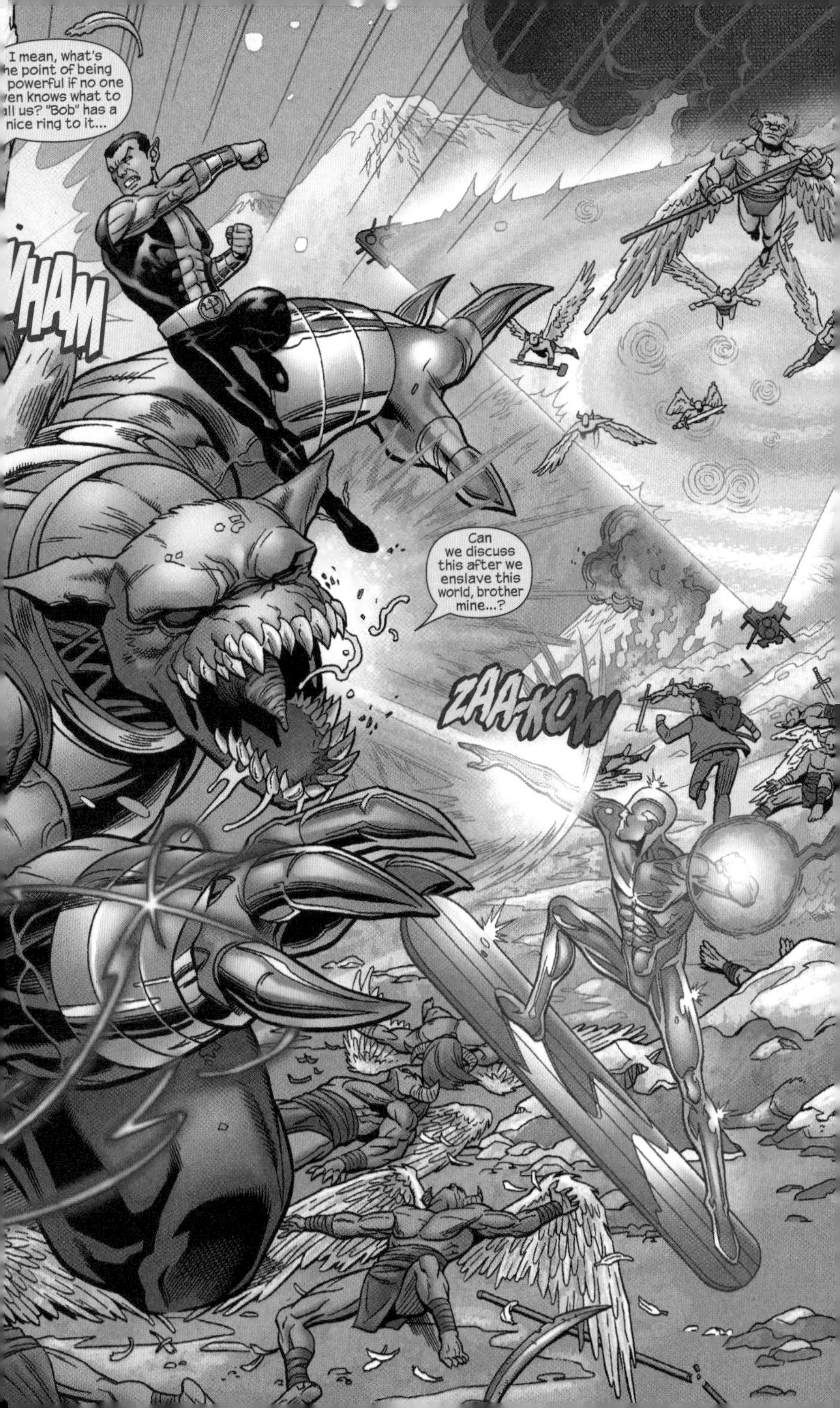
I mean, what's he point of being powerful if no one ven knows what to all us? "Bob" has a nice ring to it...
HAM
Can we discuss this after we enslave this world, brother mine...?
ZAA-KOW

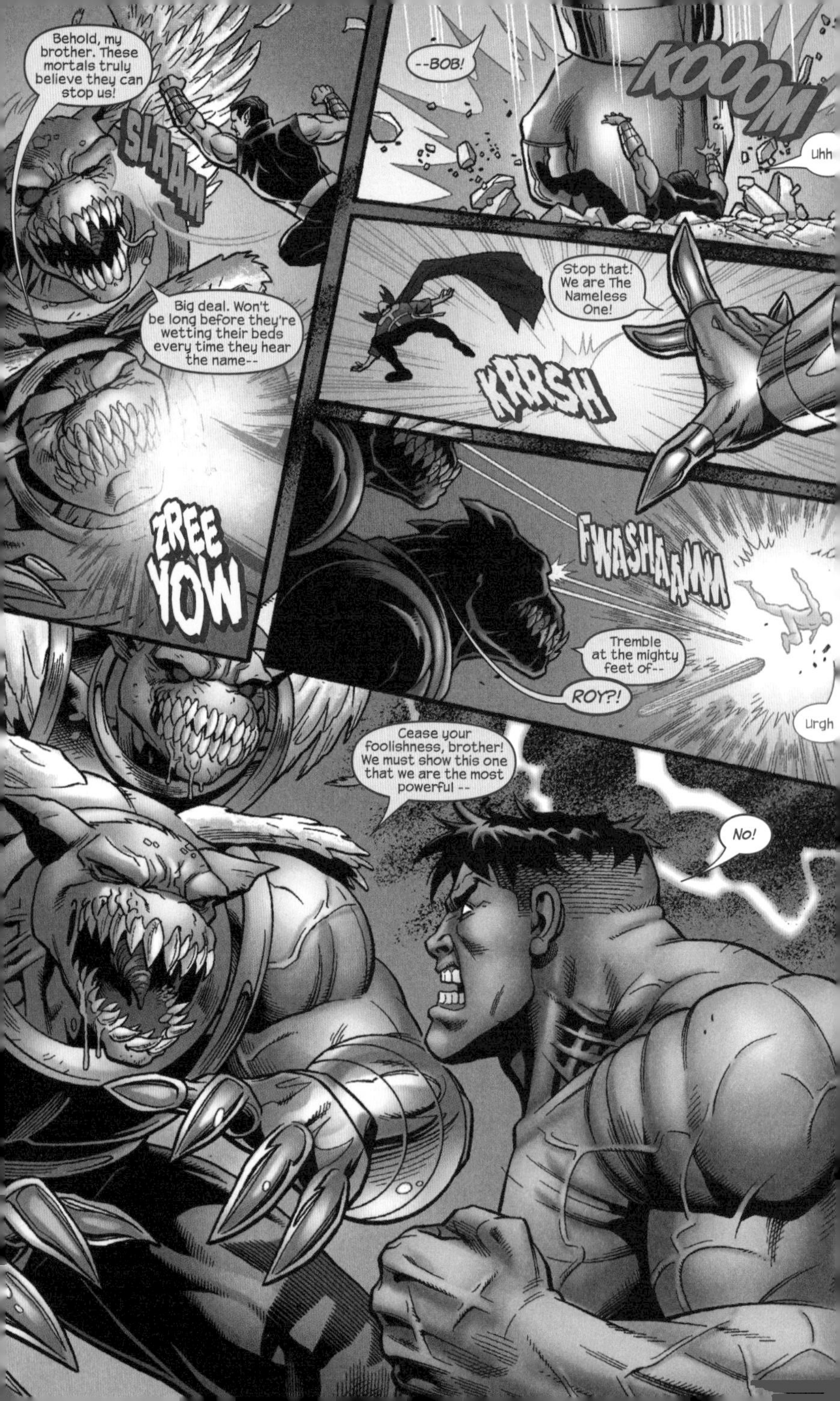

Behold, my brother. These mortals truly believe they can stop us!
SLAAM
Big deal. Won't be long before they're wetting their beds every time they hear the name--
ZREE YOW
--BOB!
KOOOM
Uhh
Stop that! We are The Nameless One!
KRRSH
FWASHAAAWA
Tremble at the mighty feet of--
ROY?!
Urgh
Cease your foolishness, brother! We must show this one that we are the most powerful --
No!

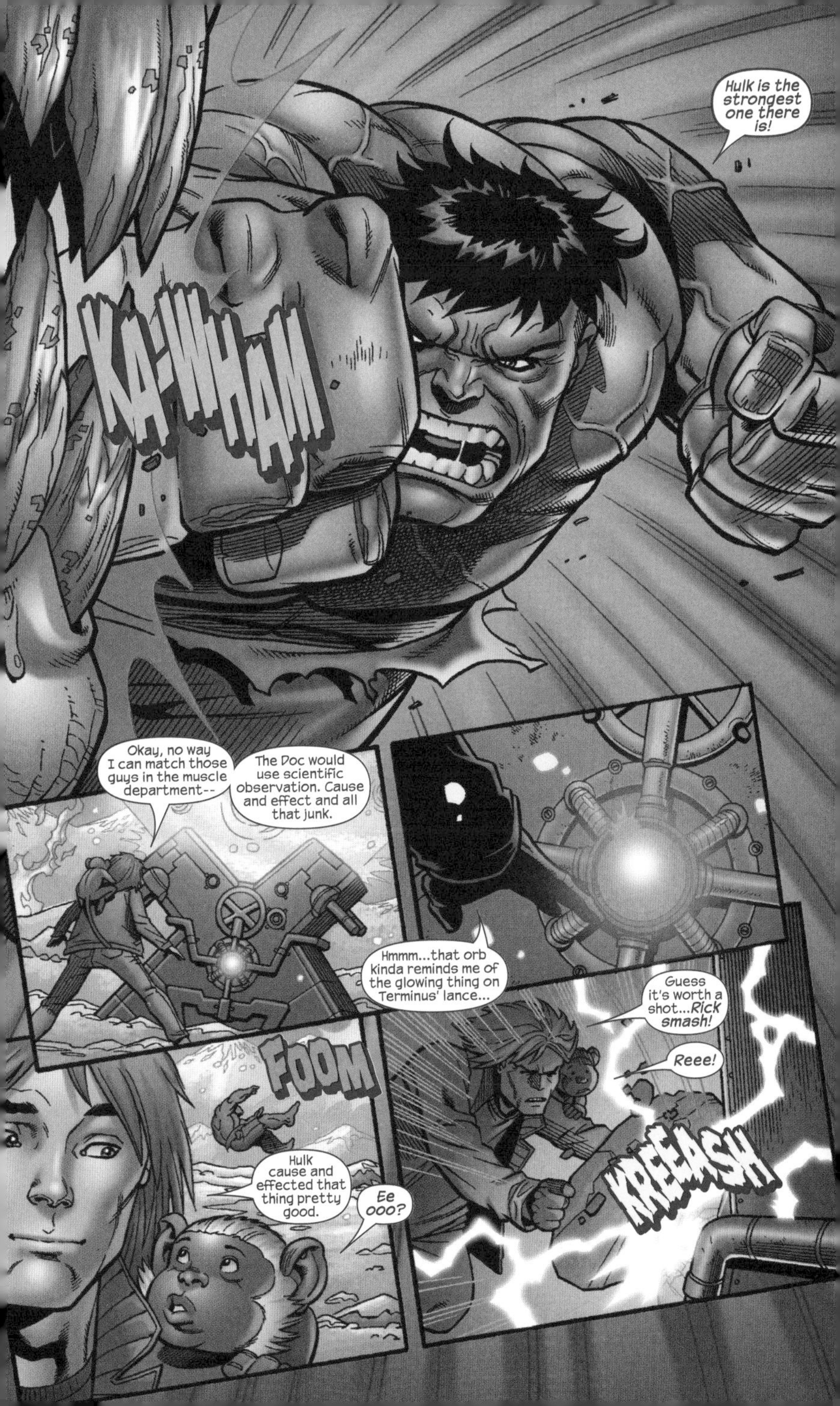

Hulk is the strongest one there is!
KA-WHAM
Okay, no way I can match those guys in the muscle department--
The Doc would use scientific observation. Cause and effect and all that junk.
Hmmm...that orb kinda reminds me of the glowing thing on Terminus' lance...
FOOM
Hulk cause and effected that thing pretty good.
Ee ooo?
Guess it's worth a shot...Rick smash!
Reee!
KREEASH

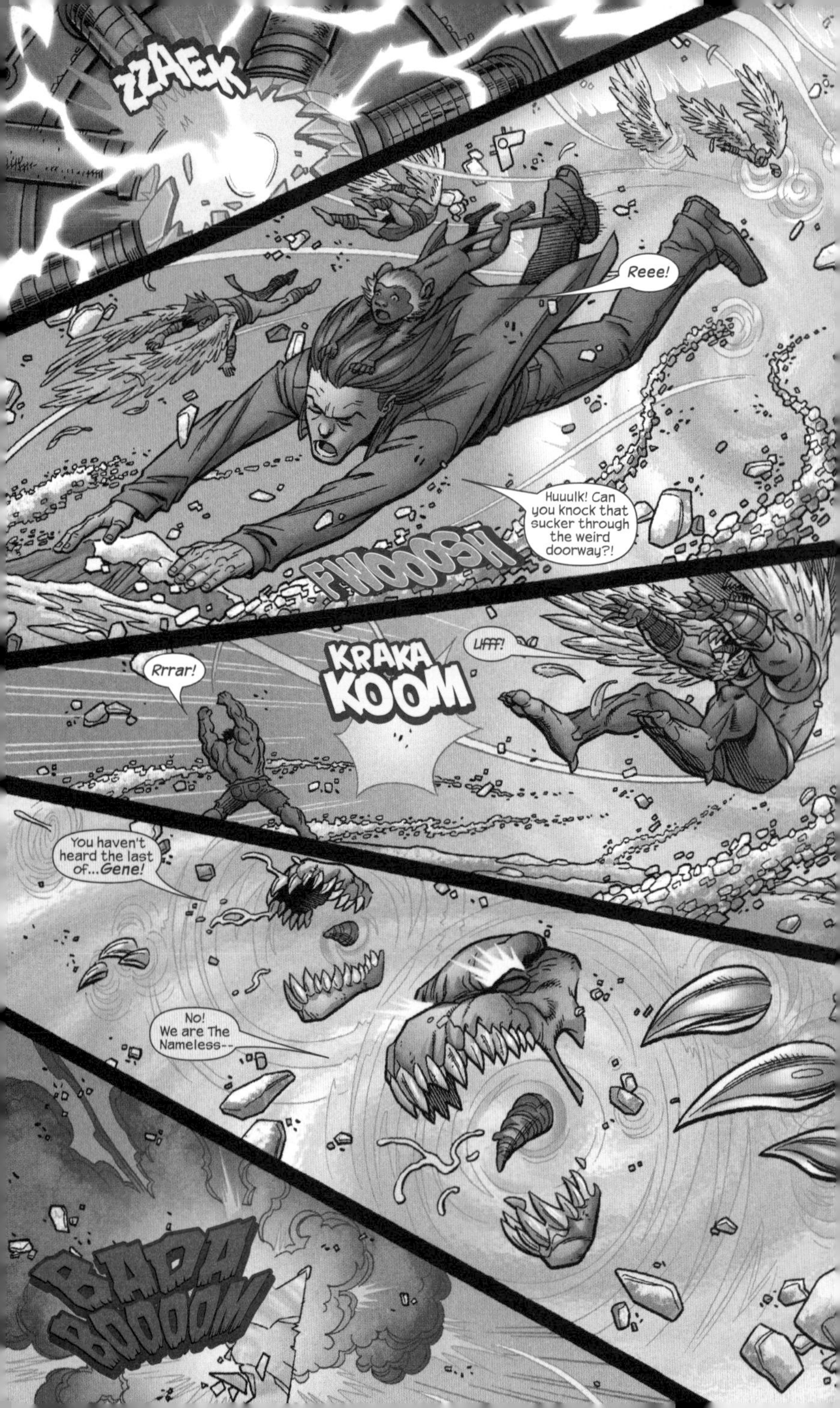
ZZAEK
Reee!
Huuulk! Can you knock that sucker through the weird doorway?!
FWOOOSH
Rrrar!
KRAKA KOOM
UFFF!
You haven't heard the last of...Gene!
No! We are The Nameless--
BADA BOOOOM

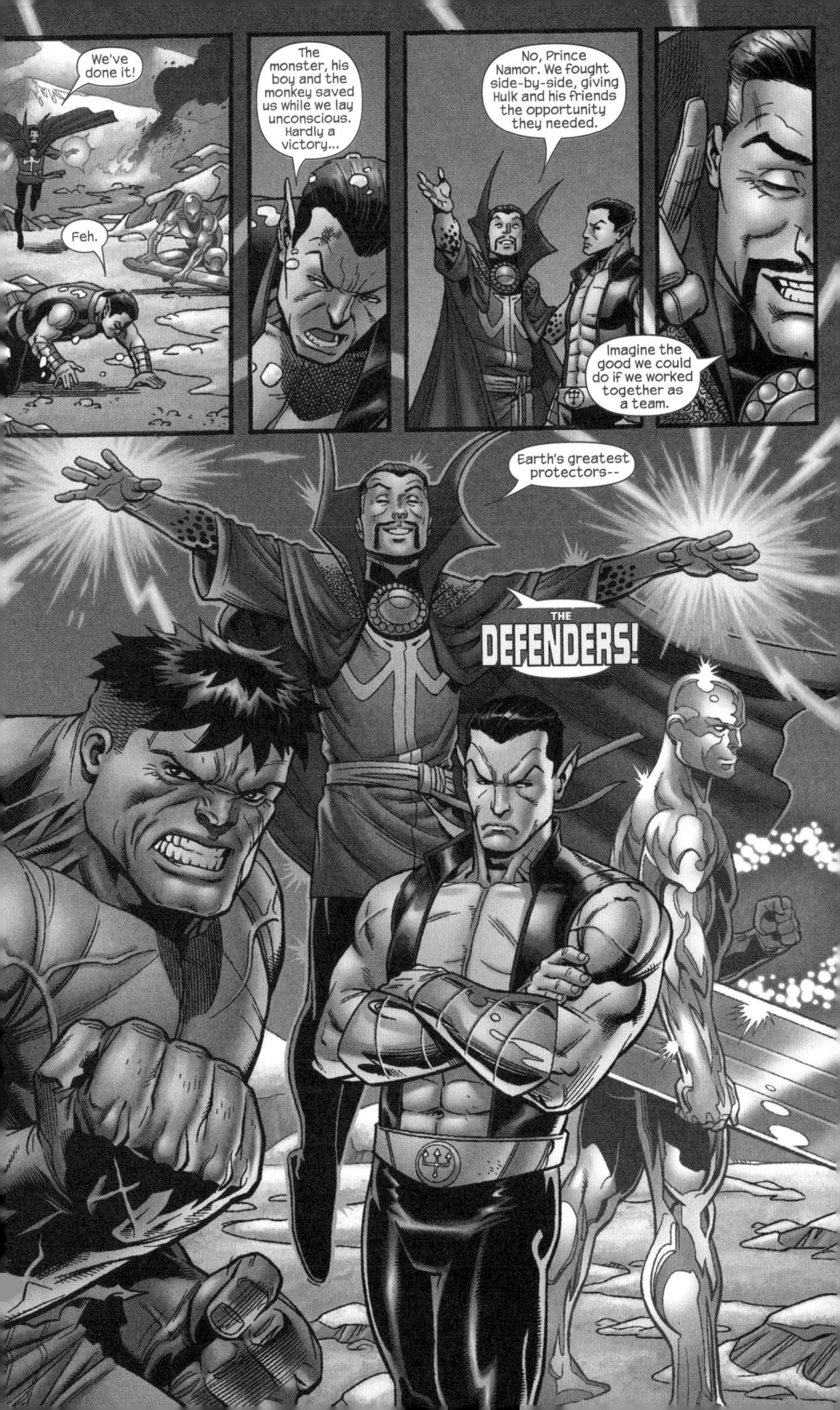

We've done it!
Feh.
The monster, his boy and the monkey saved us while we lay unconscious. Hardly a victory...
No, Prince Namor. We fought side-by-side, giving Hulk and his friends the opportunity they needed.
Imagine the good we could do if we worked together as a team.
Earth's greatest protectors--
THE DEFENDERS!

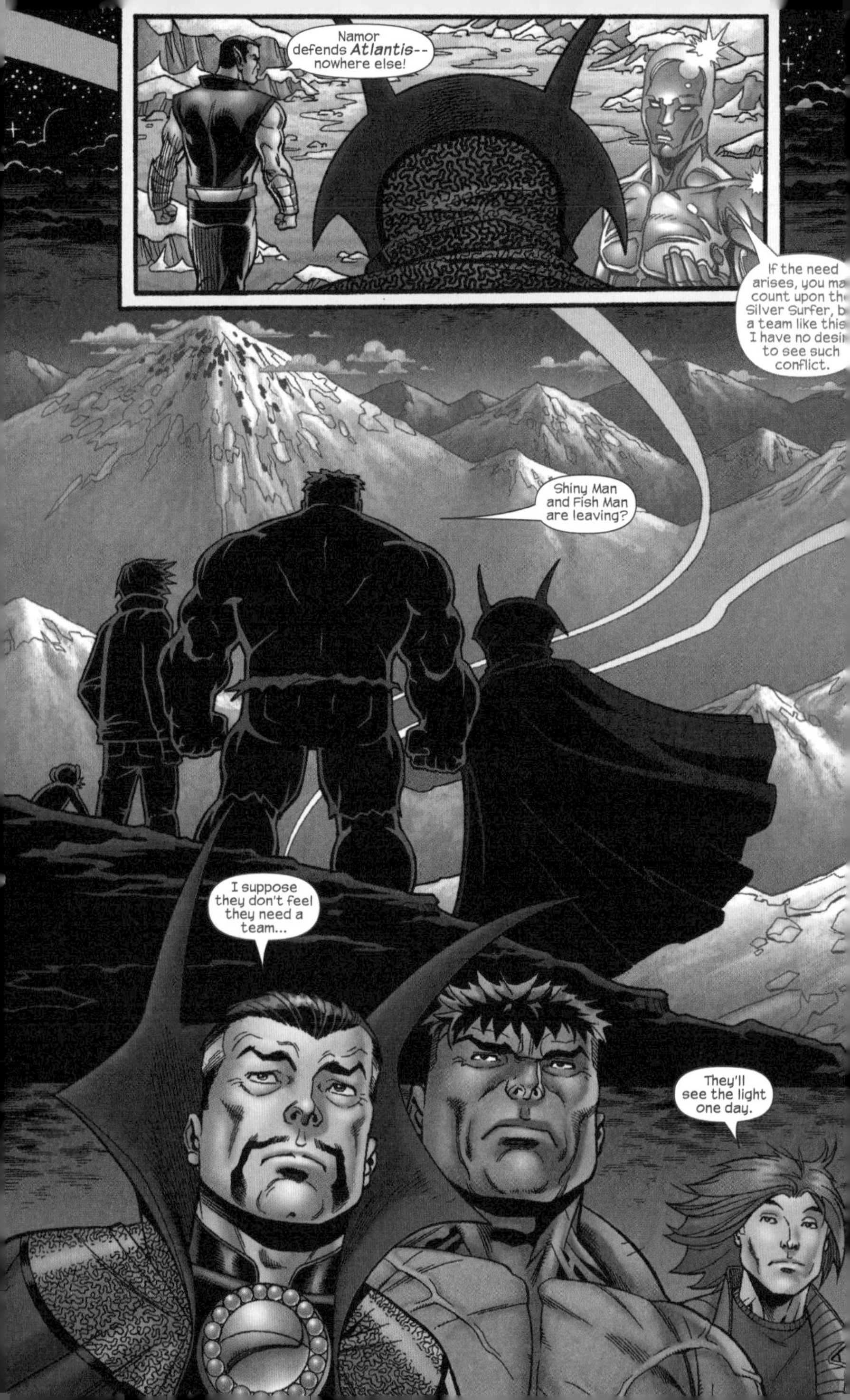
Namor defends Atlantis-- nowhere else!
If the need arises, you ma count upon th Silver Surfer, b a team like this I have no desi to see such conflict.
Shiny Man and Fish Man are leaving?
I suppose they don't feel they need a team...
They'll see the light one day.

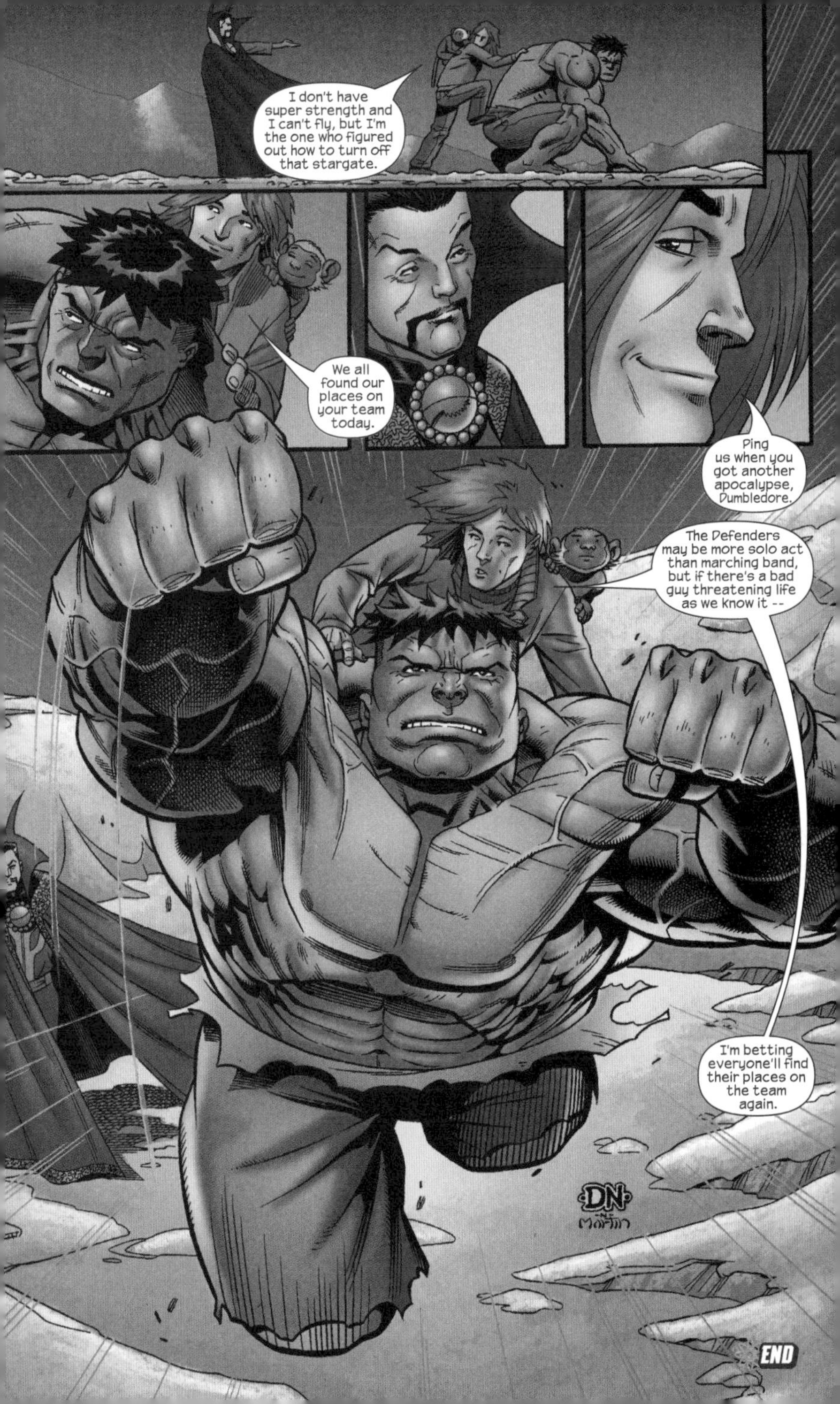

I don't have super strength and I can't fly, but I'm the one who figured out how to turn off that stargate.
We all found our places on your team today.
Ping us when you got another apocalypse, Dumbledore.
The Defenders may be more solo act than marching band, but if there's a bad guy threatening life as we know it --
I'm betting everyone'll find their places on the team again.
END

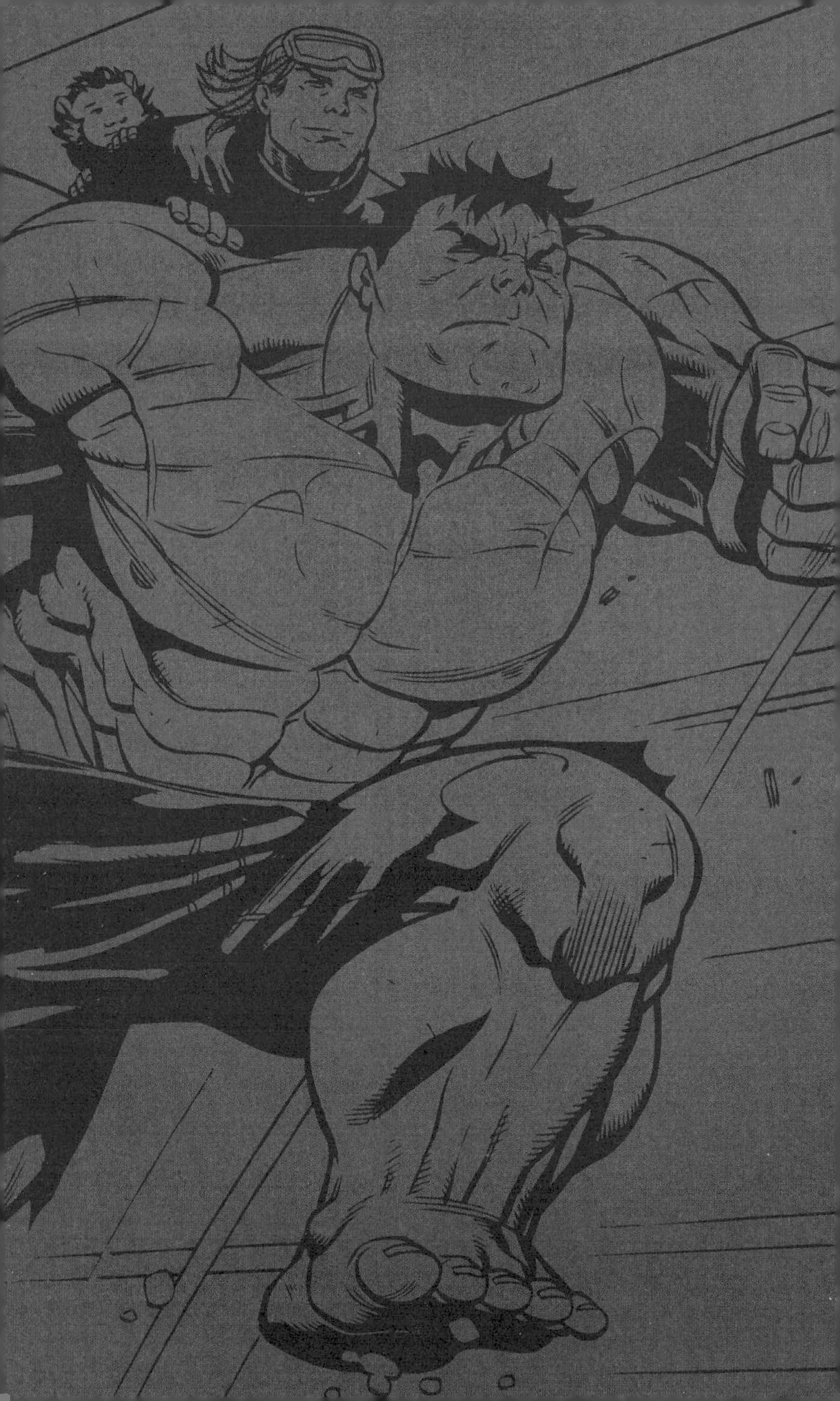